Other Works by Daniel B. Hunt

Science Fiction
The Eclipsing of Sirus C: A Dryden Universe Novel
Origins: A Dryden Universe Collection

Collaborative Science Fiction
Rise of the Europan: "Broken"

Fiction
Stories of the Midnight Sun

Poetry
The Modern Day Poet
North Wind Muse

A STEP TOO FAR

A Dryden Universe Corporate Wars Novel

DANIEL B. HUNT

A STEP TOO FAR
A DRYDEN UNIVERSE CORPORATE WARS NOVEL

iUniverse books may be ordered through booksellers or by contacting:

iUniverse
1663 Liberty Drive
Bloomington, IN 47403
www.iuniverse.com
1-800-Authors (1-800-288-4677)

ISBN: 978-1-5320-0997-6 (sc)
ISBN: 978-1-5320-0996-9 (e)

Library of Congress Control Number: 2016920085

Print information available on the last page.

iUniverse rev. date: 12/20/2016

For my mother

Contents

1

------o-o-⊚-o-o------

A GOLDEN COIN

A SHADOW moved across the fogged windowpane of the office door. The subtle change in lighting caught Paul's attention. He glanced up from his worn desk and scrutinized the figure of a man who stood outside the door. Paul watched as the handle of the door began to turn. He reached below his desk and put his hand on a snub-nosed flechette pistol.

"Rif." Paul kept his eyes on the door as he warned his partner.

Rif Slater was eating a sandwich. He sat up straight behind his desk, put the sandwich down, and cocked his head toward the door.

The door slid open, revealing a neatly dressed man in a designer suit. It was gray, and there was a bright red kerchief folded to a tight, double-pointed triangle in the man's breast jacket pocket. The tall man stood silhouetted in the doorway. He ran a hand through a thick shock of blond hair, looked at Paul and Rif, and then stepped into the room.

Paul glanced at both of the stranger's hands. They were empty. The stranger was not an immediate threat. Paul relaxed, raised his head slightly toward Rif with a nod, and removed his hand from the hidden weapon.

"Can we help you?" Rif stood up and walked toward the stranger.

Bulldog large with a chiseled chin that always needed a shave, Rif was physically powerful. He was a bit gruff and not too bright, but he was good at his job. Though he had been Paul's partner for only a little over a year, Rif was the closest thing to a friend that Paul had. Paul's move to Papen's World had not been easy. Nobody, not even small subsidiary companies like Militan Corporation, liked to lose their enforcers. But when Militan became a vassal company to the hulking, intergalactic Syrch Corp, Syrch took note of Paul's handling of a sensitive issue and offered him a position. Militan could not openly object. Syrch was just too powerful. But that didn't mean Militan had been happy. During the transition, Paul had to take extreme care to avoid getting killed. Rif had understood. He had watched Paul's back.

The stranger reached out to shake Rif's hand. "Yes, I think so." The man's voice was precise and a bit haughty.

"Take a seat," Paul said.

Rif followed the stranger toward Paul's desk. The stranger reached out a hand to Paul, but he ignored it and remained seated. Rif smiled widely, laughed softly, and settled into one of the two chairs that sat before Paul's desk. Rif crossed his legs and eyed the stranger.

"Please," Paul said, indicating the other chair.

The stranger sat uneasily, adjusted, and looked first at Rif and then at Paul.

"Is this the Security Division?" he asked.

"Maybe." Paul shrugged. He had never seen the stranger before. That made him wary. As a rule, Paul only dealt with certain people in the organization.

"Yes. I …" The man stumbled a little. "I am Dr. Warner Gibson. I work … I run the bio research station here on Papen's World."

"Well?"

"You must understand this is a little uncomfortable for me. I have never done anything like it before, and, you see, I can't say no."

Rif started to say something, but Paul stopped him with a subtle gesture.

"Go on," Paul flatly prompted.

"It's a nasty business, really," Dr. Gibson replied. "You see, the board of directors has reached a decision, and they have told me to get the job done." When neither Paul nor Rif interjected, the doctor continued. "Here—maybe this will help." The doctor moved his hand toward his inside breast pocket. He noticed Paul stiffen. The doctor's hand froze. "I have an object in my pocket. I was told to give it to the Security Division. That is you?"

"We work in the division, if that is what you need to hear." Paul's voice was rough.

The doctor dropped his hand back to his lap. "You know, I don't think either of you introduced yourselves to me."

An irritated smile flickered across Paul's face for a second. "I'm Mr. Thorne, and that … that is my partner, Rif Slater. Go on," Paul said, pointing at the man's suit pocket. "Just be slow about it, Doctor. We wouldn't want there to be any … misunderstandings."

"No. I suppose not."

Dr. Gibson reached slowly into his inner breast pocket and pulled out something small. Leaning forward, the doctor dropped it on Paul's desk with a light tingling sound. Paul and Rif looked at it. Round and gold, it was a coin. On the observable side was the circular silver-bar emblem of Syrch Corp.

Paul and Rif exchanged an uneasy glance.

"I assume you know what that is?" the doctor asked.

"It's a coin," Paul answered, trying to sound nonchalant. Although he had been with Syrch Corp for a year, he had never been given one of these coins before. He knew what it meant. Everyone knew. It was a death warrant.

"I was saying," the doctor continued, "the board of directors has made a decision. It's"—the doctor gulped air—"it's my daughter. My niece, to be more precise. They want her dead."

The words hung in the air. Paul let his eyes glide over the doctor, studying the man. There was something about the doctor's body language that seemed out of place. But Paul could not put his finger on it. Paul glanced at Rif, but the other enforcer was still staring at the coin with a look that Paul read as being one of troubled concern. Paul cleared his throat, and Rif looked up and shrugged.

Rif then looked back at the doctor and asked in a curious voice, "Your niece? They want us to knock off your niece? That seems like a hard thing to ask you to do, Doctor. Do you mind explaining why?"

"Does it matter?"

Paul replied, "I think you misunderstand what my partner is asking. He doesn't want to know why Syrch would put a hit out on your niece. That is none of our business. He wants to know why you would agree to be the messenger. You have to admit, Doctor, it does seem a little out of the ordinary." Paul reached down and fingered the coin, running this thumb over the coin's surface, trying to determine if it was legit, but he never took his eyes off the doctor. He wanted to see the man's expression and hear the tone of voice as he answered. Listening was more important at the moment than definitively knowing the veracity of the coin.

"Yes. Yes, I suppose it does." The doctor ran a hand over his face and through his hair. He took a deep breath and grimaced. "I've worked for Syrch Corp for nearly twenty years," he began. "Worked my way up from a research assistant. You know, in all that time, Syrch Corp has never asked me to do anything outside of my normal job description. Never. Oh, you hear all the stories, right? But I've never seen anything to make me think the stories were more than embellished rumors. Syrch can be a little heavy-handed when it comes to obtaining resources, I admit, but I didn't really believe they would ask me to do something like this. No ... I am shocked, but ... there is nothing I can do about it. You understand?"

The doctor paused, waiting for an answer, but when neither enforcer offered one, the doctor continued speaking, his hands fidgeting along the edge of his suit jacket. His eyes moved back and forth between the two enforcers as he spoke, and his voice lost some of its bravado, growing weak and hesitant.

"My sister and her husband worked for Syrch many years ago," the doctor said, "but they were killed in what I was told was a freak accident on one of the mining worlds. They were crushed beneath some heavy excavating equipment. It had something to do with poor computer programing. I just took it as being one of those—in the wrong place at the wrong time. Do you know what I mean? Of course I found out that was a lie. They lied to me. But I'm coming to that, please.

"Anyway, they left behind a girl, Jillian. Jillian Caldwell. And being my niece, with no other family, she became my ward."

The doctor stopped and stared at the wall behind Paul's desk. He rubbed absently at his eyes and then dropped his head and stared awhile longer at his lap.

Paul frowned. "You didn't answer the question, Doctor. Why did the board of directors pick you to deliver this order?" Paul flipped the coin back on the table where it spun, rolled in a small arc, and settled.

"I'm getting there," the doctor replied. "Please be patient with me.

"Jillian has something," the doctor finally said softly. "I don't know exactly what it is, but Jillian—Temperance, my sister, gave Jillian a cranial mesh a few months after Jillian was born. I know that is illegal, but she—my sister—was a believer in the next tech advance and thought giving Jillian the mesh would help her daughter excel. Anyway, to be short, Temperance did not stop there. She put some information in it—you see?"

"No, I don't," Paul answered. "Why don't you explain it?"

"I was told that Temperance's and Jack's deaths were an accident, remember? But I recently discovered that Temperance was stealing information and Jack was selling it. You see, I met with the board of directors last week, and they told me the true story. Syrch had the two eliminated. Do you know what that is like? I know two members of the board. I thought we were friends. But they ordered the death of my sister and her husband and then kept that information from me. I was devastated. It was like being hit with a hammer in the back of the head, and I just stood there, dumb and numb and … I don't know what else! But that was not the worst of it. I was also told that Temperance had put some sensitive information on my niece's cranial mesh. Something dangerous," the doctor explained. "Temperance was always a dreamer, a schemer. I loved her, but … I don't know why the information surprised me, but it did. And they—the board—gave me that … coin. And they told me to deliver it here in person. If I didn't … well, you understand?

"Temperance was reckless, Mr. Thorne. She caused this. But I'm not that type of person."

"What type of person are you, Doctor?"

The doctor did not answer for a while. He looked at Paul's hard stare, shifted uncomfortably, and directed his answer to Rif.

"I couldn't stand up to the board's decision in this matter. I'm a coward, you see. I like test tubes, mass spectrometers, centrifuges, and microtiter plates. Plus … the cranial mesh was defective or something. I told Temperance it was a stupid and reckless idea, but did she listen to me? No. She didn't hear one word I said. It damaged Jillian—the cranial mesh. And you can't take those things out! You would kill someone trying to do that—or turn them into a vegetable." The doctor spoke faster and faster. "I can't say I am happy about this in any way. I feel sick. But how do I say no to Syrch Corp? How? They killed Temperance and Jack. They will kill Jillian regardless of what I do. The only options I have are to die with Jillian or do what I'm told and survive. I'm just a biochemist. I am not brave enough to fight it, Mr. Thorne. And that girl, that girl, she is not right. The universe won't miss her. She is not right at all.

"Does that answer your question, Mr. Slater?" the doctor said weakly. "I am not proud of it. But that is why I am here."

"And that makes it okay?" Rif asked. His voice was cruel.

"I don't know. No. Yes? You must understand me. I tried to love her. But Jillian is … Why should I die because of something I had no control over? I just want to work in my lab!"

"Sounds like the devil's choice, Paul," Rif said. He rolled his eyes, snorted, and padded his pockets looking for a cheap cigarette.

Dr. Gibson, his face flushed, leaned forward in his chair toward Paul. "I don't want to be here, Mr. Thorne. I wish this weren't happening. I might not love Jillian. We were never close, but I don't wish her any harm. But I've delivered the coin. I've done what I was told."

"I suppose you have at that, Doctor," Paul answered. He picked up the coin and fingered its surface with his thumb again, thinking. "You didn't happen to bring a photo of your niece, did you?"

"I didn't think of that. I can get one if you need it."

"That's okay. We'll check it out," Paul assured the doctor. "Your part is done. But"—he held up a restraining hand—"where can we reach you if we need to?"

"The Forest Tower Dome," the doctor replied. "The lab is there, on the twentieth floor."

"And your niece?"

"We live nearby, on Capital Street. The oval building—you know the one—the Armory Building, in the penthouse."

"Wait a minute," Rif said. "You live together?"

"I am not a proud man. Yes."

Paul felt unsettled. He didn't like the fact that the doctor was in the lower tier of upper management and knew a couple of members on the board of directors. That would give Dr. Gibson a lot of power—power that on a planet like Papen's World was tantamount to being a duke in a monarchy. There was some type of power politicking behind this assignment. That was obvious. But Paul did not know enough about Syrch Corp's interoffice politics; he was too new to the job to judge where the dangers lay.

Paul looked at Rif, and his partner shrugged noncommittally.

"That may make things easier," Paul said in a staccato fashion. "Tell me about your niece's patterns."

"Her what?"

"What is her typical day like? What does Jillian do?"

The doctor thought about it for a moment. "There's breakfast—at around six. Out the door by eight. We go out together. She heads off to class in a private limousine, and I walk to work. She is at school most of the day, and we both get home at around four to four thirty. Watch some video vision … dinner around seven … in bed just after nine."

Paul stood. He had heard enough and wanted to discuss the situation with Rif without the doctor overhearing. "Okay, Dr. Gibson. Like I said, we'll look into it. Don't go disappearing on us. Stay in the city. Stay on Papen's World. Understand?"

The doctor stood up, and Rif joined him. The doctor looked a bit confused at the sudden conclusion of the interview. He was uncertain in his stance, and the perplexing expression on his face turned to frustration and anger, but the doctor brought his emotions under control, and a sudden look of defeat spread across his face.

"I understand."

"Then good day, Doctor." Paul indicated the door with his left hand.

The doctor shuffled toward the door. Before leaving, he turned back to Paul and Rif and, brushing a hand through his hair, said, "I know I'm a coward. I know it."

The door closed harshly behind the doctor, leaving Rif and Paul alone in the room.

"What a real winner," Rif huffed. He had found a cigarette, and it hung unlit in his mouth.

Paul shrugged. "I don't like it, Rif. It smells wrong."

"Check out the coin," Rif suggested.

"Yeah, the coin." Paul flipped it in the air and caught it again.

Moving back behind his desk, Paul slipped the coin into a barely detectable slot on his desktop. A burble of light flickered in the center of his desk as the holographic computer monitor sputtered to life. Rif came and stood behind Paul's shoulder, watching. The holographic image coalesced and settled.

Rif whistled. "It's legit."

"Well, the coin is—I'll give you that. But you didn't believe any of that cock-and-bull story the good doctor gave us, did you?"

Rif took the cigarette out of his mouth. "No. Not a word of it. But like you said, Paul, why do we care why Syrch Corp put out a hit on this woman, Jillian Caldwell? It's better not to know."

"Yeah." Paul scratched his forehead. "Yeah, I suppose you're right. The coin is good. It's a valid contract. Let's just do this and stay away from the dirt. But, um, Rif."

"What is it, Paul?"

"Why don't you stick on the doctor for a while? I don't like surprises. They're dangerous. I'll stay here and work up Caldwell. Tomorrow we'll stake her out and work up the plan."

"Sounds good to me, Paul. I could use a stretch of the legs."

Paul sat back in his crooked chair and looked at the hologram that floated on his desk. He tapped a few keys that were projected on the desk's surface and began running records.

Rif grinned, picked up his coat and hat, grabbed the rest of his sandwich, and made it to the door.

"See you later, Paul."

"Careful."

"You know me." Rif screwed his hat on and grinned.

"Yep, that's why I said it."

Rif disappeared out the door, which shut behind him with a thud and rattle of glass.

Paul stared at the door for a moment, his mind playing over the comment Rif had made during the doctor's interview. It did seem a little cruel to make the doctor bring the death warrant for his niece to the Security Division, even for Syrch Corp. Still, Paul was not surprised. He had seen enough of human behavior to know that people killed off members of their own family with wanton abandon. The doctor wouldn't be the first person to kill a family member for personal advantage. That wasn't the issue. What bothered Paul, besides the involvement of the board of directors, was that these assignments were not supposed to be delivered in this way. Syrch was a corporation and had its own bureaucracy, its own procedures. Even the Security Division was mired in protocol. But Paul could not deny the veracity of the coin. It was as real as the ground beneath his feet. Maybe it was some type of test. Maybe Syrch Corp was testing Paul to see if he would blindly obey their orders. It was, he knew, what they expected. There was no professional room for Paul to question an order.

Paul pulled the golden coin out of the reader and fingered it gently. He flipped it from side to side, studying its surface. It was the real article, no doubt about it.

What critical information did the doctor leave out of his story?

Paul didn't mind killing people. Some people deserved to die. Some didn't, but they died all the same. It was just a job. And Paul was good at it. That was why Syrch Corp stole him away from Militan. Paul always got the job done and never, ever asked why. But for the first time in his career, Paul could not help but ask. Why did Syrch Corp really want the woman dead? Why did they send her uncle to deliver the order? Why had they chosen Paul and Rif when there were several teams available for this type of action? And why now? What had precipitated the order at this point in time when Syrch could have easily killed the woman years ago, presumably with her parents?

The air in the office suddenly felt stale. Paul opened up a desk drawer and took out a small flask and a smudged shot glass. He opened the flask and poured a shot of bourbon. After putting the lid back on the flask and stashing it in the drawer, Paul sipped at the golden-brown liquor and stared at the door.

2

⚬—o—o—◯—o—o—⚬

STAKEOUT

IT **WAS** still dark. The early morning air was cold, and a wisp of rain and fog filled the streets. Paul sipped gingerly on the brutally hot coffee that he clutched in both hands as he watched the main door to the Armory Building. The unease he felt at yesterday's meeting with Dr. Gibson had not abated. If anything, it had become a sharp claw in the pit of Paul's stomach. He had found almost no information on Jillian Caldwell. Almost nothing at all. And that was most peculiar. In modern times, a person's life was a series of data points. Tracked, segregated, analyzed, and quantified, these data points self-populated throughout many marketing and government computer systems. Yet the normal checks Paul had run had come up nearly empty. From the results, he could tell that Jillian Caldwell existed but not much more. She had no shopping patterns, no bank accounts, no credit chits, no digital addresses—nothing one would normally expect to find. What Paul had found were a few scribbled jots about her birth, early schooling, and a few hints about some ill-defined medical issue. It was frustrating.

Paul looked across the city thoroughfare and through the rain and fog at the shadowed form of his partner. He knew exactly where Rif was due to the red bead of the man's lit cigarette. Paul shook his head and sighed. He had warned Rif about that, but Rif was stubborn. He liked his smokes.

Turning his attention back to the Armory Building, a tall ash-concrete building with long, monolithic lines, Paul sipped his coffee and waited. He jostled his shoulders a little to settle his pistol, which he wore under his coat in a shoulder rig, against his left breast. The metallic piece had shifted uncomfortably when Paul pulled his coat close to keep out the mist and rain. Feeling a little more comfortable, Paul leaned against the cold side of another apartment building that was just half a block from where the doctor lived. This building was built in a completely different architectural style. Unlike the grand Armory Building with its elongated windows, main doors that were arched with stained-glass windows with geographic designs, the Read Building was new-modern, made mostly of computer-controlled, electrochromic glass bound by thin sheets of silvery metal. The electrochromic glass changed its hue through the application of electricity into electrodes located between separated layers of glass. The electricity caused ions located in the chemical window coating to move, resulting in a change in the reflectiveness of the glass. The computer could make the glass any shade of gray, keep it completely opaque, or make the glass mirrorlike. Right now the glass was dark ebony and reflected the sickly streetlights that cast sullen pools of amber light through the misting morning. The shimmering light reminded Paul of Kirlov's radiation—that amber glow that surrounded framing ships as they plied through interstellar space on the impetus of Insanity Crystals. Paul had spent some time framing between the systems in his job. While he did not care overly much for the crowded ships and metallic air, he had always found the glow of Kirlov's radiation somewhat comforting.

Paul glanced up at the sky and let the rain bead on his face. The enforcer had spent several years on a desert world. The constant, cruel heat and grit of sand had been mainstays in his life. He had felt like he would never be cool or clean again. But here, on Papen's World, the rain came softly most mornings, and in the rainy season, it poured in torrents that danced and beat upon everything around. Terraformed trees bent to the winds, and rooftops chirped when the storms whipped in from the open ocean. Paul much preferred Papen's World to Telakia. He had had enough of giant dust storms that could strip a man's skin in a few hours. He realized how grateful he was that Syrch Corp had offered him this job. Who knew how long he would have been stuck on that hellhole had they not come along? And besides, the pay was better too.

Waiting during a stakeout was always a mental game. It was easy to drift off into daydreams and forget to pay attention to what was going on around. Paul mentally shook himself and tried to focus. He had lost a few tails before because his mind had wandered. While this normally did not bother him too much, as it was just part of the trade, he felt like he could not afford any slipups on this particular job. It wasn't clean. The whole situation was murky.

"Paul." Rif's voice hushed into the pickup Paul wore in his ear. It was a small, discreet device that allowed the enforcers to communicate without using any of the communication towers. A scrambled system, it gave the two men a modicum of privacy that minimized the risk of communicating while maximizing teamwork, and because it did not use any of the communication towers, it was not possible to use the towers to triangulate on their whereabouts. Historic data records on tower-based systems could be used to track Paul and Rif's movement even after the fact, and that was a liability Paul did not need. Though the range of the discreet communication system was limited, it was enough for Paul and Rif's purpose, and it came with all the nontracking advantages.

"Paul," Rif hissed again. "Hey, man, I got to pee."

Paul laughed. "All right, Rif. Don't take so long."

Rif's darkened shape detached itself from where it had been resting and moved up the street. There was a little twenty-six-hour shop around the corner. It had clean bathrooms and was where Paul had picked up his coffee.

"Get you anything?"

"Nope. Just hurry," Paul replied. "It'll be light soon. People will start moving about, and we don't want to miss her."

"Got ya."

Rif had followed Dr. Gibson for a good couple hours after the doctor left their office. But Rif had not reported anything to Paul that shed any light on the current situation. The doctor had gone to work at the Forest Tower Dome and, as the doctor had indicated, walked back home around four twenty. Paul wondered about that. He expected the doctor to do something out of the ordinary. It was not every day that your employer told you to kill a family member … or else. The doctor should be experiencing more stress, and people who were stressed displayed awfully strange behavior. But the doctor stuck to his routine. He appeared as calm and distant as a desert moon. It was one more thing that gnawed at Paul.

It would have been better if Syrch Corp had used the regular assignment protocols. Paul was sure it was a message or test of the doctor's loyalty, but that did not do much to ease Paul's anxiety. Paul felt tense. He kept looking over his shoulder, expecting to find someone lurking behind him. He would be glad when this assignment was over.

Rif came back puffing on a new cigarette and took up his position across the street. The two of them waited patiently as the system's star slowly rose, turning the dark sky into a deep, grumbling, cloud-filled gray.

Paul liked the gray. The clouds hid the eerie light of the system's ugly celestial neighbor. Papen's World orbited a typical class A star two times the mass of earth's sun. But just twenty-two light-years away was a super massive type O, Blue Giant. A super-luminous star, the Blue Giant generated tons of ultraviolet radiation that had long destroyed planetary objects in its own system. Even at a distance of twenty-two light-years, the Blue Giant cast a constant aura throughout the system and was the cause of the specialized terraforming done on Papen's World. It rained so much here, Paul knew from his mandated immigration briefing, because Syrch Corp maintained a higher-than-normal ozone layer to protect the planet from the giant's deadly ultraviolet radiation. Instead of the three parts per ten million of ozone found on earth, Papen's World maintained a staggering three parts per four million. The planet was dotted with huge, cold plasma ozone generators. All that ozone trapped a lot of heat in the atmosphere. It was why Papen's World had no polar ice, and the trapped heat also caused an increase in evaporation of the oceans. And that meant it rained almost all the time on Papen's World. Paul liked the rain and the morning fog. He felt comfortable in the shadows, and the rain helped keep the temperatures down.

Unlike in Syrch City, it was extremely muggy and hot in the equatorial zones. Paul was happy not to live in Gravesande. Gravesande, the city named after the noted Dutch professor, sat in the heart of Heyerdahl plateau just south of the equatorial edge on the central continent. It was always hot there. But here, on the upper part of the northern continent where the capital resided, the temperatures could even get a bit chilly. And that was fine with Paul. He welcomed the abundance of rain and cooling breezes. It was a better alternative to the last decade of arid skies and swirling, massive sandstorms.

Cars and trucks began moving up and down Capital Street. Shadows and rain slipped across the faces of the neatly packed buildings, and pedestrians stirred out of doors, walking under neon-lighted umbrellas and huddled in various coats and rain gear. The air was crisply cold and smelled like freshly laundered clothing. Water streamed in trickles down the gutters near the street curb, and lights began appearing in windows all up and down the strip.

Paul perked up. The time band on his wrist indicated it was nearly seven thirty, and people were moving in and out of the Armory Building. A doorman in a long, heavy coat summoned auto-driving taxis and tipped his hat to patrons as they left or entered the building.

It was Rif who saw the doctor first.

"There he is," Rif said, "great coat, at your twelve."

"I don't see anyone with him," Paul responded. He had long since dropped his coffee cup in a waste disposal unit.

The doctor was talking to the doorman. The doorman made a call on his mobile device, and soon a sleek, black limousine pulled up along the curb. There was an actual human driver.

"The doctor must be loaded," Rif commented.

"I gathered as much," Paul answered. "A perk of his job. I still don't see ... wait a minute."

Paul watched a little girl, maybe eight or ten, tentatively stick her head out of the building's door. Her face was chubby and hidden beneath the long brown fur of a hooded coat. The child looked at the rain, and even from where Paul stood, he could hear her screech and laugh as she darted out of the protective doorway, stopped quickly to give the doctor a hug on his legs, and then dashed into the open limousine door. The doorman, who was holding the limousine door, bent down and said something to the girl before he closed the door. The limousine pulled away from the curb.

"You don't think ..." Rif began.

"I don't know," Paul replied. "I lost sight of the doc. What is he doing?"

"He turned back up the street and is walking toward the Forest Tower Dome," Rif said. "See him now?"

Paul glanced further up the road as the limousine carrying the child drove by his position. He ignored the limousine and focused on finding the doctor. Then he saw him, Dr. Gibson's tall form meandering up the street. Paul stroked his mouth with his right hand.

It all made sense now—the record check results. He would not expect an adult to have such skimpy records, but a child? A minor? Minors did not have bank accounts and credit chits. They didn't buy property or get shopping-club cards. Paul thought. Had he looked at Jillian's date of birth on the records? Had he paid attention to the dates of the school records? No. He realized in a flash he had presumed the records were older. He had presumed Jillian Caldwell was a young adult.

A sense of horror filled him.

"Rif."

"Yeah, Paul. You thinking what I'm thinking?"

"It's the kid. Jillian Caldwell is just a kid. Look, Rif," Paul continued, "let's regroup back at the office. I knew something wasn't right. But don't go straight back. I've got a bad feeling."

"That sounds like good advice," Rif replied.

Paul could see Rif was already stepping away from his position and moving along the street.

"Thirteen hundred?" Paul asked. He too was moving. A bead of water rolled off Paul's head and down his neck. Paul shivered.

"Sounds about right," Rif replied. "See ya."

Paul switched his communicator off and strode quickly down the street. He moved through the growing throng of people, changing his direction multiple times and stopping in several stores to see if anyone was following him. Paul tried to look at the faces of the people around him. It was easy for a tail to change clothing, if the clothing was worn in layers, but hairstyles and faces were nearly impossible to change while actively on the job. But looking at facial features was not easy as people were huddled in coats and beneath umbrellas. Paul just couldn't tell. He did not spot a tail, but that did not mean nobody was there. It just meant that he didn't see them.

After an hour of wandering, Paul decided to get a bite to eat and collect his thoughts. So he stopped in a small restaurant and ordered a couple of eggs, sunny side up, toast, and java. He sat at the rear of the joint, facing the door. Nobody seemed out of the ordinary.

What were they going to do? He had to figure it out. Should they kill the kid? Syrch Corp would expect them to carry out the assignment. But Paul had never killed a child before. What could Jillian have done to warrant such a sentence? Even if she had something hidden away in a cranial mesh, it must be possible to wipe the interface's memory. There was something Paul was missing. He knew the doctor had been holding something back, but what?

Did Syrch Corp really expect Paul to kill a kid? It seemed incredulous to Paul. There had to be more to it. There just had to be.

3

$\circ\!-\!\circ\!-\!\circ\!-\!\bigcirc\!-\!\circledcirc\!-\!\bigcirc\!-\!\circ\!-\!\circ\!-\!\circ$

OBLIGATIONS

PAUL CLOSED his office door and plopped wearily into his chair. He left the lights off, but enough light came through the window to cast a long beam across the floor. Paul had wandered the city since leaving his partner. His hair and face were wet, and his feet sore. Outside, the storm had continued unabated, a slow plodding thing that promised more rain as the day turned to evening. Weather reports indicated that there would be a break near midday tomorrow. Then the skies would clear as one of the jet streams of air pushed the storm system further east. But the weather was the least of Paul's worries. He threw his feet up on his desk and slouched back, waiting for Rif to return.

Paul was no stranger to killing. It was one aspect of his job. He took no particular pleasure in it, but it didn't cause him to lose any sleep either. Well, not much sleep. Bourbon helped. The thing Paul disliked about killing was that he found it annoying how most people died. They threw up their arms and tried to stop the shots with their hands—as if that would actually work.

It just made things messy. Or they closed their eyes and imagined they were somewhere else, hoping that somehow that act would make them invisible and bulletproof. That response bothered Paul because it was escapism, and Paul hated it when people ignored a problem just because they did not like the implication. Sometimes people begged—"No! No! No!"—and sometimes they just sat there quietly, like cows waiting their turn in the slaughter pens, eyes wide and helpless, peeing themselves or whimpering. When people were in that state of mind, it was possible to get them to walk to the execution spot, and, as in the case with a mass killing, people would actually wait in line as if they were buying tickets to a movie. Those were the worst. Paul had only had to do that type of killing twice, and the groups were small, five people the first time and ten the next, and both times it had turned Paul's stomach. Humans should be more—should die more—it just bothered him that it was so meekly accepted. Paul had killed multiples back in the early days, before he had matured as an enforcer, when he was trying to create a reputation. But the image of the mud and the cow-eyed people and the blood and the sound of the short retort of the pistol and the thud and slap of bodies falling never seemed to leave him. Even now, years later, Paul could transport himself there and feel the wind, remember the sucking of mud on his shoes and the roar of the engine as the bulldozer pushed dirt and rock over the dead. Paul felt he had come to terms with those killings. Those people had deserved to die. But they could have done it with more honor.

It was a rare individual that was defiant. Paul kind of liked those. He felt respect for the man or woman who gave him the finger or told him to suck an asteroid before he blew their brains out. Paul could understand that. Those people had been predators of one type or another. They had a different mind-set. They understood that their luck had run dry and Paul had the drop on them. The predators knew that if it had been the other way around, Paul would have been the one fed to the cremation station and dumped in some recycling vat. It was a killing of equals, a victory of sorts, and it always left Paul feeling slightly exhilarated and strangely tired. Most people, though, were not equals. Most denied reality, begged, or died like cows.

But all the people Paul had killed had one thing in common, and that made the act of killing nothing more than what it was—no emotional drama, it was just a simple act of practicality, the effect in cause-and-effect. The people that Paul killed had done something, and that action precipitated Paul's reaction. Simple.

Paul was a professional. He was not a murderer. Murderers killed people for the joy of killing, in a fit of emotional rage, or because the murderer felt the victim was perpetuating something that could only be resolved when the victim was dead. Paul was not a soldier either. Soldiers killed people—good, bad, innocent, old, or young—because doing so helped them accomplish a military objective. A soldier's killing creed was therefore fairly simple. All the people that Paul had killed had made bad decisions. They had done something in the hopes of personal gain, but that gain caused an equal loss for the corporation. So the corporation arranged for Paul to make a little visit. In a way, for Paul, his victims had brought corporate judgment upon themselves.

But a child? Paul shuddered and tried not to imagine it. What decision had Jillian made?

Paul could not fathom what a child of that age might possibly do that would justify death. It would be different, in Paul's estimation, if Dr. Gibson had come in and said, "My niece is crazy. She killed the neighbor's kid and ate his liver. I think I'm next." But the doctor had only whimpered that Syrch Corp wanted her dead without really explaining anything. The doctor hinted at psychosis of some type, but Paul didn't believe the doctor at all. The man emanated lies. Jillian Caldwell seemed like a normal, loving kid. She had hugged her uncle before going to school! That didn't seem psychotic to Paul. Why? Why would Syrch Corp want the child dead? What possible threat was she to such a huge, intergalactic corporation?

Paul wanted answers. He had no desire to stoop to the level of a murderer. If that is what Syrch wanted, Paul was tempted to tell them to find another body-boy.

The door opened, and Rif walked into the office. Paul noticed that his partner had changed his clothing. Paul wondered if the lunk had returned home for the duds. They didn't look new. Rif often missed the subtlety of a tactic. Paul sighed. You changed your appearance on the job, not by going home and picking out a new set of pants and shirt. But maybe Rif was just ... oh, who knew? Paul decided not to mention it.

"Am I late?" Rif took off his wet coat and hung it on the tree-shaped coatrack by the door. Rif paused and looked at Paul. "You have a reason for sitting in the dark?"

"No. Not really. Did you spot anyone?"

"Was I being followed? Not that I could tell. You?"

"Nobody."

Rif wandered over to the same chair he had sat in the day before when Dr. Gibson had arrived. He sank down and stared at Paul, neither saying a word. Rif pulled out a crumpled package of cigarettes and took out a smoke. It was crushed and bent. Paul watched as Rif tried to roll it between both his hands to straighten it out. The cigarette broke, and Rif cursed. Upending the packet, Rif eased the last cigarette out. It was bent as well, but this time Rif just huffed and lit it. Taking a few quick puffs, Rif looked at the cigarette critically before hanging it in his mouth and focusing on Paul.

Paul pulled his feet off the desk and sat up. "What do you think?"

"About the kid?"

"Yep."

Rif took another puff and thought for a moment. "Not a pleasant job. Are we sure it's her?"

"I looked her up again, this time thinking she was a child. There's no doubt, Rif. Jillian Caldwell is the kid we saw with Dr. Gibson."

Rif reached behind his right ear and slowly scratched and massaged his neck. "This is going to be one for the books, ain't it?"

"What do you mean?"

"I've never killed a kid before. You, Paul?"

"No. Never."

"It can't be much different though, can it? I mean," Rif took another puff of his cigarette, "you shoot them, and they die."

"I imagine."

"Well then, I guess that is it."

Paul felt a roiling in his stomach.

"I don't know, Rif. It doesn't seem like something we should do. You know kids are off-limits."

"Most the time."

"Yeah, and good reason too. If people started taking out kids, all hell would break loose." Paul rested his elbows on his desk and put his head in his hands. "It's an unwritten rule, Rif. That's why you've never done it before—why I haven't. And the assignment didn't come through normal channels. It just feels wrong."

"You're not saying we ignore the contract, are you, Paul?"

Paul opened his desk drawer and took out the golden coin. He flipped it onto his desk. "Why not?"

Rif's face grew hard, and his voice stern. "I know you're not a Syrch baby. You didn't grow up on a Syrch world." Rif gathered himself. "Paul, you don't say no to the corporation. I don't like the idea of killing this brat either, but we have a contract. You checked its validity. That girl is a liability for reasons we do not, and don't want, to know. We don't decide who gets it. Most the time, we don't know why. But we do it all the same. If you want to survive here, Paul, you've got to get that through your thick head."

"But a kid, Rif," Paul replied. "Maybe we should decide sometimes. Maybe we should walk this one back."

"You know we can't. They'd punish us by throwing us into some shallow grave."

"I've changed corporations before."

"What?" Rif snorted. "Militan? That piss-ant corporation on Telakia? They wouldn't sneeze without a green light from Syrch, and you know it! And even with all of Syrch behind you, how many times did those … ants … try to knock you off? Remind me, Paul. Six. It was six times. Where do you imagine, in this entire, wide universe, we could hide from Syrch Corp? Tell me that, Paul! You'd have to be fucking crazy-stupid or insane to think we can walk away from this contract. And to what end? They'll just get some other enforcer to do it. You know that! Someone we know will get that job right after the division gives out two more coins—one for you and one for me."

"Rif …"

"No, I'm not done." Rif's voice dropped back down, and he sipped at his cigarette. "You listen to me for a change. I know you're a golden boy and all that, but you can't say no to this contract. That would be the end. And I don't know about you, but if it's between me and that little girl, then I'll take me. And you know I'm right."

The two men sat for a moment glowering at each other. The smoke from Rif's cigarette filled the room with an acidic yet nutty smell.

Finally, Paul dropped his eyes, reached into his desk, and pulled out his flask of bourbon. Instead of the shot glass, he reached into the larger, lower drawer and pulled out two reasonably clean half glasses and poured some into both. He pushed one across to Rif and took the other.

"It can't be that much different, Rif. Can it? I mean … the mechanics of it."

Rif relaxed and shrugged. "No. It'll be just the same."

Paul didn't believe that. But Rif was right. They had a contract. It didn't matter why. And they were both professionals. It was a hard life. Paul just had to be equally as hard.

It's just some dumb brat.

The bourbon was oaky; it had a hint of caramel and felt smooth. The liquor had a bit of a sting as it went down Paul's throat. Paul looked at the gold coin sitting on his desk. Outside, the wind pushed rain against the window, and clouds fled across the sky. Rif was right. He could do this. It was just another job.

"Okay, then," Paul said. "Let's get it over with."

4

—∘○○◯○○∘—

THE DEATH OF HONOR

PAUL SAT tensely in the passenger-side seat of the car Rif had procured. The weather report had been right. The storm broke up at midday, and the mixed light from the system's sun and the distant, hulking Blue Giant, bathed the city in their combined light. They were parked a few blocks up from the Frederick Taylor Industrial School for the Gifted, which Jillian Caldwell attended. A small, hand-sized device sat between Paul and Rif. On it was a digital display of the city road system, centered on the industrial school, and a red dot showed where the girl's limousine driver had pulled the car into the school's circular driveway. Rif was rambling while Paul tried to steady his nerves. His heart beat hard in his chest, and his palms felt sweaty. He took a series of deep breaths, held them, and slowly released. The old shooting trick normally worked to steady his hands, but this time it seemed nothing he did released the building pressure.

Paul thought he knew why Syrch Corp did not flub this job to a contract specialist. The advantage with contracted help was that they came with a set cost. Any thug could kill someone. And there were almost no additional overhead costs to using a contractor, like long-term health insurance and retirement plans. As cheap as Syrch was in its regard to labor, eking as much profit out of each project regardless of fair wages or quality of workmanship, Syrch took a much more interested approach in how it handled delicate business. For things like high-profile assassinations, Syrch Corp wanted people with a long-term interest in their personal relationship and welfare with Syrch. Contrary to what most people thought, Syrch did not believe you could buy loyalty. You earned it. Part of that hook, Paul knew, was creating a special class of corporate citizens. These executives and other specialists were surprisingly well compensated. They were reminded now and again about what it was like to work on a corporate world when you were not part of the elite and concurrently told how special they were for being so damn smart. It was a potent and heady mix. It kept the executives, managers, and specialists in line. However, that privilege came with a certain understanding. You never turned your back on the corporation. Why hadn't Syrch used contract killers? Employees were loyal—or dead—and knew how to keep their mouths shut. Paul understood this when he joined. So what had he been thinking? No wonder Rif had been so angry with him. Paul had almost done the unthinkable. He had almost said no to Syrch.

The vibration of the car was noticeable as they sat in idle. It was a nondescript, four-door sedan that Syrch built in-system. It was for domestic consumption only. The vehicle reminded Paul of the brutishness of a boxer, not the delicate balance of a ballerina—like the Elemental Spider that Lin Corp engineered. That was an elegant machine. But the car Rif had found would serve its purpose. It was exactly like the other five hundred thousand Syrch-built machines meandering through the city. There was nothing flashy about it. And that was what one wanted when one hoped to get away from a daylight kidnapping.

It was one of the odd things about the corporate universe that Paul still pondered. It wasn't like there was no civil government, no civil authority. Papen's World had a senate, lorded over by a minister president, but the CEO of Syrch Corp had the ungodly power to ignore, overrule, and replace members of the esteemed body at will. The CEO could also create laws by edict. The closest historical form that compared was that of an absolute monarchy—if it were combined with traditional mafia structures. However, the CEO for Syrch was more interested in profits and expansion of Syrch's zone of control into other systems than in ruling the rabble. Syrch therefore had in-system governors to assist in meshing civil life to corporate life, and those individuals held enormous power. But it was still a partnership. And there were still rules. Paul was consequently concerned about clashing with the civilian police, who answered to the city's popularly elected mayor. During the confusion of a kidnapping, the police might make the mistake of interfering. Knowing the baseness of this particular job, and knowing Syrch would not like the general public to find out it had ordered the killing of a child, Paul and Rif just might not get the full backing of the corporation if they were caught. It was better to do the job quickly and quietly and avoid any complications.

"Looks like the kids are getting out," Rif said. He shifted in his chair and glanced at his side mirrors. "I can see other cars stacking up for pickup."

Paul smiled tightly. "I'm ready."

He pulled his pistol out of his shoulder rig and gave it a final once-over. It was a thin weapon, almost dainty—the Malcom Mouser—with a seven-inch-long barrel that had an embedded laser sight. Paul preferred the Mouser to the heavier piece he had carried the other day. The Mouser's grip was custom fitted to Paul's hand and was coated with a rubbery substance to prevent it from slipping; it used case-less ammunition, had a twenty-five-round magazine, and was nonmetallic, making it difficult to detect using scanners. The only problem with it was its obturating ring. The obturating ring was a relatively soft material that expanded inside the chamber when the weapon was fired, forming a pressure seal that allowed the weapon to mechanically reset and seat the next round. But the ring needed constant attention. The manufacturer recommended replacing the ring every three thousand rounds to prevent a failure of sealing and the consequent stoppage of the weapon. Yet as long as the obturating ring was functioning at peak performance, Paul found the little gun to be highly reliable. To help ensure it would work on this job, Paul had changed the ring the previous night and fired about a hundred rounds. It worked like a charm.

Paul and Rif sat patiently as children got into vehicles and the chaotic process of leaving school got into full swing. It didn't take long before the limousine waiting for Jillian Caldwell began to move, the red dot of the tracking device inching its way from the school. Rif eased their vehicle into the flow of traffic and began an easy drive along the route the limousine was most likely to use. If things went well, the limousine would fall in somewhere behind Paul and Rif. There was a slight chance it would take an odd turn, but from what Paul had seen of the way the driver maneuvered the vehicle in the morning, that was unlikely. Whatever countermeasure training this particular driver had was long forgotten in the monotonous nature of daily routine. And if it didn't work out, Paul and Rif had a second plan.

Paul pulled the brim of his black woolen Homburg hat down along the ridgeline of his eyebrows. Flexing his firing hand, he seated his pistol in it until it felt like a natural extension of his hand. He prepositioned his left hand on the door release.

The traffic moved steadily. Rif was driving a little slower than the surrounding traffic, encouraging vehicles to pass on their left. In this way, the limousine carrying Jillian Caldwell slowly caught up to the enforcers.

"Two cars back now," Rif said.

"We've got some time," Paul replied. "Let's give them a chance to get closer to clear out the attack area and minimize possible injuries to bystanders."

"Yeah, okay," Rif agreed.

The two men sat quietly. Paul wiped absently with his coat sleeve at sweat that pebbled his cheek. He suspected the driver was armed. Rif had not been able to confirm that, but it made sense. Dr. Gibson was an executive for Syrch Corp, though a low-level one, and would rate a chauffeur/bodyguard. The chauffeur could not be too good at his job, though. He was either a newbie, a below-average bodyguard, or someone nearing retirement. Still, Paul would have to deal with the chauffeur quickly. Then he would pull the girl into the other car, and Rif would drive off to the abandoned warehouse where they would finish the job. Paul wanted the snatch to look like a kidnapping and the girl's death to imply it was the result of bumbling incompetence. Dumb criminals do stupid things. In that way, Paul hoped to hide the fact that it was actually an assassination.

Paul waited a few tense minutes as the limousine came nearer.

"Okay," Rif said. "We got them. They're right behind us. Does it look good to you?"

"Wait." Paul pointed quickly to a spot just up the street. "Let's do it before the next road junction. Less places for the driver to maneuver."

Rif nodded.

Paul took a final deep breath.

Rif turned on the emergency blinkers and, near the designated point, suddenly stopped the vehicle. Paul slipped out of the passenger-side door and walked briskly toward the back of the car, moving to the driver's side of the limousine. Paul could see the chauffeur staring at him through the window screen. The driver raised his hands in silent question as Paul saddled up to the driver's-side door. Without hesitation, Paul raised his weapon and pointed at the chauffeur's head. The chauffeur's eyes widened just before Paul began shooting. The glass window broke, and shards fell in rivulets against the roadway. Blood sprayed the inside of the limousine as the chauffeur's skull collapsed inward and exploded out the back. Paul used the barrel of his pistol to knock some of the broken glass aside. He reached into the limousine and switched off the engine, then pulled the driver's door open. It took Paul a moment to find the door release switch. He punched it and heard the metallic click as the rear doors unlocked. Paul pivoted and pulled the back door open. Leading with his pistol, he leaned into the car and came face-to-face with Jillian Caldwell.

Jillian was extremely young. There was a spatter of the chauffeur's blood on her little yellow and black dress. She stared wide-eyed at Paul, clutching her school backpack, a half-eaten fruit snack lying forgotten on her lap. She had a cherub face with dark brown eyes and deep, dark hair that hung past her shoulders in a heap of natural curls. Her feet were suspended above the floor of the limousine, the girl's petite legs being too short to reach the floor. Two dainty yellow leather shoes dangled on her feet. Shock and horror reflected in her eyes.

Paul tried not to look at those eyes.

Paul pushed his pistol back into its holster and reached into the vehicle, unlatching the girl's seat belt and grabbing her by her arm. She didn't resist as Paul pulled her from the car, slapped the backpack out of her arms to the ground, and quickly returned to where Rif was waiting. A few cars had stopped behind the limousine and began honking their horns impatiently. Paul ducked into the car and closed the door with one hand as Rif leisurely began driving away. Paul looked over the top of the little girl's head at Rif. His partner was scowling and rapidly shifting his eyes from the rear mirrors to the road ahead. They turned as they moved away from the scene. Paul held the girl and for the first time noticed that the girl's body was shaking.

"Why are you doing this?" Jillian's voice was thin and sweet.

Paul flinched as one of Rif's hands lashed out and cracked the girl on the face.

"No talking," Rif said. "If you say another word, I'll kill you."

Jillian cried. Paul held her tightly. There was a dull sound in Paul's ears as if he were submersed in water, and every muscle in his body was taut.

Paul and Rif exchanged a grim look.

What are we doing? Paul wondered.

Rif drove the car from street to street, changing direction often, keeping a sharp eye for the police. Paul sat quietly. The car's engine rumbled, and the girl cried.

Rif took the car to an overpass and plunged ahead. In a few minutes, he took an exit to an industrial area where he turned sharply down a neglected maintenance road. Ahead of them, a hulking and dilapidated building, its windows broken and paint peeling from its walls, sat like some ancient devil along the riverside. Weeds grew out of cement along the building's sides, and the roadway leading to it was crumbled in disrepair. The tires ground, and Rif drove past the building, deeper into the old industrial complex of several buildings that had not seen any use for twenty or more years. The car jostled along the jagged road lined by wild trees that were slowly reclaiming the industrial park's grounds. The nearby river was brown and churned relentlessly past rusted vehicles and abandoned equipment. Finally, Rif turned toward the river and pulled next to a ruin of a warehouse, its wide receiving doors perpetually open to vehicle bays that were littered with rubbish, dirt, and old leaves. Rif stopped the car.

Paul watched Rif get out of the car and stand outside for a moment, his hands on his hips. He bent down and looked back at Paul.

"Come on."

Using his left hand, Paul opened his door, pushing it harshly. It swung back toward him, and he stopped it with his foot. Stepping out of the car, Paul pulled the girl with him. She was light as a feather. Paul felt giddy, and his legs felt wobbly. He looked at Rif over the top of the car. Their eyes met. Rif seemed to be chewing on his teeth. Rif glanced at the girl and then quickly began walking into the depths of the warehouse.

Paul used both hands to lift the girl to the roof of the car where he sat her down for a moment to adjust his grip. He noticed that his hands were wet, and a flush of ammonia assaulted his nose. As he brought his head up, he noticed that the girl had urinated all over her dress. When Paul's eyes met the girl's, the electric shock of guilt ran through his arms, and for a moment he was frozen in place.

"Paul!" Rif's voice snapped. Rif was waiting in the shadow of the warehouse.

Picking the girl up again, Paul slung her across his hip and moved dreadfully toward the shadows. A slight breeze was blowing through the trees, and the sound of the river, swollen with the morning rain, mocked him. Leaves and dirt shuffled under his feet as the tang of mold and urine mixed together, swirling about him. He handed the kid to Rif and followed his partner back into the warehouse. In a corner between an old office, where a broken chair and desk still lingered, and a dividing wall, Rif stopped.

"Stand over there," Rif ordered, putting the girl down and shoving her into the corner. The girl only came up to his waist. When the girl didn't move far enough back, Rif pushed her roughly and removed his pistol from his holster.

"It's nothing personal, kid," he grumbled.

5

---∘-∘-○-◎-○-∘-∘---

CHANGES

SILENCE. PAUL'S ears were not working. He shook his head several times and looked away from Jillian and Rif. The warmth of Jillian's pee was rapidly cooling on his hands. It was pungent. Time crawled by, and Paul's thoughts ran jagged and unfocussed. A picture of the little girl's curly hair, her flushed cheeks, wide eyes, and ruined, yellow dress danced before him. He felt sick. The cruel world echoed an empty chorus of heartbeats that pounded against his temples. He closed his eyes and swore.

"Rif, don't." Paul put a restraining hand on his partner's shoulder. Rif shrugged him off.

"Rif!"

Rif shoved at Paul. "Stop it!" he snapped. "I'm doing it!"

"Rif!"

But Rif ignored Paul. He squared his shoulders and brought the pistol sights up to eye level.

Paul's pivot was lightning quick. Paul threw a quick jab to Rif's kidney, then ducked in under Rif's shooting hand and, lifting with his legs, put Rif's arm in a straight arm bar while simultaneously forcing Rif's arm up into the air. Paul was the smaller of the two men but used the surprise of the attack to his best advantage. Paul rotated outward so that he faced away from Rif. Grabbing Rif's pistol toward the front of the receiver, Paul twisted and pushed the weapon toward Rif's body. The weapon came away freely, and Paul tucked it into his chest.

Then the counterblows began.

Rif was burly, a deep-chested thug of a man with years of practice and training. He stepped into Paul while throwing a jab at the back of Paul's neck. Paul fell to one knee, and though he suddenly felt like vomiting, he braced his left arm on the ground and, using his right leg, kicked back, striking Rif in a stinging blow about three inches from Rif's knee. Though the blow created a little space, Rif absorbed most of it, and before Paul could regain his feet, Rif piled into him, smashing Paul to the ground and pinning him there. Paul struggled but could not break free.

"Damn you, Paul! What is your problem?" Rif hissed. There was a series of furious hand movements as Paul tried to shake Rif from off his back. "We had this settled," Rif grunted. He struck Paul two more times on the spine of the neck, rose up a few inches above Paul, and collapsed back down, driving his knee like a hammer into the center of Paul's back.

Stunned, Paul lost control of Rif's weapon, and the world swam and dimmed.

Rif picked his pistol off of the floor and gained his feet. "You ass!" Rif exclaimed. He kicked at Paul, landing a solid blow on Paul's ribs. All the air in Paul's lungs rushed out. Rif looked around for the girl and saw her lithe form dart out of the open delivery doors into the yard beyond.

"Damn!" Rif ignored Paul and scuttled after the girl.

"Rif, don't!" Paul wheezed. He struggled to his knees and then his feet. Stumbling through the shadows and debris, Paul lurched toward the door. He heard Jillian screech and the sound of a powerful slap. When he got to the opening, he saw Jillian cowering on the ground as Rif loomed above, his pistol moving into line with the little girl's head. "Rif, don't!" Paul pulled his weapon out of its holster and raised it with a shaking hand at his partner.

Rif glanced back at Paul. "Don't be a fool, Paul. We have to do this."

"Don't!"

There was a slight shifting in Rif's weight toward the girl, a barely perceptible rotation of his hips. Paul fired. His bullet struck Rif in the upper back with a resounding thud. Rif's arms flew wide and he reflexively fired three rounds into the air as he crumpled face-forward to the ground.

Jillian kicked away from the big man and the blood that had splattered across her legs and over the ground. A thick, rosewood-colored blood—deep and dark red—began pooling by Rif's body.

Rif moaned and struggled to roll over. The effort was too much. Instead he twisted his head and looked at the little girl. Paul moved to him and rolled the enforcer onto his back.

"Rif?" Paul shook his head.

Rif tried to smile, but the best he could manage was a feral grin. "You dirty bastard," he accused.

"I couldn't do it, Rif. I can't do that type of killing."

Rif laughed softly, his breathing ragged.

"Rif?"

Red foam bubbled out of Rif's mouth. His eyes glazed over.

"Rif?" Kneeling at Rif's side, Paul rested a hand on his partner's neck. No pulse.

Paul felt a swelling of anger. Looking up, he noticed Jillian still lying in the dirt. Her mouth and lip were bleeding, and a purple and red swell covered her cheek. "Don't you run," he warned.

Pushing himself up, Paul walked over to the girl. "Get up. Get up!"

Jillian stood, cupping her hand over her face.

Paul looked at her for a moment. He sighed. "Get back in the car."

Jillian shook her head no.

Paul snatched Jillian by the front of her dress and started dragging the little girl to the car. She tried to pull away, and this made Paul angrier. He picked the girl up and held her at face level.

"Get ... in ... the ... car."

Opening the front, passenger-side door, Paul tossed the child into the seat and slammed the door. Hobbling around the front of the car, Paul got into the driver's seat and started the engine. He looked at the body of his partner a final time before slipping the car into drive and pulling away. At the entrance to the abandoned industrial park, he stopped the car and looked at Jillian.

"Hey, kid. Put your seat belt on."

"What?"

"Your seat belt ... put it on." Jillian seemed confused, so Paul leaned across and fastened the belt around her.

"Are you taking me home?" Jillian asked.

"No."

"I want to go home," she insisted.

"No. No you don't."

"I want my daddy!"

Something sparked in Paul's head. He whipped around and hissed, "He's not your father." The words thrummed harshly. "Your mother and father are dead! Dead! Do you hear me? The man you think is your father—Dr. Warner Gibson—commissioned me and my late partner to kill you. Do you understand that? Do you! You have no father!"

"That's not true!" Jillian yelled. "You're a liar! Liar!" Wracking sobs shook the little girl. "I want my daddy! I want my dad!"

"Enough!"

Paul let off the brake and drove the car back toward the interchange. "Your mother and father are dead. They have been for years. If you don't want to join them, you need to shut up and let me think."

"I ..."

"Quiet!"

Jillian leaned her head against the door and cried.

6

--◦-◦-○-◎-○-◦-◦--

REFLECTIONS

PAPEN'S WORLD has a large, interconnected oceanic system. Part of Syrch Corp's initial terraforming effort had been seeding the oceans with diatoms to produce oxygen and provide a basis for a marine food chain. Syrch then brought in thousands of ocean species from earth and, using great reproductive vats, seeded the oceans with life. While it was primarily supposed to be a cheap oxygen and food resource, the terraforming project resulted in booming tourism. Ships of all sizes churned their way through the waters, carrying tourists from the local star system or moving manufactured goods and fishing products between the planet's six continents. It was one of the few charms of Papen's World.

In a strip of forty islands in the Great Ocean was Paul's favorite getaway spot, Bektov Island with its rough hills covered with jungle; prominent cliffs rising several hundred feet above the surf on the northern shore; and resplendent, white, sandy beaches that lounged peacefully at the water's edge. When vacationing on

Bektov Island, Paul always stayed in the tiny village of Mekajiki. Nestled in the Bay of Joy, the village offered a simple lifestyle and sported several restaurants and dives that served a variety of local seafood. True to his nature, Paul avoided the tourist trap of nearby Kuchin City. Paul thought of it as hell on earth. But a soulless day in Kuchin City, with its trite resorts and artificial quaintness, was preferable to sitting in an abandoned and leaky construction trailer in the ship graveyard near Traitor's Point. The rotting hulks of ships were strewn like chaff along the river's edge and out into Kendrack Bay. The water reeked and was tinted with rust, and even the air seemed diseased and damaged. Slick vermin scurried about, and oily dust clung to almost everything. Yet it was safe. The hazardous state of the ship graveyard guaranteed no visitors and no curious eyes. And Paul needed the privacy. He could not count on Syrch Corp's support. The public optics were too bad. Paul had kidnapped a Syrch executive's daughter, almost murdered her, and then murdered a Syrch employee. It was a tabloid's dream story. And that didn't take into account his failing to live up to the contract he had been issued. Anyway Paul looked at his situation, it reeked.

Then there was the girl.

Jillian Caldwell was sleeping on an old mattress that was tucked into the corner of the construction trailer. The mattress squeaked every time the little girl moved. Jillian was still wearing the pee-stained yellow and black dress and matching yellow leather shoes. Her hair was a tasseled mess. She had her legs pulled nearly to her chest and had an arm under her head and a dirty, old pillow. She looked cold.

Paul draped his coat over the child and then stood silently above her, watching her sleep. He couldn't go directly back to Syrch Corp and ask them for help. What would he tell them? Paul knew very little about what was actually happening. He couldn't go to the police. That would be worse. He couldn't kill the kid. And he couldn't give the kid back to Dr. Gibson either. It was a real mess.

Paul rubbed at his face, massaging his temples. He felt drained. His body ached, and his ear bled softly. Why hadn't Rif been more reasonable? Paul couldn't think of a single time in his career that he had seen such blind devotion to the letter of the contract. It hadn't mattered to Rif that the coin had been delivered by Dr. Gibson and had not been sent via courier or proffered during a one-on-one with their section chief. It had not bothered Rif too much that the assignment had been, to all outward appearances, a loving little girl. Rif had not been the brightest light, and he fell short in the area of morality—an advantage in certain lines of work. But even he should have seen the inconsistencies in the assignment.

Dragging a beaten chair into the center of the little rectangular room, Paul sat gloomily down and stared at his hands. Uncomfortable, he slouched down and looked at the blank walls of the construction trailer. He was angry: angry at Syrch Corp for giving him the assignment; angry at Dr. Gibson for being a horrid person; angry at Rif for his lack of imagination; angry at the kid for being normal; and most particularly, he was angry at himself. If he had not allowed the shock of the revelation that their target was a nine-year-old child so unsettle him, Paul could have handled the situation differently. He could have asked Dr. Gibson for more information. He could have talked to his boss. He could have forced Rif to—what? Not be Rif? Paul chuckled. It was more likely the Church of Chaos would get organized than Rif would deviate from his basic nature. Still, the mistakes were avoidable. All of them.

Paul was to blame. His lack of clarity had led to Rif's death. He was so concerned about being a tough guy and following orders that he had not evaluated the assignment.

Maybe taking this job with Syrch Corp had been a mistake too. He had been comfortable in his role working for Militan Corp. He and the CEO had an understanding. In contrast, Syrch Corp was impersonal, a vast machine of offices spread over many systems. Flat, Syrch Corp's internal business culture, was Spartan, and the central, civilian culture was not much better. The people on Syrch worlds were inoculated in the power of the corporation—much like Rif. To the people born and raised on Syrch corporate worlds, the corporation was everything. Father, mother, brother, sister, priest, and executioner, the corporation was revered and feared. Paul had not thought about those things when he accepted the position. All he had seen was getting out of a dead-end job, getting into a prime system, and all the pay and extra benefits that came with being a lackey for Syrch. Paul had been drunk on the possibilities.

Jillian stirred. She pulled Paul's coat up to her chin. Her breathing was delicate.

What was he going to do with her?

Paul felt drowsy. His thoughts lacked clarity. Paul considered getting onto the rickety bed with the sleeping girl but felt that would somehow be an unwanted intrusion. Instead he stood up and walked over to the wall. He kicked at the dirty floor and then sat down, resting his back against the wall, his legs stretched out. He had managed to lock the door so the kid could not escape, and he needed to sleep. But he sat numbly as the system's star began to set.

The trailer grew dark. Outside, the light from the distant Blue Giant star covered Papen's World with its violet aura as the small moons rotated into view. The trailer creaked and groaned slightly in the wind. Paul looked at Jillian, huddled under his coat, and felt a wave of sadness well up in him. Dipping his head, he looked at the shoes on his feet. His head lolled, and he slipped into an uncomfortable sleep.

7

⊶∘⊸○⊶∘⊸

ALLIANCE

STIFF, HIS mouth dry and dusty, Paul awoke to find Jillian Caldwell staring at him.

"I'm hungry," she said.

Paul's back and ribs hurt. The floor he had slept on was hard and cold. Paul blinked several times. He still felt tired.

"I'm hungry." Jillian was sitting on the mattress with her back to the wall. She held Paul's coat up under her chin.

Sitting up, Paul groaned. "Hungry? Well, kid, I … I have to pee."

It took Paul a moment to get his body working again. He struggled to his feet, cursed, and stretched. He could feel the beginnings of a headache. Walking to the door, he fumbled with the makeshift lock, pulled out his pistol, and slowly opened the door. The morning was a dull haze of cool mist. He looked back at Jillian.

"You stay here. Understand?" He stepped out the door and stopped, turning back when he heard the bed springs creak. "And where are you going?"

Jillian stood sullenly before the bed. "I have to use the restroom too."

Paul sighed. "Restroom is so … formal. I was just going to pee on some old, rusted hunk of metal. There are no restrooms here, kid."

"But I have to go."

"All right. All right." Paul waved his hand, beckoning. "Come on. We'll find you a private corner. Be mindful of all this rusted junk. Don't get cut by any of it or you're likely to get tetanus. It's a disease. Nasty. And no running away. We're in the middle of nowhere, kid. There is no place for you to go. Then we'll come back and eat something."

Paul had figured they would both be hungry, so he had slipped out early in the morning and bought a few sandwiches, chips, and sodas. It might not be the most wholesome meal, but it was better than nothing.

The morning bodily rituals complete, Paul offered Jillian what he had for food and absently picked at his own sandwich. He watched as Jillian ate with zest, remembering that she had not had any dinner. There had been no time. But now he had a few hours, and Paul needed to figure out what he was going to do.

"You know, kid. It's a real pickle. Do you know what is going on? Have you figured it out? No? Well, I'm a Syrch enforcer." Paul looked at the girl to see how she reacted to that news. She stopped eating for a moment, looked down at her legs, and almost started to cry. But she gathered herself and started eating slowly.

"You know what that is then?" Paul asked rhetorically. "Good. You see, Rif and I—my late partner—were given a job to do. And that, little one, was you. A valid contract." He shook his head. "It just doesn't make any real sense. As far as I know, Syrch Corp doesn't kill little kids. But it was their order. And it came from your uncle, Dr. Warner Gibson."

"My uncle? You mean my father?"

"Just eat, kid. It's not important."

Jillian continued to eat as Paul thought out loud.

"You know, I did a little job on Telakia. I killed four people to cover up a mess, and there was one more person to kill. But I didn't do it. Do you know why? Um? I'll tell you. Syrch Corp realized that the only other person involved in the profit loss was a little girl. A baby, really. And though they had to give up quite a finder's fee of credits, for which the other four had already been killed, they backed away. It must have cost Syrch billions. Come to think of it," Paul paused and scratched at his face, "I killed those other people for nothing. Syrch still lost the money. Life! But I'm off track.

"You know, Syrch's backing off of that killing is one of the primary reasons why I came to work for them. Each corporation is different. Self-aggrandizing Terra Corp—they think they are the ultimate in business professionals. And, who knows, maybe they are. Lin—they are full of themselves and think they are in harmony with the universe. I don't think I would fit in either of those organizations. But Syrch is less pretentious. Syrch is not obsessed with corporate pride, and they don't delude themselves with semireligious, universal harmony. Syrch is profit bound. What makes sense makes sense, without all the hype. There are hundreds of lesser corporations too. My point is that they all have their own culture, moral, and ethical bounds.

"Did you know," Paul asked, "that not a single one of the corporations support the contracted killing of children? Not one. You'd figure there would be at least one with a culture that allowed it. Strange. Why do you think that is? You know in corporate space, there must be tens of billions of people. What is the value of one little life when there are that many people standing around? None. Life has become cheap.

"Take me for instance. I don't suffer from any illusions. If I were to die, do you think Syrch Corp would have any problems finding a replacement? My body would still be warm, and there would be someone sitting in my office eating my stash of snacks and drinking my bourbon. Hell, if you really wanted to, you could probably shoot me and clone my replacement from my carcass. It would be cheaper too—no retirement, but you retain the skillset. See what I mean?"

Jillian did not answer.

"No contracted killing of little kids—in a way, it's mind-blowing."

Paul was quiet for a minute. Jillian, looking small and frail, took up the other half of her sandwich.

"I've thought about this a lot," Paul said. "The coin—the contract—was valid. But maybe it wasn't sanctioned. Maybe the good doctor somehow circumvented the process, or knew someone who has access, and he just took a coin. It can't be very difficult to get one programed when you have access to Syrch's own computer kit. See, now, that makes sense to me. An unsanctioned hit, getting Syrch's own muscle to handle it—slick. Really slick. And then at the end, your uncle gets to play the martyr. But why? Why would your uncle wish you dead? Are you loaded? Do you have a vast fortune or something? No?"

Jillian shook her head.

"It has to be something," Paul continued. His sandwich lay forgotten in his hand.

"Did you know he is not your father? Dr. Gibson."

Jillian shook her head again.

"He told me that your parents died in a mining accident," Paul lied. The lie was a small one, as it omitted the part about Syrch Corp having killed Jillian's parents for being corporate spies. But he figured the girl was already dealing with a lot. "He said he is your uncle and that he adopted you. Did he ever tell you that?"

"No."

Paul sighed. He had been a little blinded by the doctor's position as a Syrch executive. Paul realized he had taken most of what the doctor said for granted, though he had claimed to Rif that he didn't believe a single word the doctor had said. The executive mantle had reared its ugly head. Paul had always been less than impressed with powerful people and people with titles. He actually found their posturing a bit ludicrous and funny. But Paul had a strange sense of humor. Yet that had not protected Paul when the good doctor arrived, spouting off about the board of directors. Working for Syrch Corp seemed to have gone a little to his head, and that mistake had cost Rif his life. Paul should have been more discerning. He liked Rif. What had happened to his partner was not right. But from where he sat, Paul could not think of any way to make it right. What wasn't he seeing?

"Maybe the doctor isn't your uncle," Paul finished his thought out loud. Wasn't that part of the basic facts that Paul had swallowed? But if Dr. Gibson was not Jillian's uncle, who was Jillian?

"Jillian, do you remember your mother?"

She shook her head no.

"Have you seen your mother's photo?"

Again, no. But this time Jillian started to cry. Her mouth was full of sandwich, but that didn't keep her from sobbing. Paul was afraid she was going to choke.

"Whoa." He moved to the edge of the bed and gently took Jillian's sandwich away, placing it on the paper grocery bag that she was using as an impromptu plate. "Careful now. Calm down. Finish your food. Then cry."

Though it was difficult, Jillian swallowed the food. "He has to be my dad," she managed. She looked up at Paul.

"I'm sorry," Paul replied. "But maybe we can find out for sure."

"DNA?"

Paul looked at Jillian curiously. "Perhaps."

"He has to be. He said he loves me!"

"Maybe," Paul tried, "he does—in some way." But Paul didn't believe it.

Jillian slunk forward and leaned into Paul, wrapping her arms around him and wept. Paul looked around the room nervously and then looked back down at the top of Jillian's head. He slowly dropped his arm on her back and patted Jillian gently. He could feel her whole body shiver and shake. And he was not sure what to do. So he sat there quietly, awkwardly holding her.

After several minutes, Jillian was spent. She pulled back a little and looked up at Paul, waiting.

"We need more information," Paul told the girl. "I'm sorry this is happening to you, but we need to understand it. If I can figure it out, then maybe we can make it better. Maybe we will both survive. Does your father have any private records at home? Or in his office?"

"I don't know about records," Jillian answered. "He has a computer."

"At work?"

"At home."

"The house computer?"

"Yes."

Most houses were controlled by central computers that handled everything from energy distribution to security monitoring. Some were simple, and some quite elaborate.

"Are you keyed to the system?"

"No. But …"

"Go on."

"I can hack into it."

Paul looked at Jillian, surprised for a second time.

"Your father … Dr. Gibson … said you had a cranial mesh implant. Is that true?"

"You mean a computer in my brain? No. I don't think so. I have a wireless implant."

"Is that why you think you can hack into the computer?"

"No. I think I can hack into it because I have before. I installed a back door. I'm really good at quantitative reasoning, and I like computers. Miss Harold says I have exceptional processing speed—I can do really complicated math in my head. And computers are giant math puzzles. I like puzzles. And besides, all the good shows are filtered out by the child-content filters, so I use the back door to get around them. I don't see what's so bad about those shows anyway. My favorite is *Martian Mysteries*. Do you know that one?"

"No, not really." Paul was thinking.

"Constable Lilac Jennings and Sergeant Jack Git solve murders, burglaries, get involved with spy stuff—and Jackson Montgomery is so cute. I might marry him one day."

"Excuse me?"

"Jackson Montgomery plays the bumbling Sergeant Jack Git. He is so cute and funny."

"How old are you?"

"Nine."

Paul had no idea if it was normal for nine-year-old girls to dream about marriage and have crushes on celebrities. It definitely was not normal for them to know enough about programing to install a back door into a computer system. There was something else too. Jillian seemed to switch between what Paul thought of as normal kid speech and a more developed adult style. Perhaps that was why Jillian was going to a school for the gifted. Paul was not sure why that fact suddenly seemed important. Instinct perhaps? Something about the way Jillian had looked when she spoke about mathematics tugged at Paul's mind, but he could not put his finger on why it seemed so important. What did she remind him of? He had seen that type of expression, heard that droll tone of voice before? Though it nagged at him, there was no meaning behind the feeling.

"How smart are you?"

Jillian looked quizzical.

"Have you ever taken an IQ test?" Paul asked.

"Oh, loads of times."

"And?"

"I normally score around 180."

"Is that good?"

"I guess so," Jillian mumbled. "Einstein was supposed to be between 160 and 170."

"So you're smarter than Einstein?"

"Well, I don't know. If you add in the Flynn effect, it's not that big of a deal. You might be as smart as Einstein."

Paul doubted that very much. "The Flynn effect? Oh, never mind. Look, kid." Paul scooted back a little. "Would you be willing to break into the doctor's computer for me? Maybe he has some files on it that explain his real relationship to you. It might help explain"—he made a helpless gesture—"all of this."

"He's my dad." Jillian's lips began to tremble.

"Maybe there will be something on the computer that explains why he told me otherwise," Paul offered, ignoring Jillian's statement. He tired another tact. "You said you like puzzles. This is a puzzle too, but I'm missing a few pieces. If I can get more information, then I'll be able to figure this out, and hopefully that will help me fix this mess."

"And I can go home?"

Paul looked at the little girl and shrugged. He wasn't going to lie to her. Even though Paul was not sure how he would fix their situation, he knew one thing. He couldn't give Jillian back to the man who had so easily brought in the coin that had marked Jillian for death.

"So you're not going to kill me? Please don't kill me," she added more softly.

Paul looked at the girl and leaned back. There was a burning sensation in his body that he could not readily identify. It made him feel uncomfortable, almost guilty.

"No, Jillian. I'm not going to kill you. But other people might try. And the only way to stop them is to figure out why a hit was put out on you by Syrch Corp. If we can get into your home computer, then we have a chance. I need your help. Will you help me?"

Jillian was quiet. Paul could tell the girl was thinking, but to what end Paul could not tell. Finally she nodded and mumbled a yes. Reaching out, Paul ran his hand over Jillian's head in what he hoped was a comforting manner. Jillian looked at him, and he smiled, but Paul thought their chances—his chances—were not so good. Syrch Corp would be angry. The corporation did not like people who failed them. And at this moment, Paul felt like the biggest failure of all time. It would surprise him, Paul realized, if he survived the day.

8

THE ARMORY BUILDING

PAUL STOPPED outside the main doors to the posh Armory Building. He pulled the collar of his coat up, pushed the brim of his Homburg down, and reached back, taking Jillian's hand. The little girl was standing next to him as vehicles drove by on Capital Street. Being early evening, people moved along the sidewalks, heading out for dinner or a night's entertainment. Capital Street was just off center of the most popular restaurant and shopping area. Two blocks to the west, the city sported high-end dining, while a little further near Carl Nyberg square, more affordable establishments lined the streets, nestled amongst many small shops and boutiques. Since the night was clear and cool, Paul knew the area would get more crowded as the evening wore on. While it meant there would be more eyes watching, Paul could also take advantage. It would be difficult for the city's security cameras to identify individuals due to rapid transit through each camera's focal points. Even with the use of advanced stereoscopic cameras that saw in three dimensions, it was extremely difficult to pick a specific face out of any given space. Much like the confusing effect of a herd of zebras milling about in constant motion, camera systems were not always able to ascertain where one person stopped and another began. Paul and Jillian could therefore mesh within the crowd and have a greater chance of maintaining their anonymity.

The doorman was a problem. But Paul couldn't just stand there like an idiot.

Paul pulled Jillian behind him. He had wrapped her in a coat he had bought to hide her dirty dress, and he had struggled to brush through her hair. Jillian was not the picture of perfection, but she would pass general observation.

"Miss Jillian's security escort," Paul said, showing his Syrch Corp credentials to the doorman. "Is her father home yet?"

"Hi, Miss Caldwell!" The doorman's voice was genuinely friendly. "How was your day?"

Jillian shrugged.

"We all have those days now and again, Miss Caldwell. No, sir," the doorman directed at Paul. "The doctor is not back from dinner yet."

"Well, I'll call him then," Paul replied, "and let Dr. Gibson know that I brought Jillian back home. Come on … Miss Caldwell. Let's get you out of the night air."

Paul had warned Jillian to behave and stay quiet. He had told her that he didn't want to have to shoot the doorman or anyone else. If she tried to get help from someone, that person would die, and Jillian would be at fault. The threat had the desired result. Jillian remained quiet.

"You have a good evening, Miss Caldwell," the doorman said.

The doorman didn't seem to know anything about the kidnapping. Paul had been counting on the doctor not being vocal about Jillian. It had been a big risk, but until the doctor knew what was going on, it would not be in his best interest to stir up the authorities. If the doctor had alerted the police to the kidnapping and spread the word around about his daughter, then the doorman would have had a more expressive and alarming reaction to seeing Jillian. So the doctor had remained quiet. It was a good sign.

Though Paul had no doubt that the driver's murder was being investigated by the local police, he also knew that the investigators would drop the case once they positively associated it with Syrch enforcement. The killing had been clean. No bystanders were injured. So it was strictly Syrch business. Of course, Paul knew that would all change once Dr. Gibson realized Jillian was alive and well. Paul's window of opportunity to move about freely would vanish once the doorman talked to the doctor and mentioned seeing Jillian. The doctor would know something was wrong. Paul gave the doctor another six hours of fretting before he contacted the police with some type of story, so this was likely the last time Paul would be able to freely move about the city. Paul had to make the most of the opportunity. After tonight, he would have to be more careful.

Paul and Jillian pushed through the revolving door and stepped into the grand entrance of the Armory Building. Art deco in style, the floor panels were of deep caramels and creams. Flecks of gold and green emerald showed in the natural seams of the marble. High chandeliers hung in the center of concave bowls that rippled across the ceiling. Deep, warm, amber marble walls, sporting geometric designs, tied smoothly into wall sconces with their cool metallic finishing. The sharpness of the reflective floors, combined with crystalline chandelier light, gave the entrance a feeling of liquidity. The bank of elevators on the left was equally as fashionable, with arching pieces of veneer in decorative patterns. Above each elevator was a different picture created out of bone, ivory, mother of pearl, and different woods. The picture above the elevator where Paul stopped depicted an old Venetian wharf. A healthy merchant in flowing robes sat upon a cargo crate. He seemed to Paul to be haggling with a cluster of less wealthy men as behind them all, in the distance, trade ships, with their sails drawn, bobbed at the docks on a quiet sea. The men in the picture wore hats with feathers, airy shirts and pantaloons, and short capes. A couple of them wore thin, dagger-sharp swords. There was some writing under the picture, but it was in a language Paul did not understand.

The opulence of the building made Paul feel a little uncomfortable, but he stood his ground, quietly waiting. There was a ding, and the elevator doors slid open revealing a mirrored interior trimmed with gold.

Paul and Jillian stepped into the elevator, and Paul pushed the button for the penthouse. The elevator beeped in annoyance.

"Would you, please," Paul said to Jillian, indicating the retinal scanner. He picked Jillian up, and she looked into the reader. A low-level red beam danced across Jillian's eyes, and the elevator door closed. The elevator began to move.

"Remember," Paul said, "you need to pack some new clothing and get changed. Once you are done with that, we will look at your father's computer. But we have to be quick about it."

Jillian nodded her understanding. She stood meekly, her hand tiny but warm, holding on to Paul's left hand. She looked up at Paul, and Paul smiled down at her.

The elevator opened directly into the penthouse. Long, sleek columns of charcoal-colored onyx framed a grand white staircase that descended from the entrance to a tiled, mosaic floor. The mosaic floor, an eight-pointed gray star filled with yellow tiles, with a smaller star embedded in its center, supported a wooden table where a dark pewter statue of a woman carrying a basket welcomed them into the home. The basket held a variety of colorful fresh flowers. To the left, an elongated room was framed in metal. White furniture filled the space, resting on a luxurious rug. The entire far wall overlooked huge windows that opened to a clean balcony and the city skyline. To the right, the marble-lined hall and arching ceiling led past a distressed vanity cabinet holding a decorative copper bowel. Above it, a sunburst mirror of polished nickel reflected a rich watercolor painting of some quaint, brick buildings by an azure sea, which hung on the opposite wall. A long emerald carpet ran the length of the hall, past several doorways that were trimmed in thin columns of matching onyx that blossomed at the top.

Jillian pulled away from Paul and began scampering down the hall.

"Jillian?" Paul warned.

"My room is over here," she said.

Paul sighed, tossed his hat on the oval table, and followed the girl. He had known that the doctor was rich, but he had not imagined the doctor could afford such a lavish place. Paul wondered, if the doctor was just a low-level executive in Syrch Corp, what were the lives of upper management like?

Following Jillian into her room, Paul watched as the little girl pulled out a suitcase and stuffed clothing in it. She paused a moment by a fancy, golden-colored vanity table with a large, oblong mirror. The vanity was decorated with wooden figures and horses. Before the vanity sat a matching, half-moon chair with pearl-white cushions. Jillian took a brush from the table and stuffed it in her suitcase.

Paul moved around the canopy bed with its billowing cover and glanced into a private bathroom. The claw-footed tub and shower dominated the space, but there was not another door.

Paul sat on the edge of the bed. "Jump in the shower, kid. I'll wait here."

Jillian picked some clothing out of her belongings and ducked into the bathroom, closing the door.

"Leave it unlocked," Paul warned. He had looked at the door when he scanned the bathroom. Though Paul could kick it in, he would prefer not going to such fuss.

"Okay!" Jillian whined back.

Paul sat silently on the bed, listening to the running water as Jillian showered. He thought the kid was doing pretty well, all things considered. Paul half-hoped that the doctor would stumble back home. Then the enforcer would be impelled to confront the man. But he was still worried about the coin and how Syrch Corp would react. If this was a legitimate contract, then confronting the doctor would not be wise. Somewhere, Paul hoped, the doctor had hidden something that would fill in the gaps in Paul's knowledge and give him what he desperately needed—a way out. Paul was counting on the doctor being dirty. Everyone had something to hide. And Paul knew he had to find it before the doctor or Syrch Corp figured out that the job wasn't done.

That thought gave Paul pause. He wondered if he could get to Lin or Terra Corp space if things went badly. He couldn't think of any transport off planet that wasn't controlled by Syrch. Maybe he could hide out on one of the deserted islands in the Great Ocean for a couple of years until things blew over. Of course, he thought wryly, there was a better chance he would morph into the Europan than there was that he could avoid Syrch on their home world. He just had to find something to clear himself. He just had to.

9

—○○○◯◯○○○—

LITTLE GENIUS

SHOWERED AND dressed, Jillian sat at the curved desk in her father's drawing room. Paul was sitting in a chair he had pulled up from the dining room, looking over the girl's shoulder as Jillian typed on a keyboard.

"It is not really a password," she was explaining. "I have the computer programed to respond to a series of strung-together subroutines that are preprogramed, symbolically, following the katakana system. You can string the subroutines together in almost any variation and get the computer to do things."

"You're programing it?"

"No. That's not what I said."

"Right."

"I'm just kind of … asking it to open up. There!" she said. "Now be quiet for a moment. Kitty …"

"Wait a minute."

"Please, the computer needs to hear my voice to unlock the back door. Oh, and I call her Kitty."

57

"Of course you do."

"Good evening, Kitty. Do I have any messages?"

The computer responded through hidden speakers in the room. "Good evening, Jillian. No new messages."

Jillian began typing again. Paul was unfamiliar with the characters on the keyboard. Instead of normal letters, oriental brush strokes were etched upon each key.

"I'm starting a search routine. You said I should look for something that is hidden. Nothing is really hidden in a computer system. People try, but being able to recover information, by definition, means that it is somehow marked for retrieval. Of course, Dad is not that computer literate. He used some commercial software to encrypt his files, but that was easy enough to get through. I went snooping once," she admitted. "But I didn't see anything interesting."

Paul watched as Jillian worked. Paul found the duality of her personality—her intellect—eerily disturbing. Jillian took to the computer like a scorpion to sand. Paul couldn't follow what the kid was doing, but he hoped she had heeded his warning and was not calling for help.

"That is strange," Jillian said.

"What is, kid?"

"Well ... the operating system has been reinstalled."

"Why is that so strange?"

"It looks like my dad shredded all the data files and then reinstalled the operating system. Why would he do that?"

"Can you recover the data?"

"No. He used something good. And it's mostly flash memory. It's not like the old days when there was a physical charge left on a hardware device even after it was deleted. Those old computers just removed the registries but left the data there."

"But if he reinstalled the operating system, how did you manage to get in? Wouldn't it destroy your back door?"

Jillian laughed. "You don't know much about computers, do you?"

"Not really."

"My stuff was not in the register or in the file allocation table. It is completely invisible. The computer itself doesn't know it is there."

"I thought you just said nothing is really hidden in a computer system."

"Right. But I wrote a ghost system that the real system doesn't recognize as being a system. Therefore, it does not exist."

"I'm not following you, kid." Paul shook his head, feeling dazed. "So there is no data there?"

"No."

"At least we know that your father—the doctor—has been covering his tracks. I guess we will have to somehow break into his office. I wanted to avoid that."

"Maybe not," Jillian offered. "Dad has a hiding place in his bedroom."

"A what?"

"It's a little hidden compartment. I've seen him use it before."

"Like a safe behind a portrait? Why didn't you tell me that before?"

Jillian shrugged. "You didn't ask. Come on, I'll show you. Good night, Kitty."

"Good night, Jillian," the computer responded.

Jillian pushed away from the desk, and Paul followed her into the master bedroom. Paul expected her to walk over to the wall and reveal some hidden safe. Instead, she walked to the ebony dresser and began examining the underside of the dresser's top that extended maybe half an inch from the body of the piece.

"There!" She pushed a button, and a section of the dresser's top shot open—a hidden, low drawer lined with green felt.

Paul walked over to look. There were a few unimportant papers and a data crystal.

"Can you download everything that is on the data crystal to a new one?" Paul asked. "I don't want to spend the time searching through it here. We should be going."

"It will take a minute." Jillian took the crystal, and Paul went with her back to the computer station.

It took a couple of minutes to make the transfer. Jillian gave Paul the copy, and Paul put the original back in the secret drawer. He had to give the doctor a little credit. The hidden compartment had a plastic mechanism and no metallic parts. The simple mechanical design of the release mechanism would make the device very difficult to detect using standard handheld search equipment.

"Come on, kid, it's time to go."

"Wait! I forgot something." Jillian ran back toward her room. In a moment, she popped back into the hall holding a small, fuzzy stuffed animal with floppy ears.

"Mr. Bunny," she explained.

Jillian took Paul's free hand. Paul carried her small suitcase in his other hand. It didn't leave a hand free to draw his weapon, but there was not much Paul could do about that. He stopped to grab his hat and then took hold of Jillian's hand again. Guiding Jillian back into the elevator, they rode to the lobby and stepped out into the night. Paul had the doorman flag them a taxi, which they took to the local transportation hub. Once there, Paul bought the two of them transit tickets on the monorail, and they climbed into one of the first-class cars. They were alone.

It was not long before Jillian's head began to loll. She rested it against Paul's right arm as the city flew by the transport's windows. The girl was becoming comfortable around Paul. He was not sure that was a good thing. What was equally strange was that Paul was beginning to feel the same way.

Paul let Jillian sleep until they came to a stop at a randomly selected station. Taking the sleepy child out, Paul flagged a new taxi. He repeated this process a few more times before taking a final taxi to where he had stashed his car. Paul didn't want anyone following him.

By the time they got back to the little construction trailer in the ship graveyard, Paul had to carry Jillian in and place her on the bed. He put his coat over her and locked the main door. He chided himself at having left the data crystal in his coat, and he gently fished it out, setting it aside, high above on an old wall-mounted shelf. Paul thought about crawling into the car to sleep, but he didn't want to leave Jillian alone. Instead he settled once again on the floor, expecting a terrible night, and thought about the little girl.

She was something—Jillian. Small and fragile, she had the calculating mind of an adult. And she had a good heart.

Paul watched Jillian sleep, her chest rising and falling almost imperceptivity. Jillian's cherub face was relaxed and, she unconsciously rubbed her nose for a moment.

Tomorrow Paul would have to find Jillian a computer. He hoped the little girl was as smart as he suspected. Though he was not sure what they would find on the data crystal, Paul was sure that it would incriminate the doctor. He just hoped it explained why Jillian was at the center of this mystery. If he could figure out why the doctor wanted Jillian dead, then he would know if his next planned step was suicidal or not. It was time, he knew, to bring in Syrch's Security Division. It was time to come clean about Rif. Paul smiled, rubbed at his tired jaw, and closed his eyes.

Maybe, he thought, it would also be time for him to die.

10

∘⟨∘⟨∘⟩⦿⟨∘⟩∘⟩∘

THE DATA CRYSTAL

MORNING DAWNED to thunder and a sheet of new rain. The sky was angry and churned with banks of black clouds. The wind whipped, and the rain skidded through the air almost horizontally. Jillian and Paul stood watching the pounding rain as water dripped from the leaky roof in several places. A small pool of water had formed on the floor, mixing with the accumulated dust, to form streaks of mud. A frontal depression of air had moved in overnight, resulting in high winds and thick rains. The squall line moved sluggishly. Lightning flashed, and the sky rumbled at regular intervals. It was so murky that Paul had to squint to see the car that was parked only twenty feet away. Paul knew that storms like these rushed out of the middle of the continent and developed when dryer air struck an opposing band of moist air from the ocean. The storms did not linger, but they were powerful, and it was always better to remain indoors than travel during the height of a squall. But Paul thought that Dr. Gibson knew that Paul and Jillian had been at his penthouse apartment. There was no doubt in Paul's mind that the doorman had told the doctor of the visit. Though the doctor would not find anything amiss in his apartment, Paul suspected Dr. Gibson would be wondering why Jillian was still alive. The doctor would be thinking about what he should do next. And Paul had to stay one step ahead.

"You ready?" Paul asked.

Jillian was wrapped up in her coat. She nodded.

Paul pulled his hat down tight. "Stay here. I'll get the car." And he stepped out into the storm, the wind ripping at his coat and the rain stinging his eyes. He splashed to his car and ducked inside, starting the engine and moving the car closer to the door. Reaching across the seat, he popped the passenger-side door open, and Jillian, water stained, dashed into the car. Her floppy-eared stuffed rabbit was clutched in her hands, pressed tightly against her chest.

"Where are we going?" Jillian asked.

"You need a computer, so … my office."

"Your office?"

"If Syrch Corp or the civilian police are looking for me, then there are two places where it would be absolutely stupid of me to go: my apartment and my office. Everyone knows that. So that is exactly where I will go. It will be unexpected."

Jillian didn't look like she understood the logic. Paul ruffled her wet hair.

"I know, kid. It sounds stupid to me too. But we need a computer, and the best place for us to find one that is secure is in my office. And if Syrch grabs us, well I'll just have to explain everything as best I can and hope for the best. Buckle up."

Paul drove the car slowly out of the ship graveyard and headed back to the city. He allowed Jillian to pick some music and concentrated on driving. Jillian sat quietly, holding her rabbit, staring at the rain and passing, blurry scenery.

The Syrch Corp building where Paul worked was industrial. It was a plain, rectangular building made of red brick and cement that looked worn and old. The façade was battered, and the interior was drab, with exposed steel and ductwork hovering over smeared cement floors. But it was close to corporate headquarters and had a large underground parking facility that met the Security Division's spatial needs for armored and specialty vehicles. There were several medium-sized weapons vaults, a shooting range, a gymnasium, and a dojo. The building was only fifteen stories high, but that was more than enough space for the Security Division. So they shared the building with several ash-and-trash operations like transport and building maintenance. The Security Division managed its field operators, who were flung throughout Syrch corporate space, from the building, and there was a special branch stationed there that, as Paul understood, worked in more clandestine realms. Most of the offices were small, and many people worked in cubicles in open floor plans. Paul and Rif's office was on the first floor, in a cubby of a space that looked like it might have been an architectural afterthought. The boiler room was located just below his office, giving the place a musty, oily spell. But Paul liked it that way. People didn't feel obliged to visit. He was out of sight, out of mind. That was another odd thing about the way the current contract had been assigned. A person had to work at figuring out where Paul's office was located. It took effort.

Paul could kick himself for putting such trust in the validity of the coin. He should have referred the doctor to the main office. Paul admitted that the prospect of the bonus payment for a successful mission had also clouded his judgment—that and wanting to make a good impression with the new corporation. He had dug himself into a hole, and bad news did not get better. He had to come clean and hope for the best. But Paul didn't have to be stupid about it. If he could get pertinent information off the data crystal, he had a chance to make the admission of his culpability less ... culpable.

The wind and rain made driving difficult. The car wanted to pull to the right, and it was difficult to see. The vehicle did have an infrared camera and heads-up display, but to no surprise, the Syrch-constructed mechanism did not function. So Paul took it easy, weaving slowly through the traffic, heading to the city center. He went through a drive-through and ordered Jillian some breakfast and himself a cup of Stem. The thick, hot, syrupy drink tasted like hell but would keep him alert and clear his mind. He tried to avoid Stem when he could. The stimulants were not identified by type, though he was sure none of them were addictive. The worst thing about Stem was when it wore off. It always made Paul feel nauseas, and he was often left with a killer headache. But he had had a rough couple days with little sleep and felt he needed the boost.

Jillian sat eating a breakfast sandwich, her legs swinging and her head turned toward the rain-filled window. She seemed like she was in a good mood. Paul wondered how that had happened. Was it part of a child's nature to not be afraid? She had seen Paul kill two men. Paul would have thought the experience would be more traumatic. But Jillian took tiny bites out of her breakfast, sipped at orange juice from a small carton and straw, and looked almost happy. Somewhere along the way, Jillian had grown accustomed to Paul. That attitude was even more pronounced today, with Jillian waking wide-eyed and talkative. Jillian's behavior reinforced Paul's original estimation regarding the girl. Besides her uncanny, mathematical mind and bursts of demonstrated technical knowledge, Jillian was just a little, normal child. Sweet. He hoped the director of security did not tell Paul that he still had to kill Jillian. What would Paul do then?

The thing about killing people was not getting to know them. As long as they remained things and not real people, pulling the trigger was easy. You had to separate the information about their lives, which was discovered during preoperational research and surveillance, from the reality of what that information implied. Married. That meant you might have to deal with two subjects. It did not mean that the subject was in love and had a life's plan. Kids. That meant it would be a hassle and you might have to deal with crying and screaming or with removal of the child before the killing was done. It didn't mean that the kids loved their parent. Saved a woman from drowning. The subject was not a hero worthy of respect. It just meant the person could swim. Owned a dog. If you hit the subject at home, you'd likely have to kill the dog too. It didn't make the subject a humanitarian. None of what Paul discovered about his targets equated to their being human. The emotion surrounding the facts of the subject's lives was put aside and never considered. However, Paul had gotten to know Jillian. He recognized how she liked to rub her feet together when she slept, how she crinkled her nose while eating, and her tendency to look up at adults with a bit of trepidation. Jillian was socially unsure of herself. Everything about her screamed for nurture and protection.

Lin Corp space? Could he get her to Lin? Paul chewed on that thought as he made the final drive down a four-lane road to the entrance of his building's parking garage. Paul let the access computer scan his iris, pulled deep into the structure, and parked.

Nobody paid attention to Paul as he led Jillian down the long hallway to his office. The building was dim, the cheap lighting not powerful enough to push aside the gray of the raging storm. Paul unlocked the door and stepped into his office. His desk was sitting by the widow on the far wall, and Rif's desk—it was just as Rif had left it. A pile of paper, folders, and pens, glasses, and old cans of soft drinks littered the surface of Rif's desk. His chair was pushed back and half-turned toward the wall. And his trash can was overflowing. Water dripped off Paul's coat as he stood, staring at the empty seat. But when Jillian shuffled into the room, he turned and took her coat, hanging it on the coat stand. He placed his coat next to it and flopped his hat onto one of the upper prongs.

"Over there, kid." Paul pointed at his desk.

Jillian walked over to the desk and looked back at Paul expectantly.

"You sit behind the desk, Jillian. I'll boot the computer. The data crystal reader will be projected on your right."

Jillian did as she was told as Paul closed the door and joined her. He activated the computer, and the holographic screen appeared in the center of his desktop. Logging into the system via iris scan, Paul called up the virtual keyboard and turned it over to Jillian.

"Here you go, kid. Here's the data crystal."

Jillian took the small, clear crystal in the center of her palm. She stared at the desktop for a moment before finding a dim, blue circular light that seemed to radiate from the desk. Placing the crystal in the center of the interface circle, she began typing on the keyboard. Paul watched as Jillian cocked her head to the left and then the right. At one point, she winced and held her hands up to her ears.

"Wow, your wireless isn't very good."

"That, kid, is because I don't have an implant. I don't think Rif had one either. Implants are a two-way street. Where something can go out, something can get in. And in my business, it's important to keep one's thoughts to oneself."

Jillian looked at Paul as if Paul were stupid. But she turned her attention back to the task at hand, sending wireless instructions to the computer through her implant, and the holographic screen began running through the files on the data crystal.

"He used the same encrypting software," Jillian said. "That makes it easy." She sounded disappointed. "What am I looking for?"

"Why don't you go and sit down over there now," Paul suggested. "It is hard to explain because I don't know exactly. But I'll know when I see it. It may take me a while."

Paul settled down behind his desk as Jillian sat across from him where Rif had been wont to sit. Paul rubbed at his face and glanced at Rif's empty desk. Then he turned his attention to the computer display and slowly began searching through the files. Luckily, it looked like the doctor had not stored reams of personal photos, porn, or any other type of normal clutter on the data crystal. The electronic files were neatly arrayed under folders and subfolders. Paul sighed and started at the first root folder, drilling down in each subfolder and looking at each document. Paul could see that the doctor had been doing some type of personal experimentation, but what exactly the doctor had been attempting to do was beyond Paul's understanding. It took Paul nearly forty minutes to get to the root folder named "Misc." It contained a hodgepodge of individual files of no significance … except for one. It was titled "Journal."

Paul opened the file and was rewarded with the first words that appeared on the document's page:

The first phase has gone well. I was able to modify the genes of the embryos. I reengineered the RNA sequences dealing with human intellect. At the same time, I edited out twenty-three hereditary disease markers. I have twenty embryos. Stem cell, line editing, modified into sperm and egg, proved cost-effective. But I need to find a subject for the IVF. Four would be better. I am bound to lose some of the embryos.

Paul skimmed down the journal. His eyes caught on a name.

Temperance has agreed to carry four. She has not told Jack.

And later.

A healthy pregnancy. I had to abort three of the four fetuses, but the last one is strong. Temperance is healthy, and all looks well.

Paul flipped nine months forward in the journal. He used his finger to help skim the text, moving along each steady line.

Here at last! The baby is born. But Temperance has gone mad. She wants to keep the child! That was not the agreement. The child is mine! I have to be sure. I have to know that I succeeded. Jack thinks it is his child. Temperance lied to him. They have both turned against me!

Scanning further, Paul's heart jumped.

> *It's done. Temperance and Jack. The baby is mine. Jillian is mine.*

There was more to read, reams of words that covered, in detail, Jillian's growth and development. Paul sat back and looked over his desk at the little girl. He finally understood what she was.

While it was allowable on the civilized planets to weed out hereditary diseases, and you were allowed to modify hair, eye, and skin color, it was illegal to tamper with more subtle things like life cycle and intellect. Even attempts to enhance body strength had ended in disaster. Horrible things had happened, abominations of pain and misery. It was one of the reasons why other augmentations, juice or cybernetics, had developed so much in the last century. Science had not progressed enough that genetic modification of core functions of the body were reliable. The journal was full of self-congratulation as Dr. Gibson followed and recorded Jillian's progress. But what would she become? Jillian was a normal happy kid, but who knew what long-term damage the subtle changes in her RNA sequence meant for her? What horrible genetic curse might strike her down? Paul felt as if his heart had fallen into a void, and for a moment he sat stunned. The doctor was a madman!

Paul scrolled to the final entry, and in his mind it all became clear. He understood why the doctor had delivered the coin. He had found the answer to the critical part of the puzzle. And it made him angry. It made Paul mad.

11

DECISIVE POINT

PAUL GAVE Jillian the remote control for the video vision and tucked her into bed. They were at a small hotel, the Festival. It was not the most luxurious place in the world, but it would do. The beds were free of bedbugs, the rugs were worn but clean, and the sheets were bright white.

"But why do you have to go?" Jillian asked.

"I'll be back soon. I promise."

"Can't I go with you?"

"No. But remember what I told you. If I am not back by this evening, you call this number. Ask for Freddy. Tell him what I said."

"That Mr. Thorne needs to get a package to Lin space?"

"Yep. I've already set it up. Everything is paid. He'll come and get you. Okay?"

"Okay."

"And I stocked the little refrigerator with some food, drinks, and snacks."

"What's going to happen to my dad?"

Paul sat on the edge of the bed. "He did some bad things. I will go and talk to him and to my boss. And we'll figure out what will happen."

"Don't kill him …"

"Why would you say that?"

"You're an enforcer. That's what they do."

"You love him, don't you, kid?"

Jillian nodded.

"All right. I'll work it out some other way—if it's possible. And, Jillian," Paul added, "don't you warn your father. Don't call him. If he runs, then someone else from Syrch will get to him first. And they may not be so receptive to the doctor retaining his health. You're going to need to trust me on this one.

"Now"—he stood up and walked to the door—"don't eat everything at once. Try to relax. Here. Here is your rabbit."

Jillian took the stuffed rabbit and smelled its head, resting her chin on the toy. "I know it's not real," she told Paul. "But it was my best friend when I was little."

"It's all right, Jillian. I understand. You two watch your shows and rest. I'll be back soon."

Paul left Jillian laying under the blankets, her head propped up against pillows, Mr. Bunny sitting beside her. The video vision was on, and the air conditioner was humming.

The rain from the day before had abated. The sun had risen in the sky, and the air already felt oppressive. Paul knew it would be a humid and uncomfortable day. He sat in the car and turned the motor on, adjusting mirrors and glancing at the power level. He tapped on the car's computer screen and activated the videophone function. Syrch Corps Telecommunication Company's emblem coalesced on the screen along with a welcome message.

"Mr. Gordon Pepper, Syrch Corp," Paul instructed.

It took a moment before the call was answered by a petite woman in a business suit. Paul recognized her as Anabel Curry, Gordon Pepper's office assistant.

"Did you get your hair cut?" Paul asked. He didn't remember much about Anabel except that she was attractive, and rumor had it that Mr. Pepper and Ms. Curry were more than just business associates. That was really none of Paul's business, but it could make the difference between a good and bad outcome. Paul needed to get on her good side so she would pass him directly to the director. Women were always primping, so it was a good bet Anabel had recently done something to her hair, and just as good a bet she was not happy with the results. "It looks good." The compliment was a shot in the dark.

"Thank you, Mr. Thorne."

"You know, Ms. Curry, you never have taken me up on those concert tickets," he lied, the fabrication coming easily. A little flirting wouldn't hurt.

Anabel smiled. "What do you want, Paul?"

Paul had forgotten the woman had a great memory for faces and names.

"Who said I wanted anything?"

"You just did." She eyed Paul through the monitor and shook her head gently in exasperation.

"You wound me, Ms. Curry." Paul smiled slyly and winked at her.

Anabel laughed. "Well?"

"Is the old man there?"

"He'll be here in a few minutes."

"Good. I need to get in to see him."

"He is booked through the morning."

"It's important. He'll want to see me on this one."

"Why is it, Paul, that every time you call here it is important?"

"That is because I hate calling the boss. So the only time I do it, it is because it is important. He's going to want to see me."

"Can you give me a hint?"

"He already knows—to some extent. It's about Rif."

"Oh." The smile disappeared from Anabel's face. She breathed heavily and turned slightly, apparently going through Gordon

Pepper's daily schedule. "Why don't you just come in, Paul. I will tell him you are on your way."

"I will be there in twenty minutes."

"I will let him know," Anabel assured Paul.

"Thanks, sweetheart."

Anabel looked at Paul, her expression annoyed. Paul grinned back at her.

"You're impossible—obvious and impossible, like a child, you know?"

"Why, Ms. Curry, I have no idea what you're talking about."

Anabel laughed again and reached over to flip off the video call. "We'll see you soon," she said.

The call disconnected, Paul put the car in reverse and pulled out of the parking space. Turning out of the lot, Paul drove down the highway along the river. This part of the city was not as dilapidated as the north side. Nestled into a bow in the river, the neighborhood was designed for white-collar workers. It was a mix of small apartment complexes and individual houses on tiny plots. The north side, where Paul lived, looked like something out of an old gulag. Paul could afford to live in a nicer place, but he liked the thick seediness of his neighborhood, and he preferred putting a little money in savings versus paying it all to a landlord or bank. And with his schedule, he was rarely at home anyway. Why pay for something he wasn't going to use?

Paul spent the rest of the drive fretting about the coming interview. Mr. Pepper was a violent man who worried excessively about his own position in Syrch Corp. Paul knew that Mr. Pepper had a reputation for stabbing people in the back, and the man had been an enforcer in the olden days when the red tape was minimal and people in power were more willing to allow independent enforcement. Those had been bloody days. Mr. Pepper was not a man to mess with, and Paul was not sure how he would explain the death of Rif. Running would be foolish. Fighting would be a sure death sentence. All Paul could hope to do was put the cards on the table and let the truth speak for itself.

Deciding to park on the street and not in the garage, Paul found a spot and stopped. He took a moment to remove his pistol and his backup weapon and store them in the trunk. He did not want being armed to be misinterpreted. It made him feel naked.

Nothing seemed amiss as he entered the building's security checkpoint. Paul skated past the guards. He took the elevator up to the top floor and walked down the hallway to the director's suite. Unlike the rest of the building, the hallway on the upper floor was trimmed in marble and was crisp and clean. There were no chips in the floor, and there was no exposed plumbing. The double doors to the suite were made of some type of dark wood, and frost-etched into the two glass panes were the Syrch Corp emblem and a picture of a factory. Beyond the doors, Paul stepped into the reception room where Anabel Curry sat, polishing her nails. She stopped and looked apologetically up at Paul. She then glanced at the four toughs who were lounging in the chairs.

The four men jumped up and grabbed Paul, roughly searching him and then pushing him toward the director's closed door. Paul endured the indignity grimly. One of the men found the data crystal and took it from Paul.

"He's going to want that," Paul said.

The man grunted as Paul was ushered into the chief's office.

A gaunt man with a pale, sallow complexion sat steely behind a large mahogany desk. He wore deep blue slacks with a freshly pressed shirt. As Paul was escorted in, the director took off a pair of wire-rim glasses and placed them on his desk. He pushed back a bit in his chair and turned violet eyes at Paul. Gordon Pepper's hair was closely cropped, snowy white with streaks of gray, and when he snarled, like he was doing now, his teeth were ivory bright and his lips unnaturally red.

"Well, well," Gordon Pepper said. He looked questioningly at the men surrounding Paul.

"He was clean, sir," one of the men replied. The man took a step forward and placed Paul's data crystal on the director's desk.

"Sir, I—"

"Quiet! When I want to hear from you, I'll ask."

Paul stood silently, but his eyebrows pulled together, and his jaw clenched in anger.

Mr. Pepper nodded to the four goons, and they stepped back out of the room. A deep foreboding sound thronged in the room, reminding Paul of a vault door closing, as the men departed. Paul sat quietly, waiting for Mr. Pepper.

"Rif Slater."

Paul winced.

Mr. Pepper rolled the data crystal in his right hand. He studied it for a minute and then said, "We found him yesterday evening. And that is when we starting piecing things together. Why did you do it, Mr. Thorne?"

Paul rubbed at his eyes with his left hand, trying to ease the headache that was behind his eyes and quickly spreading back into the center of his brain.

"I had a nice chat with Dr. Warner Gibson," the director continued. "His daughter appears to be missing. You wouldn't know anything about that, would you? Wait. We have video of you and Rif outside of the doctor's residence, then again waiting outside of his daughter's school. And we have footage of you, Mr. Thorne, shooting one of our employees who had been assigned as a limousine driver and forcibly pulling the doctor's daughter out of her car. And then—no, keep waiting."

Paul closed his mouth.

"You and Mr. Slater kidnapped her—didn't you? Of course you did. But this is the part I don't fully understand, Mr. Thorne. You and Slater had some type of fallout, and you killed Slater. Was it over the money? Did you no longer want to share?"

"Sir, I ..."

Gordon Pepper held up his hand to forestall Paul. "Or was it that you grew cold feet? It was you, was it not, that took the girl back to Dr. Gibson's apartment the next day? Were you trying to bring her back? Or were you trying to live up to your part of the bargain with the kidnapping? Where—by the way—is the ransom money, Mr. Thorne?"

"Ransom money?"

"Three-quarters of a million credits, Mr. Thorne—the money that Dr. Gibson paid you for the return of his daughter. And the girl ... where is the girl?"

Paul stood with a drooping head. He suddenly felt unsure of where to start.

"It's your turn to speak, Mr. Thorne."

Paul looked at the director. He ran his right hand through his hair and glanced out the window at the city skyline. Then Paul kicked off his right shoe with his left foot and bent down. Picking it up, he shook out a small object. Gordon Pepper kept an eye on Paul. His gaze shifted as Paul tossed the object onto the director's desk where it clattered, rolled, and fell. It was the golden coin.

The truth was Paul's only way out. He told the director about the visit from Dr. Gibson, the receipt of the death warrant, the identity of the person targeted by Syrch Corp for assassination, and the subsequent story of Jillian's kidnapping and Rif's death. Paul explained his return to the doctor's apartment and how he had discovered and copied a data crystal, which Paul later hacked to see the doctor's personal journal. Paul related how the doctor had, in the journal, admitted to using his sister in an unsanctioned experiment and how, after the experiment reached fruition, the doctor had written about killing his sister and her husband so that the doctor could retain the child—Jillian. Though Paul did not fully understand the technical aspects of what the doctor had done, he understood the gist. The doctor had genetically altered Jillian beyond what was allowed by intergalactic law and practice. And Paul explained that Jillian had begun to pose a threat to Dr. Gibson. Finally, Paul denied any knowledge of a paid ransom.

"How so?" Mr. Pepper asked. "Take a seat. How is Jillian Caldwell a threat to Dr. Gibson?"

"It was an audit, sir." Paul took the proffered chair. "The doctor's section was scheduled for a detailed audit. They would have found out about Dr. Gibson's misuse of Syrch Corps' funds, laboratories, and time. They would have discovered Jillian, and that would have ruined Dr. Gibson. And though he could destroy his files on the company computers and hide his research on that data crystal copy, Jillian is a walking, breathing testament to what the doctor has done."

"An audit." The director looked thoughtful.

"Yes, sir. That is my theory. So the doctor got ahold of a coin." Paul pointed at the golden coin that sat unmoving on the director's desk. "He is connected. He said he knows board members. And he—this part is a little embarrassing for me, sir—the doctor looked for the most susceptible people in the Security Division. He targeted me and Rif—me because I am new, and Rif because he was not so smart. And he tricked us into doing his dirty work. The doctor concocted his story, and we fell for it—Rif and I. The doctor picked his suckers pretty well."

"I see." The director pressed a button. "Anabel, please ask Dr. Kase to come in and join me. And find Jerry. I'd like him to step in too."

"Yes, sir."

"You appear a little tense, Mr. Thorne." The director's voice was authoritative.

Paul smiled, hoping it looked polite and not grim.

In a few moments, a young man with dark hair, short and pudgy, entered the office. His face was rosy, as if he had just climbed up a hundred stairs, and his breathing was thick and wet.

"Scan through this, Doctor." Gordon Pepper held up the data crystal. "Tell me what you think. Mr. Thorne here—Paul—believes the information has to do with a genetic experiment. Take your time. Jerry is on his way too."

Dr. Kase acknowledged Paul with a nod and took the proffered crystal. He sat next to Paul. Holding the crystal up to his face, the doctor blinked, and a blue beam of light came out of the doctor's left eye, caressing the data crystal.

Paul jolted and looked more closely at the doctor. While the doctor's right eye was fresh and moist, the left eye was dry and hard, and though the azure blue of the right pupil was matched, the left pupil rotated in two tiny sections as the eye adjusted and focused. Paul never liked cybernetic enhancements. While he could understand them in cases of accidents, disease, or defects, many people chose to have body parts removed and mechanically enhanced replicas installed. Paul suspected the doctor had been one of the self-enhancing types. Watching the doctor scan the data crystal from his cybernetic eye was strangely repulsive and fascinating at the same time. Paul couldn't turn away. He wondered what the other man was seeing, how the cybernetic implant read the data, and how it translated that data into the doctor's brain. Then Paul began to wonder what other augmentations the Syrch Corp doctor had. Paul felt uneasy.

"Ah, Jerry," Gordon Pepper said as a second man entered the room. This man was tall and stern, with graying hair, thin eyebrows, an angular nose, and a tight mouth. The man moved as though he were perpetually angry, hunched around the shoulders, his strides purposeful and sure. And when he spoke, his voice sounded like a knife scraped across burnt toast.

"Anabel said you wanted to see me, Gordon?"

"Here, this coin, did we issue it?"

"Well, let's see. It looks … Yep, it's ours. But I'll have to check the computer to see if we actually issued it. Where did you get it?"

"Paul Thorne—Jerry Fletcher. Jerry—Paul. Paul is a new enforcer."

"I see."

"Paul, why don't you tell Jerry where you got that coin?"

"The coin? It was … I was given it by Dr. Warner Gibson. I put it in the reader, and it checked out fine."

"Gibson? Gibson? Hey, Gordon, why does that name sound familiar?"

"Dr. Gibson runs one of our research divisions. You remember him—snooty blond man."

"Oh, yes. How did he get the coin?"

"That is what I was hoping you could tell me."

"It'll take some research."

"Well, get on it, Jerry—and in a hurry. I need to know how it was managed."

"You think it's a stray?"

"That is what Paul says. And I suspect he's right. We haven't issued any on Papen's World in the last sixty days or so. Paul said Dr. Gibson claims it was given to him by the board of directors."

"The board of … well, that's just silly, Gordon. Only the system governor or the CEO can issue a coin. And it always comes through us. The board is …"

"The main business mechanism, I know. Of course, I suspect Paul, being so new, did not know that. Did you, Paul?"

"No," Paul mumbled.

"And … is there something you wanted to say, Kase?" The director turned his attention to the plump man who had been motioning slightly with one hand.

"Of course, it is only preliminary, you understand," the pudgy doctor said. "Obviously it is about a long-term experiment in genetic manipulation—RNA splicing and the like. And, I take it, it's about a female human. A girl. But we would have never … I have to study it some more."

"Okay, you two get on it. But I want some answers soon. And, Mr. Thorne, you have the girl?"

"Yes, sir."

"Bring her in."

"What? Why?"

"Because I said so."

"What will happen to her?"

"The doctor will examine her."

"And?"

"And what, Mr. Thorne?"

"I can't just ... she's ..."

"Oh, I see," Gordon Pepper smiled. "We need to make sure that Syrch's equities are covered. That's all."

"That's all?"

"Of course."

But Paul felt an itch behind his eyes. He didn't believe the director for one moment.

12

---◦◦◯◇◯◇◯◯◇◯◦◦---

SNATCH

THE TEAM had its orders.

"Okay, let's go." Shiloh Trenton's voice was a gnat in Paul's ear. The team leader was dressed in a dark pantsuit, her short, blond hair tied in a ponytail with a silk ribbon. Where Paul wore a tiny transceiver in his ear, Shiloh wore none. She had a communicator embedded in her skull. Paul recognized that having an embedded communicator gave Shiloh a more natural look and allowed her to blend seamlessly into the environment, but he had seen the things go bust before. Having someone saw through the thick bones of the skull once to insert the device was one thing; having them saw your skull open a second time to fix it was quite another. Yet Shiloh liked to look like a conservative businesswoman, and a visible earpiece just got in the way. Come to think of it, Paul had never seen Shiloh dress down. She was always conservatively dressed. The only splash she made was in her makeup: bright cherry lipstick; blended purple and blue eye shadow that sparkled; rich, black eyeliner; and slightly dusted skin that made Shiloh's face look soft and new. The overall effect was a sharp contrast between her skin, vibrant lips, and deep, pouty eyes.

The enforcers moved together toward the building's door. Paul slipped nearer to the front of the spearhead formation until he was just behind and to the left of Shiloh.

Paul had worked with Shiloh before. She had an annoying habit of talking to people indirectly. It was one of the little foibles of Shiloh's curious personality. Though Shiloh was not what Paul would call model-pretty, Shiloh was attractive. Paul had a thing for pretty faces.

Paul wondered if Shiloh was still angry about the incident last year. He hoped it wouldn't cause any problems. Paul's plan was to ignore it and hope it didn't come up.

Shiloh led Paul and the three other enforcers into the Forest Tower Dome.

The corporation had decided to have a chat with Dr. Warner Gibson. Gordon Pepper, the chief of the Security Division, had called in a specialty team for the snatch, and Paul managed to talk his way into joining them. It was just Paul's bad luck that the team was led by Shiloh. About ten months ago, Paul and Shiloh had done a compliance visit with the president of the Otherworld Bank. It was one of those big, multisystem banks that fed off of Syrch Corp's largess. But the bank got greedy. Almost everyone, given enough time and enough temptation, got greedy. And they always thought Syrch Corp was not looking. Fools. The bank's president, an arrogant, fat, and miserable man, took a chop to the throat from Shiloh when he tried to blow her off. Shiloh had him choking for twenty minutes. But it got the man's attention, and after the fit had passed, the bank president did exactly as he was told. Shiloh and Paul, full of the day's adrenalin, retired to a dingy bar for a drink, and things got a little friendly. One thing almost turned into another before Paul, half-drunk and sorely tempted, stopped it all. So getting picked up on the snatch team had not been an assured thing. Maybe Shiloh harbored some bad blood. To complicate matters, Gordon

Pepper seemed to want to distance Paul from the operation. But Paul was having none of that. He eventually wore down the director. But Shiloh? She had not said a single word. She had just smiled. A flicker of regret ran through Paul.

How did the German-speaking worlds say it? *Lange, schlanke Beine* ... Shiloh sure had those. It was a pity she was wearing slacks. Paul would have liked having something interesting to look at.

Paul also felt a little angry. He didn't like the limits placed upon the mission.

"Interrogation? Is that it?" Paul had asked the director. Paul tried his best to keep his voice respectful, but he was not absolutely sure he had kept his disappointment from showing.

"The doctor is still a Syrch asset. And the system governor feels the doctor is valuable."

"But ..."

"And Ted agrees."

Ted Longbar, the current chief executive officer for Syrch Corp, had weighed in. Syrch had finished a preliminary look at Dr. Gibson's research and was intrigued. And that had ended the discussion about the doctor's punishment. The CEO had spoken. So Paul adjusted his sunglasses and walked next to Shiloh as she strode to the elevator.

"Remember the rules of engagement, Thorne," Shiloh warned Paul.

"Got it. I can't waste him, not even just a little."

"Do you always talk with your mouth, Thorne?"

"I find it works better that way."

"I don't need you ... messing this up."

"Right with you, sweetheart."

"You'd better be."

Paul had to admit it. Shiloh had moxie.

The Forest Tower Dome looked exactly how it sounded. Shaped like the letter L, the structure took up almost an entire city block. A honeycomb-pocked dome rose above the shorter end of the building where an arboretum of rare trees huddled in the light of the windowed dome. Not all the Earth-imported trees had thrived on Papen's World. But in the protective shelter of Syrch Corp's arboretum, people could come and get a feel for what forests on Earth must have been like sometime in the distant past. Paul had been surprised by the building when he first came to Papen's World. He had not thought Syrch Corp would spend any money on meditation gardens, but Paul found smaller versions of the arboretum in many places throughout the city. There was some primal desire in humans to be close to nature—well, he reconsidered, Earth nature. Paul figured it had to do with six million years of evolution for which there were almost no records besides cave paintings and the occasional skull or artifact. The human race grew up in the wild. They needed that connection. Feelings of alienation fostered by the metallic, industrial environment—particularly on many of Syrch's factory worlds—led to a loss of mental ability, depression, falling productivity, and ultimately dropping profit margins. And of course, Syrch Corp was all about profits. So spending a little money on mental health could be justified by the board. The arboretum was also an important symbol of Syrch's power. The dome proclaimed to everyone that Syrch was a wealthy and powerful corporation. But Paul could not linger under the reaching trees.

The doctor's office was on the long leg of the building on the twentieth floor, high above the dome. The top ten floors of the building were all hermetically sealed lab units. It was where Syrch did most of its most sensitive biological studies. Paul knew that was code for where Syrch tried, and often failed, to reverse engineer the biotech products of Terra and Lin Corp. Syrch was a distant third in a two-party race when it came to biotech. Terra had the upper hand in biotech, as Lin Corp's natural predilection was to look inward to find perfection, while Terra's was to improve upon the human form. "Improve," though, was an important distinction for Terra Corp. They were not into fundamentally changing human forms, and they, like their cousins Lin and Syrch, had agreed upon strict DNA manipulation rules as a result. That is part of what made the doctor's work so distasteful. The prohibition against fundamentally changing what it meant to be human was a major shared cultural value across all of human space. And previous experimentation had been gloriously unpleasant. Playing God had unleashed many a short-lived horror. Science just didn't understand how all the genes fit together and hit-and-miss experimentation was, in Paul's view, a sorry way to advance the science of gene manipulation in humans.

How much had the doctor manipulated Jillian's DNA? That was still unclear to Paul. He feared Jillian might suffer a terrible fate as her manipulated traits grew into adulthood. She was just a good kid trying to find her way in a hostile universe. The child had not done anything to deserve it. But the doctor had wanted Jillian dead, so Paul suspected Jillian was the product of mass manipulation, and that thought increased his concern for Jillian's long-term health.

Shiloh led the team through the building, up the elevator, and into the atrium of the twentieth floor. An air-locked door separated the atrium from the main laboratory space, but Paul could see people in white, knee-length lab coats moving about behind the separating security glass. Shiloh scanned her iris in the security reader, and the door opened with a hiss.

"Hey, you can't just come in here!" An alarmed and relatively irritated man in a lab coat said as he hurried forward toward the group of enforcers who pressed into the open floor plan of the lab. "You haven't been through decon! Nobody is allowed in here who has not been through decon!"

"Dr. Gibson, please," Shiloh said.

The man looked at the group of enforcers, his voice suddenly becoming a bit uneasy. "What? He ... are you ... is he expecting you?"

Shiloh pressed a hand onto the man's shoulder and forcefully shoved him out of the way. "Where is his office? It's toward the back, right?"

"Yes, but ..."

The enforcers moved rapidly between tables of experiments and office cubicles. All work stopped as the workers turned to watch the enforcers advance. So much for keeping it subtle. Paul was convinced he, Shiloh, and the other enforcers would be the talk of the cooler and lunch tables for the next few weeks. Maybe that wasn't a bad thing. Maybe that was all part of the Security Division's messaging: don't screw with Syrch Corp or you'll be next!

The enforcers scooted past the startled employees toward the far end of the floor where five doors lined the outer wall. The three doors to the right appeared to lead to small offices, likely for section chiefs or team leaders. A spacious conference room where Paul could see a large table surrounded by chairs was immediately to their front. But Shiloh focused on the far left door, which the enforcers knew led to Dr. Gibson's office. The door was closed. Shiloh rudely opened it and strode boldly into the room.

Dr. Gibson looked up from the pile of printouts he had been studying. The doctor was standing at the corner of his desk. His eyes flashed with anger, but this quickly turned to a look of cautious curiosity. He stretched out fully, straightening his back and looking down at Shiloh. If this was supposed to cow the woman, Paul could see it was ineffectual and, Paul thought, a little dangerous. Shiloh looked steadily at the doctor, her body weight pushed forward in an aggressive stance.

"How dare you barge into my office." The doctor's voice was low and pointed. He did not sound like the weak and simpering man Paul had met a few days earlier. Like the rest of the staff on the floor, the doctor wore a bleach-white lab coat. It had the Syrch Corp emblem embroidered on the right breast pocket. Beneath the emblem was the doctor's title and name.

"How's it going, Doc?" Paul ignored both of them and flopped in an open chair. He slid the chair forward a few inches and then propped his feet pretentiously upon the surface of Dr. Gibson's desk. "Do you mind if I make myself comfortable?"

"Get your feet off my desk!" Dr. Gibson's voice was harsh, but he recognized Paul, and the expression on the doctor's face changed from anger to uncertainty.

"I don't think it's your desk, Doc. I think it belongs to Syrch. And they don't mind. How is the breathing coming along, Doc? I see you are still doing it."

"Paul," Shiloh warned.

"Have you two met? No? Shiloh Trenton, this is Dr. Warner Gibson. Dr. Gibson, this is Syrch Senior Enforcer Shiloh Trenton. Don't let her looks fool you, Doc. She's ... I'm not quite sure how to say it."

"Capable?" Shiloh offered.

Paul smiled at the team leader. "I was thinking more along the lines of mean as hell, but capable will do too."

"What do you want?"

"That didn't sound very friendly, Doc. After all, you and I are old acquaintances. But it's her show. I'm here for the ambiance."

"Well?"

Shiloh grimaced. She took two quick steps around the corner of the desk and finger-punched Dr. Gibson across the carotid artery. The effect was instantaneous. The doctor's eyes rolled upward, and he staggered, his body turning away from Shiloh stiffly, and the doctor tumbled to the ground, dragging papers off his desk where they fluttered in the air before settling on top of the man.

"Neatly done," Paul said nonchalantly.

"Do we understand each other, Dr. Gibson?" Shiloh loomed over the man as he groaned and moved sluggishly. "Get him in his chair." This was directed to the other members of the snatch team. Two of the enforcers moved around the desk, took Dr. Gibson under the arms, and lifted him into his leather swivel chair. They had to hold him there to prevent him from slipping out of the seat and back onto the floor. "And you ..."

Paul held up his hands in deference.

Shiloh turned back to the doctor. "You stole a coin from Syrch, Dr. Gibson." Shiloh leaned in close. Taking a handful of the man's golden hair, Shiloh forced the doctor to look at her. "Now all of us are going to take a trip downtown. My boss wants to talk to you. And it would be best if you checked your attitude at the door. Understand? My boss is not as understanding as I am. You take that tone with him, and he's likely to break every bone in your body. So you owe me. That's right, Doctor. You owe me for saving your miserable little life. Now are you going to be good? Yes? Great." Shiloh turned her back on the doctor and started toward the door. "Get him up and down to the cars."

The enforcers half-carried, half-dragged the doctor toward the door. Paul followed neatly behind. In the outer office of cubicles and long, marble-covered workbenches and laboratory tables, the disturbed, white-clad scientists watched nervously as Dr. Gibson was pulled between two enforcers toward the exit. Shiloh walked before the enforcers, angry, as if daring any of the lab workers to interfere. Nobody did. They meekly averted their eyes, staring at tables and beakers and scientific equipment, but not one of them made any move to intervene.

Paul followed the snatch team out of the door and into a waiting elevator. There was a bounce in Paul's step. He hadn't felt as good or had as much fun in several days. As the automatic doors closed behind him, he pushed back in the elevator and surreptitiously looked at Shiloh.

"What is it, Paul?"

How did she know? "Like I said, just enjoying the ambiance," he replied.

Paul was not sure, but he thought he saw the edge of a smile threatening the crease of Shiloh's lips.

13

THE INTERVIEW

THE HOLDING area reminded Paul of the starkness of a hospital. White walls, sterile, artificial rubber flooring of yellow with a deep orange trim, and a series of security doors with small window viewers and food trays lined the hall. The air tasted flat and stale, full of the pungent smell of dried sweat. Someone alternated between mumbling and crying behind one of the closed cell doors while a mopping robot hummed along, a tall, thin drum held up by a rotating disc and crab-like arms. Halfway down the hall on the right, the portraits of the Syrch CEO, the in-system governor, and Gordon Pepper, the white-haired Security Division's director, hung in a descending order of relative power. Paul knew the only time anyone would see his portrait on a wall was at his funeral—and maybe not even then. Enforcers were not the most popular people in the universe, rarely had family, and a more typical end for an enforcer was an urn—if they were lucky. It was much more common for them to end up in a recycling pit, churned into nutrient pulp for the fields. Paul was not sure that was such a bad thing. At least he would not have to worry about being dug up by some fanatic in a hundred years to suffer countless indignities. The possibility of being abused after death had occupied the energies of the elite for millennia, but not a single tomb or vault had ever been built that protected their corpses from the clawing hand of vengeful humanity. But nobody would mess with Paul's remains. Paul had no doubt that he would be forgotten ten minutes after his death. He was one of the small people. Insignificant. There was no god of Valhalla or heaven waiting for him. Only the sudden, endless nothing of eternal silence loomed in his future.

Shiloh Trenton led the way. She had let her hair down. Blond locks swung purposefully as she made her way to cell number seven. The two of them had orders to bring Dr. Gibson up to Gordon Pepper's office. That seemed a little strange to Paul. Why didn't they use one of the interview rooms? That was why they were there. Dragging Dr. Gibson up to the director's office seemed counterproductive in making the doctor talk. It smacked of coddling.

Shiloh opened the cell door. Dr. Gibson was sitting on the edge of an unadorned cot. He had removed his lab coat and his silk suit jacket and was tapping a foot on the floor. Based upon the expression on the doctor's face, Paul figured the man was fuming.

"Doctor," Shiloh said. "We've come to get you."

"Where are you taking me?"

"Now, now," Shiloh said, "I thought you and I had an understanding."

The doctor reached a hand to the side of his neck. A meandering, purple and black bruise marked the spot where Shiloh had struck him. "Yes ... we do."

"That's better. We're going to talk to Gordon Pepper."

"The security chief?"

"One in the same. He has a few questions to ask you about your experiments—your personal experiments and about your niece."

"I have no idea what you are talking about."

"That's right. Lie to him. I understand he likes that. Have you ever visited a slave mine, Doctor? No. If you're not careful, you might get that opportunity. Or he might just shoot you. Mr. Pepper is difficult to predict."

"I don't know why we are wasting our time," Paul said. He leaned casually against the wall. "It seems like a bother."

"Well?" Shiloh asked.

The doctor stood up and brushed at his hair with his right hand. "He better have a damn good explanation for why he is treating me this way. I have friends."

"That's nice."

"Follow me, Doc," Paul said, leading the way out of the cell.

The doctor followed, and Shiloh came last. The three of them made it back down the stagnant hallway to the central lift where they briefly waited for the next elevator. Then it was up to the top floor, a quick stroll to the director's door, and soon they were all sitting around a circular conference room table with another man. Paul recognized the older man as Dr. Jerry Fletcher, the security director's top scientific adviser.

"Anabel," Gordon Pepper called to his secretary. "Can you bring in some drinks? Tea, coffee, Stem, water, anyone?" The director frowned. "Just bring in a little of everything, Anabel."

"Yes, sir."

Anabel brought in the drinks and a tray of cookies. She put the serving platter down and served the guests and finally the director.

"Thank you, Anabel. Can you catch the door behind you?"

Paul sat opposite the security director at the end of the oblong table. To his right was Shiloh Trenton. The senior Syrch enforcer was stirring sugar into a cup of hot Stem, but Paul could tell she was keeping a close eye on Dr. Gibson, who sat to her right near Director Pepper. The doctor was picking at a cookie and had opened a bottle of water, which he sipped now and again. He looked at each member of the gathering in turn, clearly trying to ascertain the situation. To Paul's left was the security director's chief science adviser, Dr.

Jerry Fletcher. An older man, he was still regal, with thin eyebrows, a sharp Romanesque nose, and salt-and-pepper hair. The doctor was flipping through a neatly bound paper report and marking it in the margins with a red pen. But Paul was mostly concerned with the security director himself. Gordon Pepper had greeted everyone warmly, like they were all the best of friends, and that made Paul nervous. Paul figured this meeting was as much about Paul's activities as it was about Dr. Gibson's illegal experimentation on Jillian. Paul had killed his partner. And he had failed to abide by the contract that had bound him to performing the hit on Jillian. To make matters worse, if they could be any worse, he was new to Syrch Corp and did not know anyone powerful enough to shelter under. Everyone else at the table had their personal network and was therefore at least somewhat protected. He was the lone wolf, out on the edge of a wood, in danger of stepping on a deadly coil-spring trap. And though he could sense it hidden somewhere, he did not know where it lay in the foliage. If he took the wrong step, the trap would spring, and Paul would find himself flayed and skinned and boiling away in a resource reclamation vat.

"Should we get started? Thank you for joining us today, Dr. Gibson. I've taken a rather sudden keen interest in your work. I am particularly interested in this." Director Pepper produced a golden Syrch coin and slid it across the table to Dr. Gibson. The doctor leaned away from the coin as if fearing its touch. "Would you like to explain?"

"I assume you already know," the doctor replied. His voice held a bit of his previous brass, but the haughty edge was muted.

"Yes, well," Director Pepper admitted, "it did take us a little while to track it down. Unfortunately, Jasvinder Dhawan suffered an accident shortly after we found out she had been the one to give you the coin. Pity. She was a lovely woman."

"Accident?"

"The board member was accidentally shot in the head. Twice. But accidents happen. I am sure I will get a negative comment in my annual ratings statement because of it, but it just couldn't be helped. That is why they call them accidents, is it not?"

Dr. Gibson looked down at the coin. Paul saw a bead of sweat start at the edge of the doctor's hairline and begin a slow roll down his cheek. The doctor unconsciously wiped at it.

"I see."

"Syrch Corp does not take kindly to theft, Dr. Gibson. It finds the theft of warrant coins to be particularly baleful. I hope you understand why and take that lesson to heart … Good. Now, we are all a bit curious about your other work, Doctor. No, not the deaths of your sister and her husband, though I admit we have opened a preliminary inquiry into their sudden demise. What we are most curious about is your niece. Forgive my manners. I think you remember Dr. Jerry Fletcher, don't you? Yes. He has been telling me the most interesting things about your special project. In fact, the CEO personally called me. He is interested too. I asked Ted for his advice, and he told me to look into it. If I found everything to be in order, then I have the option of charting a way forward. But if I find that things are not going to work out, Ted gave me full authority. Full authority. Oh, I almost forgot." He reached inside his breast pocket and pulled out a second golden coin. Holding it up, the director slowly rotated it in the bright light of the room. "Look what else I have. A second coin. Should I give it to young Mr. Thorne? He looks like he is a bit unsettled and could use the distraction."

Paul leaned forward in his chair. But his eagerness died away when Paul realized that the coin could just as easily contain his name. He sat back and forced himself to relax.

"Of course I'll cooperate in any way I can, Director."

"Gordon, please."

"Yes … Gordon … I'm happy to be of any assistance."

"Dr. Fletcher?" Director Pepper turned to his science adviser.

Dr. Fletcher was somewhat taken aback. He looked up from the report he had continued to review as the director spoke, cleared his throat, and spoke in his raspy way. "The experimentation—I've been reading about your work, Dr. Gibson. It does not exactly meet the legal definition under the DNA sequencing protocol established by the League of Planets, of which we and the other major corporations are signatories. But I feel—we feel—there is a certain amount of poetic nuance in the nature of your work. And I feel—we feel—that it is in Syrch Corp's best interest to consider further pursing your line of inquiry into RNA resequencing."

Paul looked sharply at the security director. The man's lips were pursed together in a serious line. Paul opened his mouth but felt a sharp kick under the table. Shiloh was leaning toward him with a tight smile and a warning in her eyes. Paul kept his thoughts to himself.

"Was there a specific area that interested you, Dr. Fletcher?" Dr. Gibson asked. He had visibly relaxed.

"If I may?" Dr. Fletcher asked the security director. Director Pepper nodded, and Dr. Fletcher continued. "Syrch Corp proposes assigning you to lead a team of focused research to refine and develop your findings—under certain conditions."

"Yes?"

"I've got this, Jerry," Director Pepper answered. "The team's work will be strictly confidential. Any disclosure will result in summary execution. All work will be kept on Syrch's secured servers and systems. Any deviation will result in summary execution. And you will remain on Papen's World unless given express permission to travel, and then you will only travel under the protective umbrella of the Security Division as the division sees fit. Any failure to abide by the travel prohibition will also result in summary execution. Do you think you can work under those terms?"

"That's it?" Paul interjected. He felt another sharp pain in his shin. Shiloh kicked him a second time for good measure. "Excuse me, sir. I was out of line. Please accept my apology."

The director shifted his gaze back to Dr. Gibson. "Do we have an agreement?"

"And the girl? Jillian?"

"Ah, Jillian. Yes. You are not to see her, Doctor. You are not to communicate with her in any way. She is no longer your concern."

"I just go back to my lab then?" Dr. Gibson's voice was relieved and confident.

"No." The director stood up, and everyone stood up with him. He put a hand on Dr. Gibson's shoulder and said, "We are going to build you a new lab. A private one. You and Dr. Fletcher will have much to discuss with your other colleagues as you develop the plans and oversee the building of the facility. The Security Division will naturally be involved ... but we are involved in everything. And you will get a chance to shine. I think you've made the right choice, Doctor. I'll excuse you now." He picked up the golden coin that had remained in front of Dr. Gibson for the entire meeting. "No souvenirs," he quipped. "And not you, Thorne. You stay behind for a moment."

"Yes, sir."

Paul watched as Drs. Gibson and Fletcher, followed by Shiloh Trenton, left the room. He soon found himself alone with the security director, feeling angry and wary and worried about Jillian.

"I ought to have you shot!" the director exclaimed. "In all my time ... You are one lucky bastard, Thorne."

"Am I? I don't feel very lucky."

"It doesn't matter what you feel. We've decided not to retire you, though for the graces I don't know why. We've decided to keep you on the job. We've decided," Director Pepper said vehemently, "that you are to have no—and I repeat—no more contact with Jillian Caldwell. You are not to bother Dr. Gibson. And you are to keep your head low and stay out of my line of sight. Understand?"

"Yes, sir. Clearly."

"Now get out! Go home. Get yourself together."

Paul left the office, stepping out of the shadow of the security director's anger, past the pretty Miss Anabel Curry, and into a waiting elevator. He had the shakes. His arms and legs were trembling. Paul rubbed at his eyes and felt tired, bone weary. All he wanted to do was break something and fall into a deep, forgetful sleep. But his mind was working, churning, scheming. It was not right. What had just happened was not right. Paul kicked at the door and struck the wall with his head. It couldn't end this way. Paul left the building and picked his way back to his apartment, careful to meander, always with an eye to his six. At home, Paul found his flechette pistol and set it on the living room table, then poured himself a tall glass of bourbon. Paul never expected life to be fair. It was harsh and cruel. But he did expect more. He expected more from Syrch Corp, from Director Gordon, and from himself. Paul drained his glass and cursed.

Syrch Corp had Jillian. And they were not going to let her go.

14

❨❨❨❨◉❩❩❩❩

A GUILTY SOUL

WAKING UP sober after a night of heavy drinking, the deed done and Jillian in Syrch Corp's control, made Paul wonder at the wisdom displayed by humanity's forbearers at having crawled out of the primordial soup. Paul groaned, rolled over, and jolted at his own stink. He shuffled to the bathroom and back to his rumpled bed, throwing himself onto the tumbled sheets and comforter. Paul rubbed slowly at his eyes and then stared sullenly at the white ceiling of his bedroom. He glanced at his clock. It was nearing noon. He knew he should get up but found he lacked the motivation. Instead, he rolled onto his side and stared at the opposite wall. For the thousandth time, Paul thought he should buy some art. Maybe that way the room would not feel so empty. But he had never found anything that appealed to him. Most people hung family photos on their walls, or maybe photos of colleagues at a celebration, and if the person was particularly vain, perhaps they covered their walls with award certificates and college diplomas as little testaments to how much they mattered in some way, though

Paul knew their lives were just specks in an endless sea of space and time. What a clutter must be other people's lives! Paul was not hemmed in and surrounded by the past. His future, like the wall, was a blank canvas. He liked it that way. Sometimes though, it was nice to imagine himself at the center of a small family with little mementoes around the house and a nagging but pretty wife. But then he thought about all the backstabbing bullshit in most marriages and the astronomically high numbers of divorce. Paul didn't need that type of headache. He had enough problems without manufacturing more.

Paul closed his eyes and let his mind float and tried his best not to think about the pounding behind his eyes. He sat up, dangled his feet over the side of his bed, and then once again trudged into the bathroom looking for something to take the edge off his headache. He popped a pain pill and used his hands to lap up some water from the sink, and, arms braced on the bathroom counter, he looked at his drooping image in the mirror. He had looked better. His beard was a scraggly shadow, and his eyes were surrounded by dark circles while the sclera, the normally white part of the eye, was fractured with red veins. His hair was tussled and wild, and it looked like there was some dried drool on the corner of his lips. Paul splashed his face in cool water, wetted down his hair and shaped it with his fingers, brushed his teeth, and swished mint mouthwash to clear his palate and get the taste of dead sock out of his mouth. Stumbling into the kitchen, he brewed some Stem and made toast and eggs. Sitting at the edge of the counter, he ate and drank and wondered when he could legitimately go back to sleep.

Fumbling at his empty plate, Paul pushed it into the sink and slunk into the living room with a second cup of Stem and collapsed on the couch. How was it that Rif was dead and the only consequence had been the imprisonment of a little girl? Dr. Gibson had actually been given a type of promotion! And Paul's burgeoning career was likely ruined too. Paul had been manipulated and abused. It would have been better if he had just shot Jillian and been done with it. Why did he have to get so righteous?

Paul rested the hot mug of Stem on his chest, sipped at it, and thought about all the other ways he could have handled the situation. He should have gone straight to the Security Division when the coin was first presented. But he had wanted to show off, wanted Syrch Corp to be impressed with their new enforcer. What an absolute disaster—a moronic disaster!

Pawing at the remote control, Paul switched on the news and listened mindlessly to a bright-toothed man who was babbling about an ongoing trade mission from Syrch Corp to the League of Planets. The newscaster went on and on about negotiations for twelve new cargo ships, speculating Syrch would beat out both Lin and Terra for the contract. While Lin and Terra produced fine spacecraft, Syrch had access to new, high-quality material that allowed them to undercut Terra and Lin prices. Paul knew all about that. He had been mixed up in the business of securing that material for Militan Corp, one of Syrch's puppets. Paul noted there was no mention of those killings in the news story.

The newscaster went on to say that because of the labor structure for Syrch, the ships could be produced much quicker by Syrch than by either of the major competitors. Yet the League of Planets was still being a bit squishy about the unfortunate events in the Eper system. It was therefore not clear if the League of Planets would accept Syrch's offer.

The Eper system had made headlines in much of human space. Syrch Corp had been wrongly accused, according to the newscaster, of strip mining the fourth planet in the system without having properly conducted a full biological study to determine if there was any native life. Syrch Corp maintained, the newscaster continued, that they had completed the survey and that the late discovery of a four-legged creature called a Quadcat on the planet, though it did not resemble a cat in Paul's estimation, was the result of criminal staging by an unscrupulous yet unnamed competitor. Obviously, if the creature had been truly native to the planet, Syrch's own biological study would have discovered it. Syrch would therefore not have destroyed the creature's habitat with massive strip mines. Syrch Corp had, during the course of the resent week, asked the League of Planets to send an investigative team to Eper to root out the people or corporation responsible for illegally introducing the obviously "genetically altered, nonnative species" onto the planet in hopes of disrupting Syrch's Mining Services. Syrch's Mining Services, the announcer reminded his audience, provided critical resources to several habitable worlds. The newscaster then began talking about local sports, so Paul flipped through the available stations until, unsatisfied, he turned the video vision off and lay in the stiff silence.

Jillian Caldwell was in Syrch custody.

Custody was a subjective word. Jillian had been returned to her private school, though now she lived on campus in one of the two dormitories for children. She was free to go about her business, but she could not leave school grounds without permission and an escort. That was not too dissimilar to the rules for all the kids. But Paul thought it was a sign of things to come. As Jillian grew up and her friends became adults with their own lives, Jillian would still live in a protected and controlled shell. Syrch had to be careful not to let an outside doctor examine the girl. Her manipulated DNA would be easily spotted, and Syrch did not want her story getting into general circulation. Syrch would also want to reap the benefits of the experiment, and the only way to do that was to examine Jillian at regular intervals. She would, Paul thought, spend the rest of her life as a prisoner of Syrch, poked, prodded, needled, and studied. And what if Syrch decided to end the experiment? What if the anticipated value of Jillian's genes was not realized? What then? What did scientists do with a rat when they were done experimenting on it? Paul knew. They disposed of it. A lifetime of discomfort and dehumanizing followed by a fine needle and sudden death—it was a cruelty that nettled at Paul.

"How can I just sit here and let it happen?" Paul said to the empty bourbon bottle.

Closing his eyes, Paul let lethargy infuse him. Sleep or drink. Drink or sleep. He had to escape the nagging voice of guilt that rang in his mind.

Sometime later, Paul awoke, stiff, sore, his eyes trying to focus. He didn't feel any better. He walked to the window and looked out over the city. The squared roadways, the industrial high-rises and haze of smog that swirled like smoke in a vacuum, even the system's sun that rode the sky like a charioted god appeared falsely beyond his window. All of his dreams were slipping through his fingers, and the harder he tried to hold on, the more difficult it was for Paul to justify the means. Paul knew what he had to do, but it would destroy years of clawing his way up from a freelance thug to getting his foot inside one of the major corporations. Was it all for nothing? He had lived like a rat, suffered, barely escaped with his life, and done violent things. He had thought that he was a hard man, strong and sure. He did not realize that lurking behind the façade was a sense of natural justice, of what was right, and an aversion to causing harm where harm was unnecessarily cruel. Paul was no hero. He knew that. He was no innocent. Quick with a gun and distantly cool, Paul was not a murderer either. Paul was not sure what that made him, but he apparently was not an enforcer. And if not, what was he? What would he become?

Whatever the answer, Paul knew he could not sit idly and let Jillian fall into a twilighted life. Syrch Corp might not think Jillian was Paul's concern, but for Paul, she was his business, and he had to act.

Paul sighed and turned and headed back into the center of the living room. He picked up a small, handheld videophone and dialed a number. He kept the camera off.

"Yes." The voice was a high-pitched, energetic male one.

"It's me."

"I'm listening."

"It's on."

"The package?"

"Yeah, the package." Paul ran his hand along his jaw.

"When?"

"Two days, maybe three. Is that enough time?"

"I'll manage."

"Where?"

"The usual place."

"Okay, I will bring the payment. And … I'm burning bridges."

"How bad?"

"All of them."

"I see."

"Yeah, so it is going to be rough," Paul said.

"Cost more."

"I know."

"Okay."

"What's the word?"

"Dorothea."

"Dorothea? Got it. Talk to you soon." Paul disconnected.

Paul looked around his apartment. He would have to get all of his hidden rainy day funds. The decision made, he still didn't feel all that great. He felt hollow. It wasn't a particularly beautiful apartment. It was worn and ugly, but it was home. Paul would miss it.

15

──◦◦◦○◦◦◦──

BIRD'S EYE

FOR ONCE it was not raining. The sun was low on the morning horizon, and a refreshing breeze tickled through the air, stirring trash together in a small vortex at Paul's feet. He was standing on a tall building a few blocks from Jillian's school, a set of binoculars wrapped in his right hand and a small digital device in his other hand. Paul wasn't the only one to notice that this particular part of the rooftop was not under camera cover. The conduit strip for the cameras that stretched across the rooftop had the center extension arm broken off, the arm where a security camera would normally sit. To Paul's left was a stack of empty beer bottles that, no doubt, had been left by some teenage kid or the building super. Paul figured this mysterious beer drinker had kicked the camera fixture until it had broken, knowing full well that building management would see little value in its repair. That implied, to Paul, the building superintendent. Paul had to admit it was a nice spot to hide and have a few drinks. The super could sit up here all day, enjoy the view, and nobody would be the wiser.

Paul put the binoculars up to his eyes and looked across the intervening space between the building and Jillian's school. He and Rif had not done a detailed survey of the school. That amount of detail had not been necessary for the kidnapping. But now Paul had to memorize the compound; he had to understand how the staff and students moved about. Once he understood the layout and the rhythm, Paul could finalize his plan.

The Frederick Taylor Industrial School for the Gifted, FTISG, occupied a whole city block. The compound was somewhat trapezium shaped and was surrounded by a fifteen-foot-high concrete security wall that was well lit and monitored by security cameras that Paul suspected were connected to an automated threat analysis early warning system. Half of the compound sat along the ridgeline of a hill. The southern side of the property rose an undulating fifteen to twenty-five feet above the northern side. Just behind the perimeter wall, a ring of trees stood guard. Tall things with thick leaves, the trees created another layer of obscuration of the compound if looking at it from ground level. Paul thought that was a nice touch. Paul turned his attention to the interior of the compound. It appeared to be separated into three distinct areas: two square quads of dormitory buildings on the east side; a row of classroom buildings, with a swimming pool in the center of a small green area and what looked to Paul like a tennis court, in the center of the compound; and the administrative buildings, gymnasium and playing field on the western side of the compound. In all, the compound had six distinct subareas, a main entrance on the southwest side, and a service entrance on the northwest side. Here and there within the compound, Paul could make out the shape of standard guard stations, little concrete boxes with windows on all four sides to allow for full coverage of the area, and he caught the occasional glimpse of patrolling guards.

The observable security measures were fairly robust for a school. But then TFISG was no ordinary school. Their clients were some of the most powerful people in Syrch space. Paul would not be surprised if there were not some type of advanced emergency-response robots hidden about the compound too. That meant that Paul had to try to make rescuing Jillian seem normal, part of the routine. If the alarm went off, Paul would have to face the armed guards and whatever little secret combat robots might lurk in the stone-faced buildings of the elite school. The last thing he needed was a firefight while surrounded by children. Besides the potential harm to the kids and staff, Paul was sure he would be outgunned and killed.

Paul shifted his vision to a dark spot in the center of the compound, at the bottom of the looping hill. Jagged, large stones of dark metamorphic rock were strewn across a green lawn. Shaded by nearby trees, the rocks seemed to be a popular resting place for the school children. Paul saw over a dozen kids of various ages lounging on, leaning back upon, or climbing the rocks. The kids all wore uniforms: the girls with knee-length skirts and buttoned blouses, and the boys in dark slacks and white shirts. Further to the northwest, by the service entrance, Paul noticed a parking lot where several large all-terrain vehicles were stationed. Men and women in dark suits moved occasionally around them, marking them as bodyguards in security details assigned to cover some of the more precious children. That was great. It meant there were more guns down there than just the obvious guards and potential robots.

Focusing back on the eastern side of the compound, Paul looked at the northernmost dormitory quad. He counted chimneystacks until he reached the third of the five chimneys. That was where his information indicated Jillian Caldwell was staying. She had a private room on the third floor. After hours, at around nine o'clock, the girls who lived on compound were subject to curfew. That was an advantage. It could take Paul hours to search through all the buildings to find Jillian. But with the curfew, it was a sure bet Jillian could be found in her dormitory room after nine. Making a move later at night would also reduce the amount of security details significantly. They would have taken their charges home. And it would minimize the amount of additional staff—teachers, administrators, and building maintenance personnel—that Paul would have to deal with. So Paul had the timing down—maybe. But he needed to figure the rest of it out. How was he going to get on to the compound, find Jillian, and leave with her without setting off the alarm?

Paul looked at the satellite photo of the compound on the faceplate of the digital device he held in his hand. He sat back on the hard rooftop, back against a wall in a small divot of a shadow, and watched the day at the school unfold. He took notes and photos and occasional digitally sketched ideas on his device. The sun meandered across the sky.

It was peaceful here, on the rooftop, Papen's World spread out below, the hum of the city mixing with the breeze. Paul reached into the little black backpack he had brought with him, pulling out a water bladder and cup, and poured a drink. The water was cold and filtered-fresh. In this attitude, Paul watched the school all through the day and into the dark of night.

16

— ∘◦•◦∘◉∘◦•◦∘ —

THE GIRL

PAPEN'S WORLD'S star dipped below the horizon, casting the capital in intermixing rays of shadow and colored light. High clouds, portending rain, could be seen in the distance, creeping ever slowly toward the city where amber lamps began flickering on up and down streets. A tense wind blew in ragged gusts, jabbing through tree leaves, blowing trash, and shuffling through the hair of people making their final day's journeys to their homes. Every now and then, Paul could feel cool mist strike his exposed face with a chill that numbed. The storm was on the move, drawing down on the city with inevitable anger, and creatures big and small scurried to find shelter in the city's comfortable nooks and sinister crannies. Thunder rumbled, and a fantastic orgy of lightning spiraled and danced in the distant sky. It was going to be a murderer's night.

Paul stepped back into the shadow of a tall building, pulling his coat close and pushing the brim of his hat lower over his eyes.

He would wait for the storm. It would cloak him, and maybe, just maybe, he wouldn't have to kill anyone.

The car Paul had chosen was black and sleek, a muscle car built by Terra Corp and offered for sale and rental at the more fashionable locales. Two small shoulder bags held clothing and personal items for Paul and Jillian, and Paul had filled the trunk with medical gear, some grenades, a rifle, and emergency rations. He had stuffed a sleeping bag in the trunk too. Though he hoped not to need any of those items, he preferred being prepared. There was no guarantee that he could get Jillian out of town and to the designated pickup location. Things could go very wrong.

Slipping into the driver's seat, Paul pushed the chair back, closed his eyes, and waited. He shifted a little; the thin veneer of his body armor, worn under his trench coat, had bunched up between his shoulder blades. Rated for most handguns and resistant to edge weapons, the body armor was the most lightweight he could afford. There was also a slim layer of cushy material that ran the length of the body armor, which the manufacturer claimed would distribute the shock of blunt trauma over a wider area of the body, reducing damage from a punch or kick. But Paul had been punched and kicked before while wearing the armor, and in his estimation, that touted feature did not live up to its promises. But what the body armor lacked in regards to muting the effects of physical blows it made up for in its stopping power. Paul had been shot three times during the performance of his job, and each time the armor had proven up to the task, stopping or deflecting the round and saving his life. And he barely gave up any mobility in exchange for its protection. As long as someone did not shoot him in the head or foot, he would be all right—unless they used a rifle. No system was perfect. Anything larger than a handgun would punch a hole right through the armor. The other problem with a rifle was that the shot would jab all the way through his torso, exiting opposite of where it hit. Then it would meet the second side of the armor after losing velocity. Having been slowed, it was likely the round would ricochet back through Paul's torso instead of cleanly exiting. In effect, Paul could be shot twice for every round that struck home. Of course, there were energy weapons too. They would eat through or totally ignore the armor. But the armor did increase the survival odds in Paul's favor. Most security personnel, thugs, and thieves on Papen's World used low-tech weapons. They were cheap and easy and, if handled professionally, deadly. So Paul was happy to have armor designed specifically for that threat.

On the companion seat of the car, a thick blanket sat waiting for Jillian. It provided ballistic protection too. Paul planned to wrap the girl in it once she was in the car. It would be easier than trying to find a suit of armor like Paul's for the little girl. And since this was an unarmored vehicle, without the protection, Jillian would be a sitting duck should someone fire at them. Paul knew it was an uncomfortable solution, as the fabric was heavy and thick, but Jillian would just have to suffer the indignity until they were away from the city and out in deep country. If they got that far, he would let Jillian shrug out of the ballistic blanket and get comfortable for the long dash.

Paul picked up a hand-sized clear cube, found its edge, and unfolded his paper-thin tablet until it was the size of a small map. He had noted the location of the pickup point outside of the capital, behind a low-running ridge a few miles east of an old, abandoned mining station. It would take two hours of hard driving to get there. It was not the first choice for the pilot of the ship that would carry Paul and Jillian off planet. But the location the pilot had wanted to use was too far away. Paul had fretted that Syrch Corp would get airborne and chase him down if he spent any more than a couple of hours on the road. Luckily the pilot was sure of himself or enjoyed the idea of stealing from Syrch and had agreed to the change of location. If everything was going as planned, the pilot and his ship, the *Dorothea*, were already on station, having flown in low and settled behind the ridge in the heart of the giant mine. If the *Dorothea* had waited to fly to the rendezvous point after Jillian had been taken, Syrch Corp would have made the connection. Air controllers would see the *Dorothea's* T-line, know its trajectory, and would know that the *Dorothea's* flight path intersected with Paul's vector as the enforcer zipped toward the mining station. And that would be the end of that. A heavy or light cruiser would station itself above the planet, and air forces ships would dart through the atmosphere, crippling or destroying the *Dorothea* before it had a chance to pick up Paul and Jillian, or the air forces would catch the *Dorothea* as it lifted with its passengers. It would be a simple matter to force the *Dorothea* to land or shoot it out of the sky. To avoid that, Paul and the pilot had decided to move the *Dorothea* in early. Paul hoped the ploy had worked.

Pushing these concerns aside, Paul studied the map and the redlined route he planned to follow. If something went wrong and he had to change his route on the fly, he would not have time to consult the map again. Having a good picture of the terrain set in his head was Paul's best bet at being able to successfully improvise.

He studied the map, sipped on some hot Stem that he had brought in a thermos, and listened as the storm bore down on the city. The wind was already stronger, and a thin sprinkle of rain was steadily falling. As Paul waited, the storm grew stronger, the rain began to dance as it bounced on the wet pavement, and thunder and lightning tolled in the cloud-shrouded night's sky.

It was a little after eleven o'clock when Paul decided to move. The rain was thick and hard, and shadows lay in large pools around meager streetlights. The roads were nearly empty, and the sharp wind muffled the noise of sparse traffic. Paul started the engine and pulled the vehicle out of the nook in which he had hidden, turning into an arterial road that led to the main road and Jillian's school.

He approached the school from the northeast, around the large driving circle, and followed the security wall of the school toward the south, looking for anything out of the ordinary. At the next intersection, he turned right and followed the wall along the whole southern face of the school before turning right once again past the main entrance. The driving circle at the main entrance to the Frederick Taylor Industrial School for the Gifted was empty. Paul slowed a bit and was rewarded with a glimpse of two dark shapes behind the security glass of the main visitor's building. As he had anticipated, the guards were hunkered in the buildings to get out of the weather. Paul was counting on that same inclination to get him through the rear entrance where the protective details normally stashed their cars. Paul hoped the guards at the rear gate would be less inclined to stand in the rain and closely examine his identification documents, which he had lifted from the Security Division's main office just a couple of hours ago. Paul had become Thomas, but any close examination of the Syrch employee badge would reveal the hoax.

Turning right once again, Paul pulled into the drive of the service entrance and stopped far enough away that it would force the guards to come out and physically inspect the vehicle while being fully exposed to the pounding rain. He flipped the vehicle's high beams on and off, honked the horn, adjusted his hat low across his brow, and waited.

A few tumbling minutes later, an unhappy looking guard slipped out of the control building, a long flashlight in one hand, his other hand holding his hat on his head, and made his way to the awaiting vehicle. Paul rolled down his window.

The guard strolled up, shone the light in Paul's eyes, and said, "It's after hours, buddy. And you can't park here."

"I have a pickup order." Paul fumbled with his stolen identification and held up a fabricated vehicle log that indicated a pickup at the school. "Thomas. Thomas Vain. That's me. Have to bring some brat to one of the labs. Hell of a night, isn't it?"

"This late?"

"I don't make the schedule; I just drive where I'm told."

The guard flicked the light from his flashlight into the car. He tilted the logbook up and read through the lines. It was difficult because the wind kept trying to flip the pages, and as water hit the logbook, the ink began to smudge and run. The guard handed the logbook back to Paul, and Paul handed the man the stolen identity badge. Before turning it over, Paul was careful to turn the badge into the rain so water beaded on its surface, obscuring the face of Thomas Vain.

The guard took out a digital reader and scanned the identification card. A light bleeped green on the device, and a display window pulled up a picture of Vain while validating the card as valid. The guard squinted at the picture on the display and was satisfied it was the same as on the identification card. Then he shone the flashlight in Paul's face again.

"Hey, can you keep that light out of my eyes? You're making me night blind, and it's tough enough to drive in this squall."

"Yeah, all right, buddy. Hold on." The guard made a call on his radio, and the vehicle gate to the rear entrance of the school compound began to open. The gate squeaked and rumbled as it moved. "Park on the far side of the lot, okay? And do you know where you are going?"

"Yep, not the first time I've been here," Paul answered.

"Okay." The guard handed back the identification card and motioned him forward.

"Sorry I had to drag you out into the rain."

The guard smiled and nodded his head and walked swiftly back toward the shelter of the control building.

Paul pulled the vehicle up beneath the dull amber glow of the parking area's lighting and moved as far away from the control building as he could, stopping in a shadowed parking spot near the edge of the playing field. Stepping out of the car into the rain, Paul pulled his collar up close, and, slamming his car door, stepped beneath a row of trees along a concrete sidewalk and began walking east down the center of the school's compound. The playing field was on his left, an oblong thing of thick grass that was slick and shiny in the rain. He passed a low, rectangular building that sat adjacent to the outdoor pool, under low-hanging tree branches that whipped back and forth in the wind, and soon found himself near the pile of great stones that he had seen earlier in the week. The rocks were slick and dull in the night. Up ahead, Paul could see the rough outlines of the redbrick buildings of the dormitories through another row of trees that ran north to south along an intersecting sidewalk. Paul shuffled forward a bit, his feet splashing, and then walked rapidly toward the dormitory buildings, turning at the corner to his left, where the northern quad rested around a well-manicured field of grass. The dormitory buildings resembled brick brownstones arranged in a half-horseshoe pattern with one branch on the west, the toe on the north, and the third branch on the eastern side of the grassy field. A tall statue on a pedestal sat in the middle of the grassy field. The statue was one of a man in ancient dress carrying a book in one hand and a power tool of some sort in his other. The statue was facing the north, and the man seemed to be extolling some great virtue to the students who, unconcerned, were huddled in their beds, hiding from the dreadful weather.

The sidewalk changed from concrete to red brick, and Paul followed it north. At the elbow of brownstone buildings, he turned right and began counting the chimneys that billowed white steam into the night. He came to the third stoop and stopped. Turning his eyes up into the rain at the top of the building, he concluded he had arrived. He walked up the stair and pulled open the front doors, ducking into the building and out of the rain.

The entryway to the dormitory building was resplendent in rich woods panels. A half table, with a marble top over which hung an oval mirror, hugged the wall to his left, and a long, open-air stairway, with rails and a dark wooden banister, followed the wall to his right up to the landing of the second floor. At the end of the landing on the far wall, another set of stairs led to a second landing on the third floor. Paul did not see an elevator. He shook most of the water off his coat, tilted his hat back a little, and followed the creaking stairs to the third floor, running his free hand up the cool banister until he stood at the end of a short hallway lined by doors. Jillian's room was supposed to be in the center on his right. But there was no center. The hall was divided evenly with four rooms on the left and four on the right.

Paul stopped before the second, right-hand door and tried the handle. It was unlocked. He pushed his head into a darkened room. A small bed was to the left, windows with a tidy desk to his front, and a protruding wardrobe ran the length of the opposite wall. Paul pulled a small flashlight out of his pocket and shone it at the still form in the bed. It was a girl, but she had light hair. It was not Jillian. The girl frowned in her sleep and waved a hand at the light. Paul released the pressure switch, and the light died. He slowly closed the door and went to the next room. The next room had the same layout, but instead of finding a light-haired girl in bed, Paul saw Jillian's little cherub face peeking out of the top of a comforter. Her dark hair was splayed out in a fan around her head. Jillian looked peaceful, her little chest rising beneath the comforter, one hand holding the comforter's edge while the other was cocked over the top of her head at an angle.

Paul moved quietly into the room and moved to the opposite wall, activating the window blinds that silently closed, blocking the view of the statue that looked at him accusingly. He found the light switch near the door and stopped for a moment to watch Jillian sleep. He had never watched a child sleep before he had met Jillian. It gave him a momentary feeling of paternal satisfaction, and suddenly a tendril of doubt crept into his mind. But whatever the nature of the feeling, Paul soon shook it off and reached over and turned on the light.

Jillian stirred. She crinkled her eyes and tried to block the light with her arm while turning toward the wall.

"Jillian," Paul softly said. "Jillian!" He walked over and sat on the edge of the bed.

Rising in a daze from her sleep, Jillian's eyes fluttered open, rolled, and tried to focus. She turned slowly and looked at Paul, but she did not show any sign of recognition. Paul pulled off his hat and shook some water off of it.

"Jillian? It's me, Paul. Paul Thorne. I've come to get you."

"What? What ... Paul? Paul?"

"Yes. You remember me."

"Paul!" Jillian darted awake and sat up with a start. She wiped at her eyes and looked at the enforcer intently. "What are you doing here? You're wet!"

"Come on, kid. You can't stay here. You're smart. You know what's going on. You need to come with me, now. This is your chance to escape."

"But ... but I have a project tomorrow. Escape ... Paul?"

"That's right, kid. This isn't for you. It's a nice prison, but it's a prison. You don't deserve this."

"My dad?"

"The doctor? He's not your father, Jillian. You know that now, don't you?"

"I thought ... He doesn't want to see me?"

"He didn't send me, no. Syrch has him setting up a new lab for new experiments. He is not thinking about you."

Jillian looked down sadly. She pulled her other hand out from beneath the comforter. She was gripping her stuffed bunny.

"Come on, kid. It isn't all that bad. Is it?"

Jillian nodded.

"It'll get better. I promise, Jillian, but only if you come with me now. Leave this place. Let me take you to where you will have your own life. Trust me."

"Trust you?"

"You did before."

"Yes ... yes, I did ... but you killed that man."

"He was going to kill you."

"He was your friend."

"Yes. In a way—and no."

"And they said I should not see you anymore."

"Who? Syrch? Of course they said that. They don't want you to have any friends, Jillian. They want you all for themselves."

"Are you my friend?"

"I like to think so."

"Why?"

"You know, kid, I have no idea. I just am."

"Will you get into trouble?"

"Only if they catch me."

"I don't want you to get in trouble."

"I'm a big boy, Jillian. I can take care of myself. But for now, you need to get dressed. Put on your coat. We need to leave before the guards become suspicious."

"Where are we going?"

"To a spaceship."

"A spaceship?"

"It'll be fun. Look, I can explain it all later, kid. Right now, let's get moving."

"You're my friend?"

"I am the only real friend you have. Ready?"

Jillian nodded. Paul helped her out of bed and turned his back as the girl slipped into a blue dress and shoes. Paul held her coat open as Jillian struggled into it. She took a small yellow backpack out and stuffed in a few of her more cherished belongings and was soon ready to go. Paul knelt down in front of her and looked her in the eyes.

"It's good to see you, kid."

She reached out and gave the enforcer a hug. Paul tensed at first but then slowly put his arms around her and hugged her back.

"Let's go."

Standing, Paul turned the room light off, and, taking Jillian by the hand, he and the girl stepped back into the silent hallway. They made their way down the stairs, along the wood-paneled walls, and back to the dormitory entrance. Opening the door, Paul peeked out into the rain. There was nobody else about. So with Jillian in hand, he descended the short flight of stairs to the sidewalk and guided

Jillian back the way he had come. The wind was still harsh, and though the rain had let up a little, it still splashed in puddles and skipped along the ground.

"Will I ever come back here again?" Jillian asked.

"If you want. When you are all grown up. But you'll do it by choice. It will be your decision."

"I'll miss my friends."

"I know. But you'll make new ones."

"Will I?"

"Of course."

They passed the rock pile, and Jillian shifted her backpack with one hand. Paul led her past the playing field and into the shadows where his car was parked. He removed her coat and wrapped her in the protective blanket, handing her bunny back to her and buckling her into the companion seat. He closed the door and took a moment to look around the empty parking lot. The guards were still huddled in the control building. Thunder rolled, and Paul dropped into his car and pulled back to the vehicle gate. He waved at the guards as they let him out. He turned right up the street and headed to the interchange, his eyes glancing back and forth from his mirrors to the road. Nobody followed. No alarms rang. Jillian settled back into the seat and was soon drooping into sleep. Paul merged on the highway leading out of town and accelerated. He didn't know how long he had before Syrch found out he had taken the girl. He had no time to waste.

The storm continued to broil, the rain pounding, as Paul stared intently at the road ahead, thinking they might actually get away.

17

—◦○◦○◦◉◦○◦○◦—

FLIGHT

THE RAIN had stopped and started again. Paul was driving diagonally away from the highway toward the rendezvous point. Jillian was sound asleep next to him, breathing softly, her head lolling now and again as she sought a comfortable position. Paul glanced in his rearview mirror. There they were, two tiny dots moving quickly behind him. He did not believe in coincidence. It was after one in the morning, and he had not seen any other cars on the road. Yet suddenly two cars, traveling together at a high rate of speed, appeared in the rearview mirror. He was convinced Syrch had been alerted to Jillian's disappearance. He was now in a race for his life and Jillian's freedom. Paul pushed down on the accelerator, and the car sped forward, the sound of its passage reverberating in the damp air.

The hulking forms of derelict buildings eased out of the shadow of night almost imperceptibly. At first, Paul was not sure they were real. The abandoned mining complex was arrayed in the morning mist like humps of whales, seen from a distance on a stormy sea.

The tallest building appeared to be just over eight stories, but most of them were a scatter of low-set forms strewn about the dark as, beyond them, a long ridge of torn dirt hid the vast pit of the strip mine that Paul knew was there. He pushed the vehicle forward, the engine revving with a solid roar as he flew from pool of light to pool of light on the poorly lit road. The car rumbled, throwing water up as the soaked ground refused the rain, pushing it into meandering waves that skimmed across the pavement. The rear end of the car suddenly eased to the side, and Paul let off the pedal and fought to steer the car through the near catastrophic slide. He cursed, cautiously slowed the car, and looked into his rearview mirror at the two black dots gaining on his position. In a sudden flash of lightning, he caught a fleeting glimpse of something darting across the sky behind him. It was solid, low to the ground, and moving laterally across the edge of his vision where it disappeared into the background of black cloud.

Raven? The airship had briefly looked like a dark-winged Raven gyrocopter. They were ultrafast attack helicopters that served as scouts and weapons platforms. A favorite of Syrch, the slim, two-person craft were widely used enforcer aircraft. It was very capable of flanking Paul, swinging up in front of him, and positioning itself between Paul and the waiting spacecraft. It likely would not fire on Paul's vehicle. The weapons it carried were brutal things not designed for subtle work. Firing at Paul would only endanger Jillian. And Syrch wanted Jillian. Would it fire on the spacecraft? That was a possibility. But it wouldn't be necessary if it could keep Paul from getting Jillian on board. However, if there was nothing left of the *Dorothea* for Paul to board, then the game would be over. Paul hoped the pilot of the *Dorothea* had seen the Raven too. The pilot was supposed to be good, experienced; hopefully he knew how to take care of himself.

Paul cursed, but nobody had told him it would be easy.

"Jillian. Jillian!" he said a little louder. "It's time to wake up. Jillian!"

Jillian's eyes fluttered, and her body moved slowly. She stretched and then pulled at the protective blanket that trapped her. Jillian panicked for a moment as the tangle of heavy, protective fabric constricted her movement. But then her head lolled toward Paul, and it seemed as if her mind was finally clearing itself of the esteemed nectar of deep sleep.

"Jillian?"

"Are we there?" The rain thudded on the roof of the car and splatted against the window as the windshield wipers worked furiously to keep the windshield clear. "Are we there?"

"Almost. But we have company."

"Company?"

"Enforcers behind us," Paul said. "And … maybe to our front. It's about to get a little ugly, kid. Are you up for it?"

"I don't know. I'll try."

"When we get closer to these old buildings, we're going to have to be ready to move. The mine is a huge pit just on the other side of that distant hill. And this car won't handle the access roads well. It'll get uncomfortable, and then we are going to have to walk."

"Okay."

Paul looked at the rearview mirror. The pursuing cars were not getting any closer. He figured they were fifteen minutes behind and wondered if that would be enough time to get to the bottom of the pit where the *Dorothea* was waiting. The pit was huge, Paul knew. A flowing bore in the heart of the planet, it was a massive six miles long, three and a half miles wide, and over six hundred feet deep. The sides of the mine were terraced. The terraces wound around the pit, following the contours of the dig, and were wide enough to allow the slow traffic of huge machines along the various levels. But it would take Paul a long while to drive the contoured road, all the time exposed to threats from above. So Paul had planned not to drive down into the mine. There was another faster but more frightening option.

Paul drove past the first of the old mining operation buildings, concrete slab walls with cheap, corrugated roofing that glistened in the car headlights with rust-red streaks and graffiti. It took another few minutes to reach and pass the eight-story central administration building situated at a fork in the road that broke to the right and, Paul knew from his survey, ran in a looping arch next to the main road, forming a D shape that, after passing the entrance to the pit itself, moved back down the ridge to rejoin the main road. Paul eased to the right fork, and the vehicle began climbing the ridge, passing other outbuildings and abandoned equipment. Paul was looking for a side road that would take him and Jillian back along the southern tip of the pit to the wheelhouse. The wheelhouse was surrounded by several smaller, brick and concrete buildings that served as the central hub for miners as they descended down into the pit or returned to the top for meal breaks or before ending their shifts and going home. Paul took the next right and looped back in the direction he had come, ignoring the following turn onto the main access road to the mine and zipping back in the direction he had come. In a few minutes, he was veering to the left. He knew the mine's gaping hole was a hundred yards or less off his left shoulder, but it remained hidden within the rain.

A dark blur moved rapidly toward him from the mine side of the road, and Paul heard the distinct chopping sounds of the gyrocopter as its blades whipped the air with a thrumming, popping noise. Suddenly a sharper peppering sound, like a tiny cannon in rapid fire, reverberated in the air, and lights flashed from the Raven's twin miniguns, throwing lead in front of Paul's car in warning. Paul ignored the threat, slowed, and drove the vehicle off the road into the muddy ground that lay a few feet below the roadway. The car slid as it careened off the road, and Paul fought to control it as the wheels slipped and churned on the muddy terrain until they again found purchase on the flat expanse of land that led to Paul's right to meet the rapidly approaching rear of a row of buildings. Ahead, he could make out the shape of a large metal structure that rose above all the buildings like one of the legs of the Eiffel Tower, crisscrossed in steel and sticking at an angle toward the mining pit. Paul steered toward it, the car jostling and thudding as it struck rocks and bounded over the uneven terrain while the Raven wheeled above in an arc and fired again, rounds bouncing along the ground near the driver's-side door. Paul swerved, cursed, and glanced to make sure Jillian was all right. She was clasping her rabbit tightly and pressing against the door in an attempt to keep from getting thrown about. She looked scared.

Flipping the steering wheel hard, Paul skidded next to the nearest building and slammed on the brakes. The car came to a skittering halt. He turned the engine off and darted out of the vehicle.

"Time to go! Jillian, get out of the car!"

Jillian opened the car door as the Raven raced overhead. Jillian ducked and then stood unmoving as the whopping of the Raven's blades echoed in the rain.

Paul opened the trunk and slung the two shoulder bags together over his shoulder and then reached down and removed the sleek form of the scoped rifle he had placed there. Fumbling forward, the packs sliding along his back, he grabbed ahold of Jillian and dragged her flush with the side of the building.

"Come on!" Paul yelled as he heard the gyrocopter rotating around for another pass.

Paul pulled Jillian and got her moving, the two ducking into a narrow alley between buildings. He almost fell as his foot hit a patch of mud, but at the last moment, he regained his footing. Guiding Jillian, Paul led her to the far side of the alley as the sound of machine-gun fire again breached the night. Turning, Paul hugged Jillian to his chest and covered her as best he could as the Raven fired explosive rounds at the just-abandoned car. Concussive blasts ripped at the ground until a string of fire struck the vehicle, igniting its fuel tank in a bright-lighted explosion that temporarily blinded Paul. Jillian screamed.

Paul tucked her behind him and brought the rifle to his shoulder. He shrugged the bags off his back and flipped the power switch on the scope. Wiping water from his eyes, he looked through the night-vision scope and quickly scanned the skies for the Raven. The gyrocopter was difficult to find against the rolling backdrop of the clouded sky, but when Paul switched the scope from passive light to active infrared, the heat signature of the Raven jumped out of the darkness as a glowing ball of red.

"Cover your ears!" he warned Jillian. But he did not waste time turning to see if she had obeyed. Paul put the crosshairs on the Raven and then moved the sights four body lengths of the Raven to the Raven's front and fired three lightning-quick rounds at the gyrocopter. He figured he must have hit it, for the Raven suddenly swerved back out toward the main road. Paul could hear the gyrocopter's engines rev and strain as it darted away from the line of his fire.

"It'll come back," he said to Jillian. He slung the bags over his shoulder again. "We're going to the big building in the center of town. It has a cable lift that will take us down into the mine. Follow me and stay close."

Jillian nodded and followed Paul as he, staying near the side of the building, walked purposefully back along the main street toward the center of the small, town-like cluster of service buildings. The building he was looking for, with the iron superstructure that lurched into the sky, was near. Looking to his left and right, Paul took Jillian's hand and scurried across the road to the squat building that housed the aerial tram that was used to move people and supplies from the top of the mine to its working heart. Paul had once read that, unlike the rest of the mine, the aerial tram remained operational to facilitate geological surveys of the bedrock of Papen's World. A little premission research seemed to confirm that fact, as Paul found photos of geologists being lowered into the mine along the aerial tram's high tensile-strength, coated, steel cables. Now he just needed to get Jillian on board the gondola for the ride down into the pit while somehow spiking the control system to prevent anyone from reversing the cable's flow and pulling Paul and Jillian back into the wheelhouse. But this system had a very special setting for emergencies that allowed it to travel at a clipping forty miles per hour. Supplies could be rushed to the bottom of the pit, and someone injured could be shipped quickly to the summit, at breakneck speeds. Paul hoped he could find that setting on the control panel, as he suspected the pursuing enforcers were already pulling up the road and into the small servicing center. If he did not get down into the pit soon, he would have to fight off four to eight highly trained professionals. The chances of Paul coming out on top of that melee were small to none.

Stepping up on to the landing, he approached the square building that housed the aerial tram. He tried the main glass doors. They were locked.

"Okay, Jillian. Stay back. A little further. Good."

Jillian moved to the edge of the landing and watched as Paul tried breaking the glass door with the butt of his rifle. He rotated the rifle and fired two rounds at the doors, punching small holes through the glass and creating a web of cracks that spiraled outward from the bullet impact points. He glanced over his shoulder to make sure the area was still clear before he beat his rifle upon the door once again. This time the glass began to give, rippling into beads, and finally collapsed in a mighty blow, scattering pieces of glass all over the tile-covered floor of the tram building. Paul quickly kicked at the edging of the glass with his heavy, black boots, clearing sharp fragments from the doorframe.

"We're good," he said to Jillian.

He guided her over the mess as the gyrocopter flew overhead. Paul would have to do something about the Raven. Even if they used the emergency descend feature on the tram, they would be sitting ducks for the Raven. But Paul didn't want to kill anyone. It was one thing to defy Syrch and steal Jillian. It was another to kill one of their pilots or enforcers. And Paul already had one strike against him in regards to the later. If he could get out cleanly, maybe Syrch would forgive him. Well … maybe they would let him live. It was a hope.

The glass skidded and crunched beneath their feet as Paul and Jillian moved through the waiting area with its rows of cheap seating to the turnstiles leading into the boarding area. The control room wasn't much more than a booth located at the right of the huge, horizontal wheel that powered the aerial tram. Paul grimaced and kicked viciously at the door to the control booth. The bolt securing the door ripped through the woodened doorframe as the door crashed open, slamming back against the wall of the control booth before bouncing partially back. Paul stopped it with an outstretched hand, smiled down at Jillian, and stepped into the booth.

An old, bar-high stool sat near a control console where rows of red and blue-green covered lights were arranged in parallel on an antiquated control board. The controls were arranged in three rows and were clearly marked. One row indicated it was for passenger control, one for equipment loads, and the third was marked in red for emergency service. A large black switch in the upper left corner was marked Power while a second toggle, protected by a red, plastic cover, lay between the second and third rows of controls.

Paul looked out of the booth at the empty transport bay. There were no gondolas. He pushed the power button and was rewarded with a series of red lights that flashed on in each section of the console. Outside, Paul heard a thud and hum as the wheel shuddered. The lights across the console slowly turned green as the system cleared and became operational. There was another dull thud followed immediately by the churning of the wheel and movement of the cable through guide rails and then around the wheel itself. In a moment, a dark shape moved through the opened-faced edge of the boarding area as a saucer-shaped gondola appeared, moving smoothly up and into position. Paul pressed the stop button, and the gondola came to a halt, swinging slightly.

He moved out of the control booth, shifted the bags and rifle on his shoulder, and took Jillian's hand. He was just taking his first step toward the gondola when he heard a shuffling foot move across the floor. Paul froze, listened, and then slowly turned back toward the entrance area.

"Are you going somewhere, Paul?" The voice was feminine and familiar. He could see someone standing in the darkened space just behind the turnstiles. "Cat catch your tongue?"

"Shiloh?"

"In the flesh—no wait, Paul. No sudden moves. I don't want to have to shoot you."

"This is none of your business, Shiloh."

"Isn't it then?"

"It doesn't have to be."

"Where are you taking her, Paul? Were you thinking you could hide out here in the mine?"

"That's the general idea." Paul lied.

"Not smart."

"I never claimed to be smart, Shiloh."

"She's tracked, Paul. Or didn't you know?"

"Tracked?" Paul looked at Jillian. Syrch must have embedded a tracker inside the girl. That's how Syrch figured out Jillian was missing so quickly. "I see."

"I don't know why you did this, Paul, but it's over. Send the girl over to me, and, for old times' sake, I'll let you go. Who knows, you're a capable fellow. You might just evade Syrch and get off world."

"That's pretty decent of you."

"I'm a decent person. Well, I'm not, but you know how it is. Jillian, come here. You're going home."

"But … I don't want to go. Paul says …"

"What Paul says doesn't matter anymore, Jillian. What matters is getting you safely back to school."

"Paul says I'm an experiment. I don't want to be an experiment."

Shiloh Trenton stepped into the eerie green light cast from the control booth. Dressed in a dark skirt, blazer, and damp trench coat, her blond hair peeking out from beneath the rim of a felt fedora, she raised her hand a little. Light glinted off of Shiloh's handgun in the glow from the open control booth door. Shiloh slightly waved the handgun at Paul.

"Step away from the girl, Paul."

Paul looked back at the gondola. They had been so close. Maybe, with his armor, he could draw on and hit Shiloh before she could kill him. But with Jillian so near? And besides, he liked Shiloh. He had always liked her. How could he shoot her?

"Do you know what they'll do to her?" Paul asked.

"No. And neither do you."

"I think I know." He was trying to see around Shiloh, wondering where the other members of the enforcer team were. He didn't see anyone. "You're alone."

"Not for long."

"The Raven?"

"Yup. See, you are bright, Paul. I had it drop me, and then I just scooted along, followed you here. Come along, Jillian. This game is over."

Shiloh had the drop on him, and there was nothing Paul could do.

"Go on, Jillian. It's okay."

"But you said …"

"Yes, but she has us dead to rights. And I don't want to see you hurt." Paul's mind was moving quickly. If he could jump off the platform after Shiloh had the girl, maybe he could work his way around the building and catch the enforcer unawares. It was risky, but what choice did he have?

"But …"

"You heard him, Jillian. Come along."

Jillian stared up at Paul for a moment, her face determinately set, and then she looked back at Shiloh. "No. I don't want to go." Jillian took two steps away from Paul and faced Shiloh with anger. "I'm not going!" Jillian declared.

"You are coming, and you are coming right now!"

Shiloh moved toward the turnstiles, shadow etched across her face, her gun held leveled at Paul's chest. Just before she stepped through, Jillian darted forward and, holding both palms up to her temples yelled, "Stop! Go to sleep!"

Paul felt a pulse in the air, and he stumbled back, his head spinning. It felt as if someone had struck him with a hammer across the base of his skull. He fell to one knee and vomited on the hard floor as a black fog stunned him. The world swam and rotated, and he placed a hand on the cold ground, steadying himself but finding it difficult to resist the urge to collapse onto the dust of the floor. His ears filled with a rushing sound like waves on a mad tide, and this was replaced by a rising, shrill ringing that rose higher and thicker and louder until it made the back of his eyes ache. He covered his ears, closed his eyes, and shook his head. He felt the urge to vomit again and felt the burning of bile explode out of his mouth, splattering against the floor like wet sand on stone. His awareness pulled away from him, but then, in a sudden moment, everything whooshed back into being like air sucked into a vacuum, and as suddenly as the pulse had started, it ended, leaving Paul drained and confused. He opened his eyes and found Jillian staring at him, tears in her eyes, clinging to her stuffed rabbit, standing a few feet away from Shiloh's prostrate and unmoving form.

"What ... what the hell was that?"

"I'm sorry."

"What? Jillian, what did you say?"

"I said I'm sorry."

"Sorry? What did you do?"

Jillian shrugged.

Paul stumbled to his feet and fumbled his way to Jillian. He put both hands on her shoulders and looked at the little girl. He shook his head again, trying to clear the fog from his mind, gave Jillian a reassuring squeeze, and went past her, through the turnstile, and knelt down at Shiloh's side. Shiloh looked like a corpse, pale and wan, her eyes open and staring. She had hit her head when she fell. Blood pooled by her face in a sickly burgundy red. Paul tentatively stroked Shiloh's face. It was warm, and as Paul moved his hand near her half-opened mouth, he could feel Shiloh breathing. He sighed. She was alive. Paul gently rolled her over and repositioned Shiloh's neck, tilting her head back and extending her jaw forward, fully opening her airway. He quickly searched Shiloh's pockets and found the inevitable hand-sized flashlight. He turned the ring, activating the device in a brilliant crystalline beam. He put this by Shiloh to mark her location and then turned, unsure, back toward the girl.

Jillian had not moved. She looked frightened and alone, the alien-green light from the control booth giving her skin a sickly, sinister color. But Jillian's face was blank, and her lips quivered. She wiped at her nose and hugged her stuffed rabbit close.

Paul stood, still feeling a little unsteady, and made his way back to Jillian.

"Well, I'm not sure what just happened. But she's alive. And we have to go. Do you feel okay? Are you hurt?"

"I'm not hurt."

Paul ran a confused hand through his hair. His questions would have to wait.

"Into the gondola then. Our ride is waiting for us, and we have to get out of here before Shiloh's backup arrives."

Paul darted into the control booth and flipped the red cover of the toggle switch and then pushed the toggle upward. The far right of the control panel instantly lit, and a red light flashed and rotated from the ceiling. A larger red light flashed in the boarding area, and an alarm horn sounded. Paul recovered his two bags and the rifle that had fallen from his shoulder when he hit the floor. Then, taking Jillian by the hand, the two of them climbed into the driver's booth of the gondola. Outside, the rain still fell. The Raven fluttered in the sky, and car headlights washed across the darkness into the service complex. Paul buckled Jillian into a seat and then buckled himself in next to her.

"Hold on, Jillian," he said. "This might be a hell of a ride."

Paul pushed a lever forward and depressed the single on/off button. The alarm horn sounded again, a deep, plodding call of warning as the gondola lurched beneath the blood-red light.

18

~~—∘⊸∘⊂◯⊃∘⊶∘—~~

THE PIT

AT FIRST, the gondola moved slowly away from the platform. It swayed as it cleared the building, revealing an angry sky above a deep, foreboding drop into the mining pit. The twisted steel cable from which the gondola hung disappeared downward at a sharp angle toward what Paul assumed was the first in a series of distant and yet unseen support towers. Paul heard a succession of mechanical noises and felt the gondola pitch as the car was moved from the main passenger line to a separate line. The gondola began to swing gently, and then to Paul and Jillian's dismay, it tilted forward at an incredible angle. A warning bell rang. Red strobe lights began to appear along the long descent, the more distant ones not much more than pinpricks of blood in a well of darkness, and Paul smiled reassuringly through clenched teeth at Jillian, whose face was pale and drawn.

With no warning, the gondola fell. It zipped down the emergency cable, and Paul found himself clenching the front of the control panel as butterflies raced helter-skelter through his abdomen. Jillian screamed, bracing her feet on the hard metal of the car, her eyes wide, her face twisted as the gondola freefell through the air toward the dark opening of the mining pit, a giant wound in the planet's crust, the air rushing and the rain pounding. Just as Paul thought the car might crash into the side of the pit, it suddenly leveled out and zipped horizontally toward the first support tower. The gondola rumbled as it passed beneath the tower's control surface. Jillian screamed again. Paul felt the urge as well, but he held it in check as the guide cable again disappeared at an alarming angle below. The gondola approached the edge of the new drop, seemed to pause for a second, and then poured down the cable with frightening speed. Paul's thoughts briefly flicked to the Raven and the other enforcers, wondering where they were, but the horror of the gondola's ride pushed those worries from his mind as once again the gondola slowed, crossed beneath a support tower, and again rushed headlong down a steep drop. It was like going over a series of dramatic waterfalls in a barrel. The terrifying fall was broken by a sudden slowing before the gondola once again raced with abandon through the dark and rain, the cable singing from the friction as, again and again, the pattern repeated itself. Once a monstrously large mining vehicle, resting on two tank treads with a huge claw and bucket on one end and an elongated counterweight on the other, rose up before them. Paul thought the gondola was going to crash into the seven-story-tall machine, but before he knew it, they were past the thing, rambling across another support tower and diving once more into the open air beyond. And then the gondola slowed and evened out. Something mechanical, part of the gondola's connection arm to the guide cable, churned, and another wheelhouse, darkened like a shadow against the gray ground, welcomed them into its embrace. The gondola stopped.

Jillian vomited. The acidic smell washed over the tiny room. And she began to cry.

Paul unbuckled the girl and jumped out of the swaying gondola onto the cement floor of the wheelhouse. It was a mirror image of its sister that stood on the summit. Paul's legs were wobbly. Reaching into the gondola's compartment, he slung the two bags and the rifle to the ground and helped Jillian out of the gondola.

"I ... am ... not ... happy!" Jillian said.

Paul laughed. He didn't mean to, but the sound came out naturally, fully, filling the empty space around them.

"It's not funny!"

"No," he replied. But he laughed again. "It is not funny." Paul wiped a sleeve over Jillian's mouth, clearing the muck that clung there. "That sucked. But come on, we have to find the ship. Those enforcers are still after us. We have to move. Are you okay?"

"No!"

He ruffled Jillian's hair. She ducked away from his hand and stood defiantly, her arms crossed, her face pinched into a frown.

Rising to his feet, Paul recovered the bags and his rifle and then turned on a small flashlight. The room was dark, and the light shown through it in a long beam. Water trickled somewhere, and the air felt heavier, colder, and most impossibly damp. Hidden in the air was the deep, musky smell of dirt and rock.

"Here," Paul handed the flashlight to Jillian, "I brought two of them. You take this one, okay? But when we get outside, turn it off. We don't want the enforcers to see the light and find us."

She silently took the proffered light and bounced the beam around the room.

"Come along." He took her hand, but the girl refused to move. "Jillian? Come on."

She shook her head no.

"We don't have time for this," Paul said. "I'm sorry it was such a rough ride. But we have to find the spaceship."

The girl looked down at her feet defiantly, tucking her chin toward her chest, her eyes glaring upward at Paul.

Paul felt a flash of anger swell in him and took a half step toward Jillian. She cringed, and all of Paul's anger dissipated, followed by a sense of guilt.

"Please?"

Paul reached out his hand and waited. It only took a moment before Jillian's shoulders drooped and her lips trembled. She took his hand and shuffled forward.

"I'm sorry, kid. It was the quickest way."

Leading Jillian again, the two slipped out of the wheelhouse that lay on the southern side of the open-pit mine. The rain was still falling, but it was not as thick as it had been. From where he stood, Paul could see the terraced roads snaking their way up the side of the mine, and here and there, huge machines with tires and tank treads twice the height of a man, and bodies that rose like metallic goliaths, loomed everywhere. Some had giant buckets; some had large cutting wheels on one end, cables that ran across two towers and then fell to a counterweight on the far end; and some were simple yet massive dump trucks. There were specialty vehicles too. Paul could not fathom what their purposes were, but they were all massive machines capable of moving tons of rock and sand. The occasional whopping of the gyrocopter reverberated above, but Paul could not see it. The Raven blended wholly into the night. The ground was wet and muddy, and with each step, Paul heard the sloppy slurp and pop of his shoes. Jillian was struggling in the mud too, slipping and sloshing her way next to Paul. He had to slow down and help her as best he could while still maintaining control of the rifle and shoulder bags.

"The ship is supposed to be on the north side," he said. "It could be right in front of us or around the bend. It's a long walk, but let me try calling. Let's stop here by this old building. Stand under the awning out of the rain."

Jillian did as she was bid, and Paul took out his phone and dialed a number. He cursed as the phone failed to get a signal.

"We're too close to the wall of the mine. We need to move to the open a little."

Jillian stepped out of the shelter of the building, and the two of them began an arduous trek through the gravelly mud, Paul scanning the sky for the Raven and the dim ground of the open pit for the hulking shape of a spacecraft. He was not sure what the *Dorothea* looked like, but he figured he couldn't mistake it for some of the machines and buildings of the mine.

"I heard something," Jillian said.

"What?"

"I heard something behind us."

Paul stopped, and the two listened for a moment. Then he heard it, a squeaking noise and what sounded like the churning of a water wheel. Paul looked back the way he had come and noticed the lights on the wheelhouse were green, and the guide cable was slowly moving as the great wheel turned.

"The enforcers are coming down," he said. "But they look like they are taking the slow route. So we have a bit of time to get ahead of them. Hurry."

Jillian tried, but the mud made her movement awkward and slow. After a little while, Paul checked his phone and was rewarded by the signal indicator. He stopped by a large boulder beneath the hulking form of an excavator and dialed a number.

Paul wiped the rain off the transceiver. "We're here. No, at the bottom, south side. Can you come and get us? Yes. That's right. Good. I've got a light. I'll flash it when you are near." He turned to Jillian. "I spoke with the captain of the ship. He's on the way. Just stay still for a moment."

Paul and Jillian stood by the boulder as the rain fell. He could hear rain cascading off the top of the mine in a waterfall, rushing down the steep sides, flowing somewhere off to his far right. He stared into the dark sky to the north, straining. Paul heard the spaceship before he saw her. A deep rumble and a high-pitched whirl grew in the darkness. A great gray shape materialized out of the ether of night, slowly moving forward, the engine blast creating a growing, warm wind that ruffled Paul's coat. The *Dorothea* was a medium transport that used a combination of gravity-well generators and jet engines in the planet's atmosphere. The *Dorothea* had larger in-system engines as well, built into the spherical shape of the ship's hull on the stern. Yet the center of the ship was hollow—a ring built around a latticework structure that glistened like a giant spider's web. Paul knew what was suspended at the heart of the web: an insanity crystal. Insanity crystals allowed interstellar ships to frame from one folded edge of the fabric of space to the next folded edge, allowing the ship to travel faster than the speed of light. Like all interstellar ships Paul had ever seen, the *Dorothea* was circular in its shape, the mass of each side of the ship balanced and equal. The hull glistened in the inky darkness, but here and there lights blinked along its body.

"Stand back," Paul warned.

Paul stepped out from the protection of the boulder and flashed his light toward the ship, his thumb pressing and releasing the rubberized switch on the back of the flashlight, creating a strobe effect. It was not long before the ship responded, a long searchlight stabbing the darkness as the *Dorothea* approached, the wind from its engines growing until Paul had to lean slightly into it, and then the sound of the engines changed, growing weaker, and the interstellar ship settled to the ground.

Paul hurried to Jillian and pulled her off her feet, carrying her toward the waiting ship. Through the sound of the *Dorothea's* engines, Paul heard the familiar whopping of the Raven as it circled overhead, and from behind him, he heard the sound of distant voices. The voices were hard and sharp and belonged, Paul knew, to the enforcer team that had finally reached the bottom of the mine and was rushing to catch Paul and Jillian.

A ramp in the spaceship opened, casting a new bright light across the muddy ground. Paul blinked at it and then averted his eyes. He could follow the light without looking directly into it. It seemed like forever until he carried Jillian under the forward frame of the ship. He looked up and saw the figure of a man silhouetted against the open ramp's light. The man was singularly tall and carried a short-barrel assault rifle of some type.

"Captain Gutwein? Kurt Gutwein?"

"That's me. Welcome aboard."

"We've got company." Paul put Jillian on the deck of the ramp and motioned behind him. "Enforcers. And there is a Raven—a gyrocopter—sitting above us."

"I can handle that," the captain assured Paul. "Let's get you both on board and get my ship off the ground."

Paul followed Jillian along the sleek loading ramp and into one of the *Dorothea's* cargo bays. The bay was full of boxed supplies and neatly packed equipment. It looked to Paul like farming equipment. The ramp closed behind the three of them with a solid thud, and soon the captain was leading his guests up through the halls of the ship to an elevator.

"Let's get her off the ground," Captain Gutwein said into a communicator built into the elevator's wall.

"Aye, Captain," came the reply.

As Paul and Jillian waited for the elevator to stop, Paul felt the *Dorothea* lift and heard the engines roar. He got the disassociated feeling he often attributed to a ship turning in the atmosphere.

"This is the main deck," the captain said as the elevator stopped and he led Paul and Jillian into a long metallic hall. "We're running dark, so only the footlights are on, so watch your step. Come on up to the flight room. I've got seats for both of you there. We'll take a tour and all that later, when we have time. But right now, I want you handy." The captain directed this last comment to Paul.

"Why do you talk funny?" Jillian asked.

"Me? Me? It's you, little lady, who talks funny."

"What type of accent is that?" Paul asked. "I can't place it... German? Is it a type of German?"

"Yes. My ancestors are German, and I grew up in a German-speaking colony."

"What's German?" Jillian said.

The captain stopped for a moment, considering. "Well, how do you explain thousands of years of Earth history to a little girl in a few words? German is German." He laughed and led them along past decompression doors and into the command room. "Strap in," the captain said, indicating a row of curved seats sitting to the right of the room.

Paul and Jillian took the proffered chairs, and Paul helped Jillian with her acceleration harness. He glanced up at the two other people in the room. Both of them, a man and a woman, peered at Paul and Jillian for a moment in curiosity but then turned back to the consoles as the *Dorothea* continued a slow rise from the bottom of the pit-mine.

"There are your enforcers," Captain Gutwein said, pointing to a command screen that showed six glowing red figures standing a few hundred yards from the wheelhouse. "And there," the captain added, "is our little gyrocopter friend. Find us some open sky, Azalea. Let's push through it."

"Aye, Captain." Azalea, the woman on the right of the command room, replied.

"Azalea is my pilot," the captain explained. "She's good too. And the other is Faolan. He's my flight engineer."

Paul stowed his gear in the cabinet above the seats and sat next to Jillian, pulling his harness over his shoulders and buckling it tight.

"Is everyone ready?" the captain asked. "Good. Azalea, if you please. Get us some maneuvering room. She's a mean ship," the captain warned. "Hold tight." The captain strapped in.

The *Dorothea's* engines roared, and the whole ship shook under the power of its main engines. Paul saw the enforcers on the display scramble for cover. The *Dorothea* held its place, the hull of the ship shaking like a racehorse before the starting gate, ready to spring.

"Punch it!" the captain ordered.

The *Dorothea* leapt forward. The force of the acceleration pushed Paul back into the soft confines of the acceleration seat. Paul turned his head and looked at Jillian. She stared back, excitement and fear mingling on her face. Jillian slowly reached out a hand and wrapped it around the top of Paul's hand. He smiled, rotated his hand, and let Jillian grip his hand tightly.

"Outbound," Azalea said tightly.

The *Dorothea* continued to pick up speed, rising through the dark clouds, snapping its way through Papen's World's atmosphere and into the deeper dark of eternal space.

19

⸺◦◦◯◉◯◦◦⸺

EVASION

THE *DOMINATOR* fired a warning salvo, and the *Dorothea* bucked in the blast wave. The *Dorothea* had made it out of the gravity well of Papen's World and had started framing out of system, but its planned trajectory was denied them as the great Syrch warship *Dominator* suddenly appeared from behind the fifth planet in the Papen system and framed to intercept the smaller *Dorothea*. The *Dorothea* was no match for the thickly armored and highly armed battleship, but the *Dorothea* was lithe and quick, and Captain Gutwein decided to try to outrun the *Dominator*.

The warship fired again, and this time the fire impacted just to port. The *Dorothea* bucked and reared, and its Mobius shields sparked and crackled as it absorbed the blast. Paul was glad the *Dominator* had not been shooting lasers—at least not yet. That meant the Syrch warship still hoped to bring the smaller *Dorothea* to heel.

"Captain," flight engineer Faolan said. "There is an incoming message from the battleship."

"Put it on speaker. Azalea, can you adjust our course to bring us closer to the gas giant?"

"Aye."

"On speakers, Captain."

"*Dorothea*, this is the captain of the *Dominator*, Captain Masopha Taljaard. You are ordered to cut your frame drive and prepare to be boarded."

Captain Gutwein made a rude gesture with his hand and frowned. "I've changed my mind, Azalea. I don't think I want to speak to the *Dominator's* captain."

"*Dorothea*, this is Captain Taljaard. We have ripplers in the tube. This is your last warning."

"Are the in-system engines warm?" Captain Gutwein asked.

"Yes, sir."

"Good, if Syrch's navy plans to hit us with a rippler and then board us, they will be as trapped in the flat spot as we are. I think we can outrun her long enough to get near the gas giant. Have you ever been in a ship hit by a rippler?" the captain asked Paul.

"No."

"It isn't pretty. Azalea. Faolan. Lock everything down. You two," the captain directed at Paul and Jillian, "tighten your restraining harnesses. When the rippler hits, anything not tied down is going to fly across the ship and smack into a bulkhead."

Paul synched Jillian's harness first, making it snug enough to cause her to complain. He then pulled his tight. He knew that ripplers created artificial flat spots in space and that they disabled frame drives, but he was not sure what that meant in application. But from the hard sound of Captain Gutwein's voice, Paul was sure it would be unpleasant.

"Not so obvious!" Captain Gutwein barked. "Make the trajectory a little more subtle, Azalea."

"Got it, Captain. Better?"

Captain Gutwein looked at the navigational display and pressed a switch on his captain's chair. A red T-line appeared over the digital shape of the *Dorothea*. The T-line bubbled out, showing the computer's projected trajectory of the cargo ship. The captain looked satisfied with whatever it was he saw.

"Better," the captain replied.

"Shit! Rippler in the void," Faolan said. "Brace!"

On the navigational display, a tiny dot detached itself from the hulking battleship and skipped past the *Dorothea* at incredible speed. Before Paul knew what was happening, the *Dorothea* reeled and spun, tumbling into a widening pool of golden Kirlov's radiation as the rippler activated, grabbing onto every framable corner of space-time within range, instantly eliminating every possible purchase for the *Dorothea's* frame drive, which gasped frantically like an asthmatic searching for air, only to find nothing to breathe. The cargo shipped spasmed, and Paul was thrown against the chair's restraints with immense force. The blow forced air from his lungs, and all across the command room, anything not tied down rocketed forward, striking the walls of the ship. Luckily, the captain of the *Dorothea* kept a tight ship, and most of what jetted through the air was harmless. But Paul did see a coffee cup explode against a computer bank, and something small and metallic embedded itself in the ship's hull. Then the lights on the *Dorothea* flashed and dimmed in quick succession, and an alarm klaxon sounded.

"Faolan?"

"We're fine, Captain. A little shaken but nothing serious."

"The nuclear drive?"

"Operational and coming up online."

"Good. Azalea, once they are up, push directly toward the gas giant. Understood?"

"Aye."

"Are you two all right?"

Paul had been checking on Jillian. She appeared uninjured.

"Mr. Bunny!" Jillian called out, extending her arms in the direction where her stuffed rabbit lay on the deck.

"He's fine, Jillian." Paul looked back at the captain. "We're both fine. What now?"

"Run for the gas giant. The *Dominator* will have to enter the rippler field to board us. So it will be in-system drives against in-system drives."

"Can we outrun a battleship?"

"Normally, in a cargo ship? No," the captain responded. "But this is not a regular cargo ship. We should be able to stave off the *Dominator* for a little while. Let them close the gap though, Azalea. Let's encourage them to think they are gaining and thereby discourage them from shooting our engines out from under us.

"They must want the two of you pretty badly," the captain continued, looking directly at Paul. "Do you mind telling me why?"

"Do you really want to know?"

The captain considered for a moment. "No. No. I suppose not. But that is to our advantage. They are much less likely to vaporize us."

"We're at 85 percent capacity," Azalea told the captain.

Paul watched the navigation display as the *Dominator*, as predicted, entered the golden glow of the flat spot. But where the *Dorothea's* entrance into the disrupted field had been harsh and sudden, the *Dominator* eased in like a man slipping slowly into a hot bath.

"Kill the klaxon, will you, Faolan?"

"Right, Captain."

The flight engineer pushed a switch on the console to his front, and the klaxon, which Paul had forgotten had been blaring the whole time, suddenly turned silent. The sudden stillness was a bit disorienting.

"How long before we can begin framing again?" Paul asked.

"It depends on how Captain Taljaard programed the rippler," the captain replied. "I'm betting the rippler is set to last several hours. So get comfortable. It's going to be a slow race."

In-system speeds were notoriously slow. Large intra-system freight haulers, Paul knew, could take weeks to months to travel between planets. The nine AU between Papen's World and the gas giant the *Dorothea* was slowly approaching could take as long as a year at in-system speeds. And that was while traveling four times the speed of the *Apollo* spacecraft, which topped out at around twenty-four thousand miles an hour. Using a gen-one frame drive that limped along at light speed, the same journey would take approximately seventy-five standard Earth minutes. The *Dorothea*, Paul estimated, likely had a gen-three or gen-four frame drive and could, if not trapped by the rippler's effect, make the same trip in twenty-five minutes or less. And Paul had no doubt that the battleship *Dominator* had at least a gen-four frame drive—but probably a gen-five. Still, everyone knew the gravity wells generated by planets created flat spots that made even the most sophisticated frame drives useless. Depending on the size of a planet and its corresponding flat spot, a ship could take several hours to move the last distance between the edge of a planet's flat spot and planetary orbit. In some ways, it was much easier to travel the vast distances of space than it was to travel the less mindboggling distances between a planet and its moons. Framing technology was great—it had opened up the stars for human exploration and expansion—but it had definite limitations. Once outside of a planet's gravity well— that was a different story. In a flat-out race, the *Dorothea* had little chance to outpace the *Dominator*.

It made Paul wonder why Captain Gutwein was so focused on getting near the gas giant. Both ships would be stuck in the planet's gravity well and would have to use their nuclear engines, but the *Dominator* had more shielding and much, much more firepower than the *Dorothea*. What advantage was gained? Wouldn't they be in the exact same predicament they were in now? It didn't make any sense. Paul hoped Captain Gutwein knew what he was about, because from where Paul sat, the Syrch warship had them dead to rights. Even if the *Dorothea* was faster than the *Dominator* in flat spots, as it appeared, that wouldn't protect the cargo ship from the battleship's massive weapons, and the moment the *Dorothea* stepped out of the flat spot, the *Dominator* would do exactly that—dominate. Paul was already trying to enjoy his last minutes of freedom before being arrested and thrown in some radioactive slave mine where he would spend his last days in a miserable existence. And that was if Syrch didn't just shoot him. The amount of time and suffering Paul would spend all depended upon how pissed off Syrch was at him and how much Syrch wanted Paul to suffer.

Paul watched the navigational display as the *Dominator* moved incrementally closer to the *Dorothea*. At least that ploy appeared to be working. The Syrch battleship was not firing at the *Dorothea* to cripple her.

Paul unstrapped Jillian to allow her to recover her stuffed bunny, and both of them used the toilet. Paul got Jillian out of her wet clothing and noticed how sleepy Jillian appeared. And though Paul was loath to part with Jillian for any time, it became obvious that she needed to sleep in a bed. So Paul asked the captain to show him where Jillian could rest.

"The ship's living space is compacted into this section of *Dorothea*," Faolan, the engineer, said. Captain Gutwein sent Paul and Jillian with Faolan to find sleeping quarters. "The state rooms, kitchen, and gym are all on this ship module. The other three modules are used for engines and cargo."

The engineer led them down a carpeted corridor, past several closed doors, and stopped midsection, opening a door that revealed a small but comfortable state room.

"Do you need help getting her settled?" Faolan asked. He was a friendly man of medium height with dark hair and eyes. His face was shadowed with beard stubble. He wore a standard workman's jumpsuit that was stained with oil and grease. And his smile was carefree and warm.

"No. I've been on an interstellar before. I can manage."

"Use the decompression bubble," Faolan warned. "You know … just in case."

Paul acknowledged the suggestion with a nod of his head. Jillian thanked the engineer in her slight voice and sleepily allowed Paul to put her under the covers of the small but comfortable bed that was attached to the bulkhead in the back of the room.

Jillian's eyes fluttered, and she yawned. "Are you angry with me?" she asked Paul.

He pulled back and looked seriously at Jillian. "No, silly. Why would you think that?"

"Because of your friend?"

"My friend? Oh, Shiloh. I will ask you about that when we have time. But no, I am not angry with you for … whatever that was. It was very helpful. Nobody had to hurt anyone."

"I thought you might be angry."

"At you? Never." Paul pulled the covers up and brushed his hand lightly over Jillian's hair. "Jillian, I'm going to activate the decompression bubble."

"What's that?"

"It is just a clear membrane that will surround the bed. That way, if something goes wrong with the ship …"

"Something will go wrong with the ship?"

"I don't know. I don't think so. But this is just in case. Everyone uses them when they sleep on a spaceship. And when it is in place, you'll see a red pull rope in the center of it. To open it, you just pull on the pull rope. As long as the ship is safe and pressurized, it will open. And then see there on the wall?" He pointed behind Jillian. The girl rolled over and glanced at the small communication box that was embedded in the wall. "You can still use that to talk to people on the ship. You know how to work it?"

"Yes."

"Good. Then I'll let you get some sleep. Ready?"

"Okay."

Paul stood up, pressing the long, flat switch that activated the decompression bubble. A metal arm detached itself from the wall and dropped down until it was centered above the bed. From the end of the arm, a fine filament began to emerge and slowly sink toward the edge of the bed where it latched itself on the bed frame. Paul heard the unit seal, and he checked to make sure it was properly functioning. Satisfied, he turned to leave.

"Paul?" Jillian said weakly.

"Yeah, kid."

"Will you stay until I fall asleep?"

He nodded. "Sure, kid."

Pulling up a chair that sat under a small desk that rested between two thin wardrobes, he sat down and waited. Jillian smiled and closed her eyes, and her breathing slowed. Paul remained unmoving, watching, until he was sure she had fallen asleep.

Paul felt amazed by Jillian. She was tiny, and everything about her emanated a need for protection. It was irresistible. *Is this how a father feels? Do they feel like they would fight the entire universe to protect their children?*

With this question in his mind, Paul quietly dimmed the lights and left the room. He felt a mixture of anxiety and a deep sense of determination. He had to do something to keep Jillian away from Syrch Corp. But for the first time in a long while, he felt incapable of directly affecting the course of events. He had to rely on Captain Gutwein. And that made Paul uncomfortable. In his experience, people always let him down.

20

◦=◦=◦-○◯○-◦=◦=◦

GAMBIT

A HALF-EMPTY cup of Stem sat before Paul. He picked it up and drained the rest of the drink. He was exhausted, but the *Dominator* had closed the distance and now loomed off the *Dorothea's* starboard side. The two ships had left the golden radiation of the rippler's flat spot behind. This had been followed by a short frame to within reach of the gas giant where both ships had reentered normal space, caught in the giant's natural flat spot. The battleship's captain warned the *Dorothea* about being boarded while the *Dominator* positioned itself to cut off the *Dorothea's* escape vector. The *Dorothea*, pressed on one side by the indomitable mass of the gas giant and on the other by the irresistible presence of the *Dominator*, moved steadily forward. It was no time for Paul's mind to be sluggish and dull. The Stem helped.

Paul looked at the *Dorothea's* captain, Captain Kurt Gutwein. Tall without being lanky, the captain sat stiffly in his chair, his eyes flashing over the navigation display and a computer-generated trajectory that seemed outlandish to Paul. But he didn't want to interrupt the captain at this critical juncture, so he kept his concerns to himself. The flight engineer, Faolan, was sitting hunched over his flight station. And the pilot, Azalea, who wore dark slacks and a frilled pink blouse, concentrated on flying the ship. The captain had demanded extreme precision on their flight path. They were threading a needle.

"Keep her steady," the captain said.

"Slow and steady," Azalea answered.

"Captain," Paul said.

"Call me Kurt. We are not so formal on the ship."

"Kurt, right. Forget it." Paul shifted uncomfortably.

"What were you going to ask?"

"It's not important," Paul replied. "It can wait."

"Do you see?" Azalea asked.

"Jump ship. Boarding party," the captain replied.

"Yep."

"Push her up a little. Make them drift."

"Aye."

A small craft had detached itself from the *Dominator* and was approaching the *Dorothea*. It was a jump ship, specifically designed for ship-to-ship transport of invading marines. Azalea adjusted the ship's engines. It was a subtle adjustment, and it took a while before Paul saw the effect on the navigation screen. The jump ship fell a little behind the *Dorothea*, forcing the jump ship's pilot to adjust.

"Crap! We need to get closer to the planet. I need the *Dominator* to get clearly inside the well." The captain changed the navigation display so it depicted the gas giant's gravitational well. "See if you can suck that ship deeper in toward the planet and then bring us back into alignment with the *Dominator's* nose. Shimmy a little too."

Azalea nodded and adjusted course. She pushed the engines a bit more and occasionally tweaked the *Dorothea's* trajectory while doing something that sent vibrations throughout the ship.

"We're fine," the captain said to Paul.

"Are we?"

"The shaking makes it looks like we're straining our in-system engines. We're not."

"A setup?"

"A feint, yes."

"Feels real."

The captain smiled. "Good."

"Captain, *Dominator* took the bait."

"I see. Good work, Azalea. Now let's add some steam and pull up right at her nose."

"We could fire at the jump ship," Faolan suggested. "Slow it down a bit. It's getting awfully close."

"Don't do that. Right now we haven't hurt them at all. We're just running. But if we shoot at them, it will change the equation. They might just shoot back."

"The jump ship's nearing docking range though, Captain. Whatever you have in mind ..."

"Patience is a virtue, Faolan. Keep steady, Azalea."

"Aye."

Paul watched as the *Dorothea* picked up speed and slipped just in front of the *Dominator*. It was a very dangerous maneuver. If the *Dorothea* lost speed or the *Dominator* picked up speed, the two ships would collide. The mass of the *Dominator* would plow through the smaller *Dorothea* to dreadful effect. And though Paul suspected the *Dominator* would survive, it would not go unharmed and would have to limp back to the high docks in Papen's World orbit.

The *Dorothea's* maneuver once again caused the approaching jump ship pilot to slow and adjust his course. The jump ship began to rotate as it prepared to dock along the bottom of the *Dorothea's* hull. Paul could picture Syrch's marines in their bulky combat suits, holding flechette and plasma rifles, standing up and hooking to the door in anticipation of forcefully docking with the *Dorothea*. The jump ship would blow a hole in the evading ship's hull through which the marines would pour, quickly overcoming the crew and ending Paul's attempt to get Jillian out of Syrch Corp's home system.

Paul wondered if it would be any use to resist the marines. He could take half a dozen down. But that wouldn't do anything but leave Paul dead and make the crew of the *Dorothea* accomplices in murder. Kidnapping—though Paul thought of it as a rescue—was bad enough. Syrch Corp would bring its brand of justice against the captain and his crew if any Syrch Corp employee was severely injured or killed. None of them would leave the ship alive. No. If the marines breached the hull and boarded the ship, Paul would not resist. So everything that Paul had done to get Jillian to safety depended on this moment, on the skill of Captain Gutwein and on whatever gods or goddesses watched over and protected children. It was now, Paul knew, or never.

"Throttle back, Azalea. Let's make them nervous."

Azalea complied, and the *Dorothea* began to slow. The gap between the encroaching *Dominator* and the *Dorothea* slowly shrank, and the collision alarm began sounding. Azalea silenced it.

"More," the captain coaxed. "Closer … closer …"

"The *Dominator* has checked its speed," Azalea announced. Paul thought he heard the sound of triumph in her voice.

"Captain," Faolan warned. The jump ship full of marines was making its final approach.

"Now!" The captain barked. "Now, Azalea!"

The *Dorothea* suddenly accelerated. Its engines, freed from a constraining hand at last, kicked into full power, and the cargo ship darted before the looming battleship. At the same time, the *Dorothea* began a hard ninety-degree climb away from the gas giant, cutting right in front of the trailing battleship and narrowly missing one of the larger ship's control towers. The jump ship that had been about to dock with the *Dorothea* found itself in the path of the oncoming behemoth as the pilot for the *Dominator* instinctively increased the battleship's speed in pursuit and tried to emulate the smaller ship's maneuver. The jump ship rolled back upon itself in a successful bid to avoid colliding with the *Dominator* but found itself cut off from the *Dorothea*. The *Dominator's* attempt to follow the sharp trajectory of the *Dorothea* was failing, the arc of its turn elongated, creating an instant spatial gap between the Syrch warship and the fleeing cargo ship.

"Frame! Frame! Frame!" the captain yelled.

"But we're still in the planetary well!" Paul interjected. He could clearly see that both the *Dominator* and the *Dorothea* were within the outer rim of the flat spot created by the gas giant.

"No we're not! But they are!"

The *Dorothea* shook, and the frame drive came to life. The insanity crystal burned bright, and the sudden glow of Kirlov's radiation, that golden hue, spread like an elixir over the cargo ship as the frame drive found purchase within the fabric of space-time and suddenly jumped to light speed. In the span of a few seconds, the *Dorothea* was 110 million miles from where the *Dominator* struggled in the malaise of the gas giant's flat spot. The warship was soon lost to view as the gas giant and Papen's system faded away and the *Dorothea* continued to increase its speed. Faster and faster until the cargo ship was at maximum speed, its gen-three frame drive moving the ship at three times the speed of light into the safe vastness of space.

Captain Gutwein laughed.

Azalea cheered.

Faolan looked like he had just avoided being a meal for a lion.

And Paul, quietly stunned, sat immobile.

"Holy shit," Paul whispered.

21

⊶∘⊶◦⊶◦◉◦⊶◦⊶∘⊶

TIANJIN SYSTEM

❝I DON'T understand how we got away," Paul said.

"Let me tell you how my old professor explained it," Captain Gutwein answered. "You see, planetary gravity wells are conical bubbles within space-time. They are not spherical as you might otherwise believe. In addition, planets are not resting on a folded sheet of space like you have been taught, but rather planets are incased by an energy tensor field of dark matter in four dimensions.

"Please explain, you say? Okay.

"Heavily massed matter-objects, like planets, create a conical warp of space-time much like a bubble surrounding another object. And that is because matter-objects don't just have gravity, they generate gravity as a gravity field. A planet's gravity well is made of the gravity field projected by that matter-object's mass. This means the gravity well of a planet resting in space-time is not just below the planet like a bowling ball sitting on a stretched fabric, but the gravity well exists on the sides and on top of the matter-object—the planet—as well. Get it? The more mass an object has, the more of a gravity field it creates, and the more of a gravity well it has in space-time. The larger the gravity well, the larger the flat spot. Larger planets have larger flat spots. We all know that.

"Yet matter-objects are dual natured. Like a negatively charged magnet, matter-objects push 'space'—space being primarily dark matter—away while dually showing a positive charge that pulls other matter-objects toward each other. We call that mechanism gravitational pull. Matter-objects have, in essence, a simultaneous negative and positive charge. The matter-object pushes at or repels dark matter—the tensor field we call space that in turn wants to expand into the matter-object's location—and pulls at matter-objects. Confused yet? Wait. Here is the kicker.

"Since dark matter has no mass, matter-objects sluice through dark matter within the dark matter vacuum. That vacuum is the energy tensor field of four dimensions I talked about earlier."

"You mean space," Paul said.

"Exactly! But it is not the same with the relationship between two matter-objects. Gravity affects matter-objects through acceleration. More simply, gravity's pull causes acceleration. A large-massed matter-object will overcome the field of a lessor-massed matter-object and pull it toward the larger-massed matter-object. And the more the mass of a matter-object, the more acceleration it creates on other matter-objects. It is this interaction that prevents the matter-universe from collapsing into a single, giant ball of mass. Understand?"

"No. And I don't think I want to."

"It gets better. Now, a smaller matter-object traveling too close to the gravity field of a larger matter-object—say a meteor to a planet—will collide due to the lack of inherent resistance to the larger massed matter-object's gravitational pull and the overcoming of the tension created in the dark-matter tensor field as it is squeezed between two matter-objects. But a smaller matter-object going quickly has an enhanced resistance to the gravity-generated field of the larger-massed matter-object. Speed allows the smaller matter-object to overcome the gravity well generated by the larger planet. The matter-object picks up energy (i.e., speed) and is deflected back into the dark-matter vacuum void. The objects do not collide. Either that or the smaller matter-object obtains enough speed to avoid a collision but does not have enough velocity to completely escape the larger matter-object, consequently resulting in what we consider an orbit. Not enough energy or speed to escape but just enough not to get sucked into a collision course with the larger matter-object."

Paul stared blankly at the captain. "I have no idea what it was you just said."

"Frankly, neither do I." The captain laughed. "I flunked that course. And it is just a theory. All I know is that I have a lower mass than that battleship, and that let me get a sharper angle of deflection through the gas giant's gravity well. And since the *Dorothea* does not have as much mass as the battleship, I was able to skip the rim of the gravity well—its flat spot—and escape it, the flat spot threshold, faster than our hulking friend. So I was out of the flat spot quicker, at a sharper angle, and was able to frame before the battleship could. And that is how we got away."

"Okay … I think I will take your word on that, Kurt."

Paul, Captain Gutwein, Faolan the flight engineer, and Azalea the pilot were sitting in the galley sharing a pot of normal coffee. The captain was glowing with the success of the *Dorothea's* escape while Faolan still looked a little sick, and Azalea—attractive now that Paul had the luxury of looking at her closely—had a pleased smile on her lips, but her mind seemed distant in that quirky way of starship pilots, as if she were here but at the same time was elsewhere and everywhere. Paul knew enough about pilots to know that their relationship to their ships was more than just physical. Pilots had special implants that allowed them to communicate with the ship on an almost spiritual level. At least that is what Paul had been told. They were a strange group as a whole—pilots. Living on the edge, always connected to their ship's mainframe computer, they all seemed to prefer the company of their ship to the company of other humans and appeared to have only one foot in the real world. It was as if their souls were elsewhere.

"But more to the point at hand," the captain continued, "where are we delivering you? The word from Freddy is that you would tell us when you got on board."

"That," Paul answered. He took a sip of coffee. The inevitable headache from drinking too much Stem had started. Paul felt lethargic, and his head was throbbing. "Tianjin. The Tianjin system."

"I see." The captain looked concerned. "Are you sure it's the type of place to take a little girl?"

Paul put his cup down and shrugged. "It's a transit point, not the final destination. And being an independent system ... well, chances are we will find someone to take us on the next leg of the trip."

"And where would that be?" the captain asked.

"Maybe that is something you don't want to know—just in case Syrch catches up to you."

"Why change ships at all? Why not let me take you to ... wherever it is you are going?"

"You ask a lot of questions."

The captain smiled, leaned back, and sipped at his coffee. "It's not every day that I have a run-in with Syrch enforcers and a Syrch battleship. I suppose it has made me a little curious. Not too curious, you understand, just a little."

"Mostly cost," Paul admitted. "To answer your question, I only have so much money in my rainy day fund, and the best chunk of it went to paying your fee. I have to find ... less expensive accommodation. Tianjin gets a lot of cruise ships full of tourists going to enjoy some of Tianjin's more interesting attractions. They have reasonable rates."

"Fair enough—on both accounts. Tianjin ... that's ..."

"Two hundred and sixty four hours, more or less, or eleven standard Earth days," Azalea interjected. "I can be more precise if you like. I ran preliminary navigation data through the ship's computer. You know"—she tapped her head—"wireless interface."

"Do you ever disconnect from the ship's systems?" Paul asked.

"What? Why? The universe is so small and boring without the interface. You're stuck here in the room. I'm here too, but through the ship's sensor arrays, I'm also aware of the rest of the universe—at least the rest of it to the limits of the sensors."

"And you don't find all that information distracting?"

"It can be, but you learn to filter," Azalea explained. "It's like this. You have toes? Of course you do—you do have toes, right? Good. Are you always aware of them? Or do you only notice them when they hurt or when you consciously think about them."

"I'm thinking about them now. Thanks for that," Paul said.

"You're welcome. But most of the time your toes are just there. It's comfortable and natural. That is what it is like being hooked into the ship systems. Now, imagine someone cuts off your toe. How does that make you feel?"

"Like shooting someone."

"It can be like that when I'm cut off from the ship. It creates a hollow space in my mind—an echo of sorts. It is uncomfortable."

Paul yawned and rubbed at his face with his hand. "I think maybe I get it. But my brain is shutting down. I think I will go and grab some sleep. Captain, if Jillian wakes up before I do, can one of you give her something to eat?"

"We're not a day care."

"I never assumed you were, Captain. But ..." Paul bristled at the captain.

"The captain's teasing—mostly. Don't worry about it," Azalea said. "We'll look out for her."

"Thank you. She's—I don't know. It's hard to explain, and I'm too tired to try."

"Get some rest." The captain stood. "Azalea, finalize our route and put us on course for Tianjin. And, Faolan, see what you can do about changing ship's markings—and change our transponder. Dump the old one. I don't want it on our ship."

"Thanks," Paul said. His anger had died as quickly as it had come. The captain had an odd way at humor. Paul stood, turned, and left the other three behind in the galley.

The ship was quiet. Paul could not hear any mechanical noises, and for some reason Captain Gutwein did not pipe in ambient noise, a practice that was common on other spacefaring vessels. Instead of finding the quiet refreshing, the deep silence amplified the pounding in Paul's head. The dullness spread out from his temples, back toward his ears where it then filled the base of his skull. The back of his eyes hurt too. But the growing thudding in his head did not stop him from quickly checking in on Jillian. She slept, blissfully unaware, in nearly the same position that Paul had left her. The only difference was that her stuffed bunny was bundled at the end of the bed by Jillian's feet as if Jillian, in some dream-swept fit of rage or grief, had thrown the bunny to the foot of the bed. Paul stood for a moment looking at the little girl, rubbing at his temples, feeling the power of adrenalin and Stem that had kept him active and alert melting away. He was exhausted. Leaving Jillian, he found the next available stateroom. He managed to get pain medication from his bag and swallow it before he collapsed, fully dressed, on the little bed.

Paul closed his eyes. Tianjin. A system where the avant-garde mingled with underworld crime bosses and spoiled rich kids, it lay outside of the control of Lin, Terra, and Syrch Corp. And though it had no home planet, the system consisting of nothing more than a large asteroid ring around a dim star, it had a voice with the League of Planets. The system had little inherent material wealth. That fact alone seemed to guarantee its independence. But, Paul suspected, the free-for-all, laissez-faire economic zone was a favorite haunt for the rich and powerful, and that too kept the corporations at bay. After all, what fun was it to be rich if there was no place in the universe where you could use your wealth to play? And where the rules for play were loose, the games were just so much more interesting.

Paul had never been to Tianjin before. But he had heard stories. He wondered, as he drifted off to sleep, if any of the stories were true. He hoped so.

22

---⊷⊶◯◉◯⊷⊶---

GOOD-BYES

THE ***DOROTHEA*** docked on the near-dwarf, planet-sized asteroid Plaza One. The massive asteroid was located within the center of a dense ring of asteroids of various sizes, odd shapes, and seemingly random movement. Some of the asteroids spun end over top, others side to side, and some had their own definition of rotation that defied description. Plaza One was named after the singular multidome complex of the same name that rested in a pocket of depressed rock, grit, and ice on the asteroid's equator. The asteroid had a slow spin that resulted in seven standard Earth-hour days and nights. Pockmarked with craters big and small, Plaza One was the most planetlike heavenly body in the Tianjin system. The other asteroids around Plaza One were filled with individual homes, from the rustic to the extreme, shops, hotels, and entertainment domes. Each had its own miniship dock where in-system ships from commercial ferries, to personally owned jetties, to luxurious private yachts flitted back and forth in a constant parade of movement. It was dazzling to the eyes.

Paul had awoken only to find Jillian seated comfortably in the galley eating some pasta and cheese and a great crust of garlic bread. The captain and pilot were there, chatting aimlessly, engrossed in the little girl in a way that, for a moment, made Paul feel a pang of jealousy. In the days following their escape from Papen's World, Paul noticed the crew of the *Dorothea* grow ever more fond of Jillian, inviting her to sit in the pilot's seat or taking her on a tour of the ship. But Paul knew it was a good thing to have the crew of the *Dorothea* enamored with Jillian. The more the crew liked Jillian, the less likely they were to turn Paul and Jillian in to the first Syrch Corp employee the crew spotted, hoping for some reward money.

It was during those quite days of transit, framing through the universe on the *Dorothea*, that Paul had a chance to talk to Jillian about what happened to Shiloh back at the mining pit on Papen's World. It was not an easy conversation, but eventually Paul worked out that Jillian believed she had the ability to order people to fall asleep.

"I've done it before," Jillian said, her head hanging and her voice small and remote, "at school. The first time it was an accident."

"An accident?"

"I told the guinea pig to go to sleep, and it did."

"A guinea pig?"

"It was in Mrs. Taylor's science class. They were giving it some drugs to make it stay awake—an experiment. And it looked really sick. It had lost fur, weight, and just sat around doing nothing. I felt bad for it. It wasn't its fault it was a guinea pig. So I told the guinea pig it was okay to go to sleep, and as soon as I said it, the guinea pig went to sleep."

"And this made you think you could force people to go to sleep?"

"No."

"I'm sorry, Jillian. I am trying to understand. No?"

"It was Rachel—Rachel Thomas. She was picking on me. And I just kind of got this idea that maybe I could make her sleep like the guinea pig. I was really angry. So I tried it, and it worked. But Rachel fell off the slide and broke her arm. I didn't mean for that to happen. I just wanted her to stop being so mean."

"So you told her to go to sleep, and she did?"

"Yes."

"Does anybody else know about what you … did?"

"My father."

"Dr. Gibson. I see. That means …"

"What? What does it mean?"

"I don't know, kid. It just gets me thinking. Are you sure there is not more to it?"

If Paul had not seen Shiloh drop comatose to the ground at Jillian's command, and felt the exertion of the command like a hammer to the back of the head, he would have found Jillian's story difficult to believe. But the proof was there. He had seen it. It made Paul wonder if there was more to Dr. Gibson's attempt to kill Jillian than Paul had suspected. Maybe the program audit of the doctor's laboratory was not the underlining reason behind the doctor's actions as Paul had concluded. Could it be that the doctor knew about Jillian? The doctor's laboratory had passed inspections before. Had the doctor become afraid? And afraid of what? Of Jillian? Or was the doctor afraid that Syrch Corp, when they found out what Jillian could do, would severely punish the doctor? Who really knew what happened when you messed with the DNA of a person's mind?

Jillian shrugged. She kept staring at the ground as if she had done something wrong, and she flinched when Paul moved, making Paul wonder if the doctor had beaten the girl.

Paul tilted Jillian's head upward and looked in her eyes. "Jillian, I don't want you talking about this to other people, okay? Okay? Good. I have to think about it for a while, try to make sense out of it and what that might mean about Syrch Corp and its determination to get you back. Do you understand?"

"I think so."

"You're a good kid, Jillian. Don't ever think otherwise."

That had been the end of the conversation. Paul had purposely not brought the subject up again during the intervening days before their arrival in the Tianjin system. The topic obviously upset Jillian, and besides, Paul had the distinct impression that Jillian did not understand this … power … any more than Paul did. And though Paul tried to think of a different rational reason why Shiloh collapsed at the child's command, he couldn't. Paul was not the type of person to ignore the evidence so clearly before his eyes, but at the same time, he found the supposition too fantastic to truly wrap around his mind.

Looking out of the port window at the busy shipyards of Plaza One, Paul focused back on the problem on hand. He had to find both of them passage to Lin Corp space. He was sure that Lin Corp, with their near-religious focus on self-awareness, purity, and balance, was the perfect place for Jillian. But where? Where would he go and whom would he talk to? In Paul's drive to get Jillian off of Papen's World, these larger questions had remained unasked and unanswered. And though Paul had thought about the next step in getting to Lin Corp space, he was no closer to finding the answers he needed.

"We will be sad to see Jillian go," Captain Kurt Gutwein said as he stepped into the room near the decompression hatch. The *Dorothea* was settling into its berth, and soon Paul and Jillian would be saying their good-byes.

"She has liked it here," Paul answered.

"And we've enjoyed having her. She is …"

"Special?" Paul offered.

"Yes. That is exactly the word. Special. Are you sure there is nothing else any of us can do?"

"No, Captain, you've done enough."

"You better go and get your bags," the captain said as the *Dorothea* clanged and settled. The ships engines cut out, and the familiar yet subtle vibration that the engines generated throughout the ship suddenly stopped. "But come to the galley, will you? The crew has gathered to say good-bye."

"We will," Paul assured the captain as he headed back to his stateroom.

Truth be told, Paul had very little to carry. He had broken his rifle down into parts, which he hid in his bags, but that was more of an attempt not to draw attention than it was to hide the rifle from Tianjin's authorities. There were very few import restrictions on small arms weapons in the system. But a handgun, tucked in a belt under a shirt, was one thing. Carrying around a powerful rifle with a precision scope was quite another. People would surely remember Paul if he stepped into the space lounge carrying such a weapon. Besides that, he had only the two small bags that he had hastily packed before the mad dash off Papen's World. He might get Jillian a few more items now that they were landed and near all the shopping that Tianjin had to offer. But for now, they were still traveling light.

Grabbing his bags, Paul hurried to Jillian's room where he found her talking to her bunny, Jillian's feet dangling from the bed, her bag neatly packed besides her.

"Ready?" Paul asked.

Jillian jumped down from the bed. "Yes." She picked up her bag and handed it to Paul. He slung it over his shoulder. "Good-bye, room," Jillian said. She touched the wall near the door and smiled a bit sadly.

"The crew is waiting to say good-bye over in the galley."

"I'll miss them. Will you miss them too?

"I … I suppose I will, Jillian. They have been nice to us."

"Did you know Azalea is always interfaced with the ship? She told me so. And," Jillian's feet made small sounds as the two of them walked toward the galley, "she knows everything about the ship—everything! Well, she didn't know about the condenser coil in the recycling line, but she knew everything else!"

"Condenser coil? What condenser coil?"

"The one that was plugged up and causing the system to strain."

"How did you know that?"

"Azalea said I could interface with the ship and watch her work."

"Did she now?"

"I've never seen a ship's pilot work. It was amazing. I learned so much."

"And the condenser coil?"

"Oh that." Jillian stopped and looked up at Paul. "I was helping Azalea with a systems scan, and I noticed an irregularity in a sister system that implied the condenser coil was clogged."

"It's not on some type of switch or something?"

"No, silly. Only major and some minor components of the ship are regulated. Not a condenser coil. That won't hurt anything; it'll just make parts of the recycling system work harder, that's all."

"Silly me."

"But I found it, and she sent Faolan to check. He said I was right! He replaced it. Isn't that great?"

"It is great. Wonder how Azalea missed it."

"She said I am really smart."

"You are really smart, Jillian. Come on," Paul said, "we need to say our good-byes and find a place to stay—a hotel."

"I've never been in a hotel. Well," she continued, "except that one on Papen's World when you left to talk to your boss. Other than that, I've never been in a hotel. Will it be a nice one this time?"

"I think so. Have you ever been on a spaceship before this one?"

"No."

"There you go then, kid. Lots of new adventures. Life is full of them."

Paul led Jillian down the corridor and into the galley where the captain and two crew members were waiting. The captain was smiling though the corner of his eyes were tense; Faolan was rocking back and forth from his heels to his toes, clutching a small parcel in his hands; and Azalea held a small gift bag, and there were tears in her eyes.

"Jillian!" Azalea put the bag on the table and gave the girl a hug. "It's been wonderful to have you on board."

"Thank you. I've had fun."

The captain cleared his throat and looked at Faolan.

"We—the captain and I—made you a small gift, Jillian. You know," the engineer said, "something for you to remember us by." He came around the table, awkwardly returned Jillian's hug, and handed her the parcel.

"Can I open it now?"

"Of course you can," the captain replied.

Jillian put her bunny on the table and quickly opened the poorly wrapped parcel. Inside was a cardboard box, and inside that was a small model of the *Dorothea*.

"I love it! Thank you, Faolan. Thank you, Kurt."

Both men smiled.

"And I made you something too," Azalea added. "Well, I had the fabricating printer make it, but I designed it for you. Actually, it's for your bunny."

"Mr. Bunny?"

"Of course. Here you go, dear."

Jillian took the small gift bag from the pilot and looked inside. She reached in and pulled out the first item, which turned out to be a bright blue, bunny-sized shirt. It had a monogram for the *Dorothea* on the right breast pocket. Next came a pair of ebony boots and finally a small matching hat with a strap to keep it from falling off of Mr. Bunny's head.

"Let me help you put them on him," Azalea said.

The two of them chatted as they struggled to get Mr. Bunny into his new set of clothes. When the bunny was dressed, Jillian held him out at arm's length and laughed. She gave the bunny a long hug. She hugged Azalea and each of the other crew in turn. Then Jillian stopped, looked at the three crew members of the *Dorothea*, and became sad.

"I wish we didn't have to go," Jillian said. "Will I see you again?"

"You never know, Jillian," the captain answered. He cleared his throat. "The universe is not as large as it once was. I am sure we will meet again. Friends always do."

"Is that true, Paul?"

"I suppose," Paul replied. He didn't know. Paul didn't have friends, at least not in the traditional sense. There were people he worked with that he liked, or bosses he admired, but he never had anyone over to his place for dinner, and he didn't fraternize with anyone after work. Paul spent all his nonworking time alone. "I suppose it is."

"We'll walk you to the hatch," Azalea said, taking Jillian's hand.

The five of them left the galley, Jillian clutching her fancy-dressed bunny in one hand, with Azalea clutching her other. The three of them chatted amicably with Jillian as Paul followed behind, stuffing the small model of the *Dorothea* into Jillian's backpack, which was slung over his shoulder. At the hatch, the three of them hugged Jillian once again before Paul took Jillian's hand from Azalea and the two of them stepped out of the hatch and into the pressurized ramp that led to the reception lounge. As Paul began walking away, the captain stopped him and handed him a small note.

"The medical center information you asked for," the captain explained.

"I almost forgot. I appreciate it, Kurt."

"Jillian has a …"

Paul grimaced. "Yep. Someone I worked with warned me."

"I thought that was illegal."

"Being illegal never stopped anyone who didn't care about the law," Paul said. "It never stopped me."

"Well, that may be so, Paul, but it just—it makes me sick. Look, if we can ever be of help to Jillian, you let us know. I mean it. I am very fond of that little girl. Good luck to both of you."

"Thanks, Captain."

Paul and Jillian walked down the long ramp, turning once to wave at the crew before the two of them disappeared behind the next airlock door into the open reception area on Plaza One.

23

————◦◦○◉○◦◦————

UNDER THE
BANYAN TREE

THE BANYAN Tree was an exclusive club located on the northern side of the Plaza One habitation dome. Paul sat in a corner booth, Jillian beside him, watching the crowd mingle between the dance floor and tables that sat in a semicircle around a protruding stage where a group of six musicians played a harsh backbeat in syncopated rhythm and blues, part of a musical resurgence in this arm of the galaxy. The guitar player was moving through a basic twelve-bar blues progression as a female singer meted out a sad love song in a voice that ranged from a whisper to a pounding, ragged thing. Jillian was entranced, glancing upward through shy eyes and tapping her little hand against the tabletop as she nibbled on her dinner, some type of vat-grown protein rolled into a long finger and breaded and fried, cheesy noodles, and quadraphonic-grown mixed vegetables. The food was hot, with steam rising from her plate, carrying the luscious smell of subtle spices. Paul's food smelled just as good, and he picked at it as he eyed everyone.

People were dancing on the club's marble dance floor as a myriad of soft-colored lights flashed languidly on and off. The room was buzzing with conversation, and Paul watched waiters and waitresses dip through and around the crowd with trays of food and drinks precariously balanced in their hands. Paul and Jillian had been on Plaza One for a little over a week, Paul discretely inquiring about booking transit to Lin Corp space while simultaneously investigating the information that the *Dorothea's* captain had provided at Paul's request. Paul liked the crew of the *Dorothea,* but that did not mean he trusted them. He wanted to be doubly sure the doctor that Captain Kurt Gutwein had recommended was not somehow connected to Syrch. It had taken a few days, but Paul was fairly sure the doctor was exactly what Captain Gutwein had said: a competent man who worked outside normal bureaucratic wrangling—if the price was right.

They had been lucky so far—Paul and Jillian. Jillian's tracking device had not seemed to alert any Syrch Corp's operatives that Jillian was on the asteroid. Paul had hoped to get the tracker device removed from the girl before that happened. But their luck had just changed.

A small group of two men and one woman slipped in the main door, fading quickly into the gathering. Paul watched as one of the men, a midsized bruiser in denim slacks and leather jacket, paired off with the woman—young and determined in her tan tactical pants and pullover blouse with a Florentine, low-cut neckline beneath a unbuttoned black blazer that was pointed and cut in a way to emphasize her figure. They moved to the left as the other man, older perhaps, with a hint of a beard and cleanly shaven head, moved in the opposite direction. Paul didn't think they were Syrch Corp enforcers. They were good, but they were not that good. Their behavior made them stand out like three pinpricks of light in a dark sky. Perhaps someone of less experience would not have noticed the little mistakes the trio made, the way their eyes flashed occasionally about with intensity, the way they kept pace with one another and how they kept track of each other with a simple nod or look. It was forgivable, the telltales, but Paul thought that slight, nearly immeasurable difference was what separated the professional from the wannabe.

Paul pegged the trio as independent operators—operators skulked in the Tianjin system picking up the refuse that managed to avoid Syrch's or anyone else's network of thugs and spies in exchange for a fee. The amount of money such independents got depended on the amount of interest. Being an independent was normally, as Paul knew, a fair way to manage to live, but it was a hard living. Independents worked outside the law and had no corporate umbrella to protect them when things turned bad. And that seemed to be a universal imperative. Things always turned bad.

Paul sipped at his beer and watched the three slink through the crowded tables in a pincer movement, their eyes searching faces. Then suddenly the trio stopped and seemed to lose interest, blending back together near a table within easy line of sight of Paul and Jillian, seating themselves and pulling out menus and pretending as if they were in their own little world, insensible to those around them and just as oblivious to Paul and Jillian. The band transitioned to the next song in their lineup, a more robust and rocking beat that encouraged the dancers to a quicker pace as the vocalist launched into a long wail that echoed as the lead guitar cried and the trumpeter emphasized each major beat of the bass drum that thudded like a breathing heart as piano notes, played vivacissimo, sharply punctuated the rising musical blend. The result was a primal sound, harshly alluring, that recalled dark caverns, pools of water and light, and the crowd responded, cheering around their little red candles that sat distinctively in the center of their tables, like voices lit in a sea of shadows. Jillian reacted too, feeling the energy of the place come suddenly alive, smiling widely and laughing, looking sheepishly over at Paul, her face glowing with excitement, happy to be safe, with good food, with the performers and their wild creation ringing in the air. Paul smiled back, ruffled Jillian's hair, and continued to slowly eat his dinner.

Paul considered a bold approach. He found that people in his line of work who had less experience often tried too hard to be sneaky and sly. They spent an undue amount of time coming up with complicated plans, considering all possible outcomes, and fretting and worrying about things that they could not possibly control. In sharp contrast, Paul tended to be blunt, opting to kick the door in or smash the vase, forcing people to respond to his high-energy attack in such a way that left the target in a weakened and vulnerable position. The enforcer was much less likely to spend days creating an opportunity to rough up a victim, simply electing to knock politely on their door and then, when the door was answered, suddenly beating the victim into a stupor. Oh, he knew there were times when tact and planning were important, but he also knew there were times for action, any action, raw and cruel and devilishly driven. Paul felt this was one such instance. It would serve little purpose to attempt to sneak out of the club and then spend hours trying to lose the independents, who even now were cautiously peeking at him while trying to look as if they were not. The trio was likely well connected to local street cops and low-level thugs and probably had a network of whores and thieves that proliferated throughout the Tianjin system. Coupled to Jillian's implant—the Syrch Corp tracker—it wouldn't take the independents too long to pick up Paul and Jillian's trail again. And here, in public, where people expected one to act with decorum, a confrontation would serve to put the independents on their heels. Paul might even kill one or two of them just to send a message. But then there was Jillian. Paul looked at the little girl, enjoying the show without a care in the universe, and felt a pang of fear. If he started a shootout, the girl would be in play. And she could get hurt. She could get killed. Paul knew he should confront the three independents now before it got out of control, but how? How could he do it in a way that kept Jillian out of the line of fire?

He took another fork full of his food and let the satisfying taste fill his mouth, savoring the flavor and appreciating the chefs at the Bayan Tree, considering his next move, his eyes scanning the room for additional threats. It had been a while since Paul had eaten anything so delectable.

There was an excited roar in the other room, the one adjacent to the lounge where Paul and Jillian ate. Paul glanced at the main doors and heard the sound again. It occurred to him that someone was winning big at one of the gambling tables. Gambling was big business on Plaza One, and the Banyan Tree club was no exception. The main floor was chock-full of flashing, chiming slot machines, video poker, and other games of chance. Long felt-green-covered craps and roulette tables were dispersed amongst different card game tables, their dealers smartly dressed in the blue and white colors of the club. The gambling was one of the reasons Paul had opted to stay at the club, with a room on the fifteenth floor, as it was an age-old ploy to attract patrons to the establishment with inexpensive rooms while taking advantage of human laziness that lured them into the gambling dens of the club where they lost big. The club didn't make any money on the rooms or food. However, the owner or owners, whoever they might be, were making a killing on the gambling. But Paul didn't gamble. So he and Jillian enjoyed the relatively inexpensive rooms while Paul plotted their next move.

In Tianjin, illegally gained money moved too. Paul had no doubt that the Banyan Tree had an illegitimate side where money was laundered through crooked winnings. It was an old game. The person with the stolen cash showed up at the casino and entered a high-stakes game. The house would consistently win until, with one or two big bets, the crook made the money back—minus the pre-agreed-upon fee. And then, when cashing out the chips, the house would pay taxes and record all the money as winnings. In an instant, the cash was legitimized. The problem the crooks got into was when they decided to cheat the tax collectors. If there was something that had remained constant in the course of human history, it was that tax collectors always got their money. Once criminals started down that line, the money-laundering scheme was broken up. But those were the stupid crooks.

Smart criminals looked upon taxes as the cost of doing business. The smart ones were in it for the long haul. They were not looking for one major score but were content to make a smaller profit over a longer time. Those profits grew, and then a place like the Banyan Tree became a major generator of wealth. Paul didn't mind the crooks. They were, in a certain light, more honest than politicians and business tycoon. Crooks, politicians, and business tycoons were just different flavors in the same machine that made some people rich and others poor. But politicians and tycoons lied about what they were doing. They wrapped their activities in political doubletalk and legal rules. Paul preferred the company of crooks to politicians and tycoons, but he could deal with any of them. Now religious leaders? Paul had no respect for them. They were conmen, grifters preying on people's fears to gain wealth and power, and, in Paul's opinion, religious leaders were the lowest type of life form. Paul would jump into a nest of Ligmi wasp-spiders before he would sit down with a priest, reverend, or bishop.

Dinner ended, and Jillian grew sleepy, drowsing in her chair, the band having finished their set to be replaced by soft recorded music that trickled out of hidden speakers throughout the room. Paul called to his waiter, and the young man meandered over, stopping for a moment to place two new drinks at one of his assigned tables.

"Yes, sir? Can I get you something?"

"I understood this to be a family place," Paul said stiffly.

"Is something the matter?"

"I brought my daughter here specifically because I was assured it was family friendly. Is there a house detective?"

"Excuse me?"

"A house detective—the security guy. I would like to speak to him or her immediately."

"I don't …"

"Look, son, are you going to get the house detective or are we going to have a problem here?"

"No. No, I'll ask the floor manager."

"You do that, kid."

The waiter stumbled off, obviously confused and concerned, returning a short time later with a middle-aged woman in tow. She was a bit plump but was impeccably dressed.

"Hello," she said. "I understand you have a problem?"

"I don't have the problem; you do. What I have is a complaint. And I need to see the house detective. Are you the house detective?"

"No. I'm the floor manager, Miss Lillian Archibald."

"Well, Miss Archibald," Paul leaned menacingly forward, "I suggest you get the house detective or security supervisor or whatever you call that person in this quadrant of the galaxy and get that person here now. I didn't come all the way from Sol only to have people like—that—hanging around the same place my daughter and I are eating. What am I paying you all for?"

"I don't understand."

"You wouldn't, Miss Archibald. You are not a security expert. That is why," Paul huffed, "I have been asking for the house detective for the last fifteen minutes. Now am I going to see that person or do I have to take matters into my own hands?" Paul stared at the woman until she averted her eyes.

"I'm sorry, but yes, right away, sir." Miss Archibald's voice was anything but pleased. "Security? Security? Send Mr. Richards to the main dining room please." The woman spoke into a small handheld device. She smiled reassuringly at the surrounding guests who, having heard the commotion, had turned their eyes toward Paul, Jillian, and the two employees of the Banyan Tree Club.

"He is on his way," a metallic voice answered.

The waiter and Miss Archibald stood awkwardly while Paul did his best to look upset, scowling and placing a protective arm around Jillian. The excitement of the moment was lost on the little girl whose eyes were closed in sleep. It took a moment for the house detective to arrive, thirty years or so old, dressed in a cheap suit, with a solid chin and close-cropped hair. Mr. Richards moved in a way that warned Paul that the other man had been trained in hand combat—likely, by the looks of it, boxing. When Mr. Richards spoke, his words were concise and his voice even and sure.

"Is there a problem here?"

Miss Archibald started to answer, but Paul cut her off. "What type of cheap place are you running here?" Paul asked. "Come with me. I want to show you something."

Paul gently laid Jillian's head on the cushion of the booth's bench, slid around the other side, and walked boldly toward the group of three operators who were busily trying to look unobtrusive.

"What type of place allows punks like this to sit around breathing air?" Paul asked the house detective. "That's right," Paul said to the balding man who looked menacingly up from the table, "you and your pals. Low-level stick boys and girls, I'd say."

"Watch it, mister," the bald man replied. He stood up, pushing his chair back. He was about the same height as Paul.

"Now, is that a way to talk to your betters?" Paul asked. Paul suddenly pushed the bald man back, having slipped a foot forward behind the man's leg, tripping the bald man back into the chair he had just vacated. At the same time, Paul's hand shot forward and plucked an automatic out from beneath the bald man's jacket. Paul flipped the weapon carelessly from his right to his left hand, pressing it back, handle first, toward the house detective. "Do you always let dime-store thugs into your place?" Paul asked the detective.

"Why I ought to ..." The bald man hastily began pushing himself up from the chair.

"If you get up, son, I'm going to knock you right back down on your ass. And you two, hands on the table."

"You heard the man," the detective said. Mr. Richards held the bald man's weapon awkwardly in his right hand, as if he was not exactly sure how it had appeared there. "Keep your hands where I can see them."

"Do you know these … people, Mr. Richards?" Paul asked. "I'm surprised such a nice place like the Banyan Tree Club would let half-pint thugs just hang around in your dining area. You know, I bet they're picking a mark."

"Is that it?" the detective snapped. He stepped forward and quickly frisked the other man one-handed, finding another pistol, which he deftly withdrew from the man's concealed holster. He put both weapons on the table before turning his attention to the woman. "On the table, sweetheart."

The woman smiled brightly, but there was nothing friendly in it. "By all means." She put her smaller pistol on the table besides the other three. "No harm done."

"Right," the detective said. "Now get up and leave. We don't like your kind in here."

"I'll remember you," the balding man hissed at Paul.

Paul cracked a droll smile and shot back, "I'll remember you too."

The house detective and Paul watched the three operators skulk out of the dining room without so much as a glance back.

"Rob is at the door," the detective said. "He'll make sure the three of them go out of the building." The detective turned to Paul. "I'm sorry about that Mr.?"

"Harlamor. Paul Harlamor." The familiar lie came easily. Paul had used the last name of Harlamor before on Telakia. If anyone ran a data check, they would find a fabricated dossier that went back years.

"How did you know?"

"I spotted them casing the place. It's a professional thing. Terra Corp. Here on vacation with my daughter." Paul pointed back at his table where Jillian's feet could be seen sticking out from the end of the table.

"I see. Well, I am sorry about that, Mr. Harlamor. Can I buy you a drink for your troubles?"

"I appreciate the offer, but it's time I got Jillian to bed. She's had enough excitement for one night."

"Are you staying here in the hotel?"

"Yes. Fifteenth floor until the end of the week."

"Enjoy the rest of your stay then, Mr. Harlamor."

"Thank you, Mr. Richards."

Paul went back to his table as the floor manager and waiter left. He sat for a while watching the house detective get a serving tray where he stacked the three pistols before covering them with a napkin and moving them out of the room. The small disturbance Paul had caused was quickly forgotten, and it was as if nothing had happened at all. But Paul was already wondering where he and Jillian would go. They couldn't stay at the Banyan Tree Club anymore. He doubted that the three operators would let the incident pass, and if the trio had picked up on Jillian's tracker, then it was only a matter of time before others would too. It was time to go and see the doctor and get the thing removed.

"Come on, Jillian," Paul gently woke the girl. "Time to go to bed."

Paul got the girl up and back to their room where he placed her in bed, tucking her under the soft comforter after slipping off her shoes. He put Mr. Bunny next to her, turned down the light, and then slowly began packing her meager possessions. Paul would let her sleep for a few hours, but that was all he dared. Leaving Jillian to her dreams, Paul went into his room and packed his gear. He turned the Do Not Disturb sign on and sank into the white leather couch, an alarm clock on the small coffee table before him, his pistol resting lightly on his lap. He had managed to confront the independent operators without putting Jillian in immediate danger, but Paul knew it was just the start of their troubles.

24

---o--o--O--o--o---

CALAMITY

THE ALARM rang. Paul sat up and looked bleary-eyed at the clock. Reaching forward, he caught his pistol that was threatening to fall off his lap with one hand, and with the other he silenced the alarm. It was midway through the sleep cycle and time for Paul and Jillian to move. Paul took a moment to allow his mind to clear, sitting quietly in the dark, his legs feeling a bit cramped from having slept on the couch. He rubbed a hand over his tired jaw and yawned, then forced himself to get up and stretch, flipping on the lights and taking a few minutes to freshen up before moving to the doorway to Jillian's room where the child was contentedly sleeping, still wrapped up beneath the comforter, Mr. Bunny, in the clothing made by Azalea, clutched lovingly in her hands by her head. Paul called to her and turned on the room lights. Jillian made a small, irritated noise and covered her eyes with her forearm. Paul let it go for the moment, removing Jillian's packed and ready bag and placing it on the couch next to his bags. He then walked quietly back to Jillian's room.

"Come on, Jillian. It's time to get up." He rested his hand on the girl's shoulder and shook her slightly. "Jillian. Jillian? It's time to get up."

She rolled over and looked at Paul, her eyes barely wide enough for her to see, her face a mask of confusion.

"It is time to go," he said again.

"Go where?"

"We have to find another hotel. It's not much to worry about, but I had a bit of trouble last night after you nodded off in the restaurant."

She looked at Paul without comprehension.

"Come on," he added, "I've already packed your stuff. Jillian," he said a little more stiffly.

"Do we have to?"

"Yes. It is unfortunate, but we do. It'll be okay."

Paul pulled the covers off Jillian, and she sat up, looking unhappy, her feet dangling off the corner of the bed. It took a few more minutes to get her up and moving, brushing her teeth and getting dressed, and Paul took the time required to give the girl a light snack while she watched a cartoon on the video vision. Finally, when she was ready and alert, Paul checked his weapons and then slung the bags over his shoulder, leading Jillian out of the door into the quiet hallway, down to the elevator. They took the elevator to the tenth floor. He then led the girl to a service elevator and took that down three more floors before getting off and making her walk down the fire escape stairwell, exiting on the fourth floor, which he followed across the breadth of its length before taking a second set of service elevators to the subbasement. Paul found the tunnels, used by the staff to service the Banyan Tree Club's restaurants, shops, gambling rooms, and guest rooms, and followed the exit signs past the employee lounge to the loading dock where he lifted Jillian up and carried her down concrete stairs and halfway through the underground parking area before setting her down again, taking her hand, and heading up the sloped driveway, past cement columns and a variety of parked cars, toward the exit. In a few minutes, they were standing on a sidewalk outside the parking garage, the green-tinged dome of Plaza One sparkling like jadeite in the distance, the dark expanse of space and the near asteroids in Tianjin's asteroid belt hidden from view. They walked crossways through a darkened park, past dim lampposts and a few scattered benches, to the main street near the Banyan Tree Club, where a row of clean, white buildings, all dome shaped and built to exacting standards for safety, silently stood. Paul began looking for a vehicle to rent or taxi to hire. He knew there was a Hyperloop terminal a few blocks over, but he thought that would be too obvious a way to leave the Banyan Tree and was a likely ambush site. He wanted to put some distance and randomness into his route to shake off anyone who might be watching him.

Guiding Jillian across the street, Paul continued to meander through the quiet streets, only occasionally seeing other people. While Plaza One—the asteroid—had its own natural sense of time, the ruling elite had, as was customary elsewhere in the universe, adopted a modified Earth-standard cycle, made readily possible by the unique position Plaza One maintained in that the dome, really several domes with one larger central dome. It had a sophisticated environmental control mechanism that allowed Plaza One to simulate Earth's day and night cycle. But it did surprise Paul that it was not as dark as he had expected, the sky resonating like a false dawn, a hazy and eerie light that made the surrounding streets and buildings look like creatures that were slinking back into shadow but who, by some act of magic, were frozen in the in-between space between waking and sleeping. The few people and moving vehicles that Paul saw appeared to move furtively and uneasily through the dimness of Plaza One's artificial night. Paul pulled Jillian gently down an alley between two rows of buildings, where it was darker, the sound of Jillian's feet clacking on the pavement as the two of them farther away from the Banyan Tree Club.

Paul felt proud of Jillian. Though he could tell she was sleepy, the girl did not complain as he continued to guide her through the domed city. He did have to take away Mr. Bunny, as the stuffed companion threatened to tumble out of Jillian's tired hands. Paul stopped long enough to pack the bunny carefully in Jillian's bag before taking her hand and once again walking toward a more distant Hyperloop terminal. If he did not find a taxi or a rental car before reaching the terminal, he would take the Hyperloop to the other side of the city. It was an enjoyable and quiet, peaceful walk. Paul soon stopped before a set of steps that led down from the sidewalk to the Hyperloop terminal.

"Are you ready to take a ride, Jillian?"

The girl nodded.

"Come on then. We can rest soon."

The steps led to a small landing where shadows pooled around the doors to public restrooms. Paul shifted Jillian to his left side, away from the restroom doors, and was just looking up when a blur of movement flashed in his eyes. He instinctively raised his right arm to protect his face, but the blow came hard, a quick slash of a billy club that cracked against his temple. His mind jerked away from him, and he lost his balance as a second blow caught him by the ear. He fell. Paul knew he should defend himself, but his mind refused to focus, and his body was drawn into a fetal position as a third blow rained down on his back and another on his shoulder.

"I told you you would regret it, mister." The bald man from the night before bent over Paul, peering into Paul's dull eyes. "A real tough guy, aren't you?" The man kicked Paul several times as Paul grunted, only vaguely aware of Jillian's scream.

"That's enough," another male voice said.

But the bald man kicked Paul again and again, in the ribs, in the face, and then hit Paul across the back several more times with the metal-hard whip of the billy club. Each blow shocked Paul's body. His face bled and swelled, and deep bruises and welts soon covered his back, arms, and shoulders. It became difficult to breathe as a particularly nasty kick hit with a sickening thud and ribs broke beneath steel-toed boots.

"We've got what we wanted," the second man said.

"A smart guy," the bald man hissed and threw one more savage kick at Paul's head.

But Paul did not feel the blow. He had already fallen into pain-filled unconsciousness.

25

−∘−◦−◎−◦−∘−

JUICE

A DULL sensation fluttered through Paul's mind. The sensation grew until it became an uncomfortable itch that radiated throughout his body, and he wondered at the feeling. His eyes flickered but refused to fully open, his face bloated, and the iron taste of blood mingled with sweat in his mouth. People, ethereal and unreal, hovered above him as beyond, lights flitted by in an endless parade like rails moving under a train. Paul's right ear hurt. It hurt very badly, and he felt like retching. But nothing seemed to work in his body, and his fluttering mind faded in and out of awareness like the rapidly moving iris of a camera shutter while time slowed and air became thick and difficult. Paul could feel blood trickle down his back, and something told him his ribs were not the only things broken. His shoulder burned, and when the shadowed men pressed him firmly down, pain erupted, only to be replaced with a sudden darkness.

It was a while before his ears recognized the beeping noise, a constant, steady ping that echoed in the space in which Paul lay. But that too vanished into gray until a pinprick of light stabbed like a nova into his pupil, and he again heard the sound, but it was muffled by a low groan as if an animal were slowly dying in the heat of a summer's day. A man in a white coat, his face one of concern, took shape before Paul. Paul blinked groggily, and his right eye refused to open, a balloon of blood and swelling purpling his face as his left eye strained to focus.

"You're lucky to be alive," the doctor said, but to Paul, the doctor's voice was an echo, unclear, distant. "Do you understand me, Mr. Thorne?"

Paul tried to nod his head, but something stiff and strong held his head in place. He heard another groan and realized that the sound was coming from his mouth, a grotesque gurgle that seemed too wet to be human.

"You need to heal, Mr. Thorne—go ahead and push ... milliliters ... thiopental. Heart rate? Good and run a full body ... Mr. Thorne? Mr. Thorn? Can you understand me? You've been attacked ... severely injured. We are treating you, but you need ..."

"Ji loan!"

"I ... I don't understand you, Mr. Thorne. Can anyone understand what he is trying to say?"

Paul struggled. A deep anger staggered his mind.

"Ji loan!"

"It's going to take time, Mr. Thorne. Calm down."

Paul's body quivered, and he tried to shake his head. "No ... No ... ti ... me ... J ... J ... J ... use."

"What?"

"J ... J ... use."

"I think he said juice, Doctor."

"What? Juice? He doesn't have that type of money. Is that what he said? Mr. Thorne, did you say juice?"

Paul suddenly snatched the front of the doctor's shirt, Paul's arm straining with the effort. "Terra ... Terra ... J ... use."

The doctor tried to pull back, but Paul held on, fighting against another pair of hands that were also trying to separate him from the doctor. "Terra ... J ... use."

"Juice? Juice from Terra Corp? I think you are right, Nurse. The patient is asking for a nano infusion. Risky. Painful and too expensive. You—don't—have—the—funds," the doctor articulated at Paul.

Paul almost cried. He released the doctor and flopped his arm onto his face, pointing at his one opened eye. "Sc ... an ... scan ..." he managed.

The doctor looked at the nurse. "He might have segregated bank accounts. Scan his eye for biometric-linked accounts."

The nurse took a hand scanner and passed it over Paul's eye. The doctor looked at the results.

"I see. Do you consent then?" the doctor asked. "Mr. Thorne, it's fifteen thousand credits for that treatment. You'll heal slowly without it, but it will be faster with the nano infusion. Do you understand?"

Paul moaned. "Com ... combat ju ... use."

"Did he say combat juice?"

"Clearly," the nurse replied.

The doctor scratched his head. "Let me see that scan again. There are only a few doses in the Tianjin system. They are ... hard to come by. Seventy-five thousand, Mr. Thorne. It appears nearly all that you have. Do you understand?"

"Terra?"

"I might only be able to get Lin or Syrch."

"Um ... um ... no ... Syrch."

"All right—I don't blame him there." Turning back to Paul, the doctor said, "Lin or Terra. You have to agree—give him something to clear his mind. Is that better, Mr. Thorne? You have to give me your consent to the cost and special treatment."

"Yes," Paul managed.

His energy spent, Paul tried his best to breathe.

"Okay, Mr. Thorne, relax now. Time to sleep. Go to sleep, Mr. Thorne. Keep him sedated, Nurse."

"Yes, Doctor."

His good eye closed, and Paul felt the blanket of oblivion drop across his mind.

Time lost its meaning, and the world swam, rose, and fell, and with it came moments of excruciating pain. Doctors and nurses rolled through Paul's awareness, and oceans sounded in his ears. At times he floated, and at other times he fought against the deep vastness of a terrible ocean that pulled at him, sucking him farther and farther away from the light of the sun into a turquoise death. And then the doctor was there, smiling, holding a thin and shiny syringe with a goopy liquid that looked like silver and sludge, which the doctor pressed into the IV, where it moved, alive and slippery, down the long tube and into Paul's battered arm. And then the pain that had been was nothing, and the pain that was exploded like fire, crawling slowly up Paul's arm, liquidly, until the juice hit the thoracoacromial artery and the heat poured through Paul's body with tidal force. The fire roiled, and it felt like millions of tearing ants were eating Paul from the inside out. Paul tried to scream, but his body was not his own; the nano machine-infused juice flooding his system with terrible purpose had taken control. The nano and nubots tore and scraped and rendered, and in those moments Paul wished for death, wished for an end to everything. But in his desperation, when he could bear no more, the face of Jillian rose like a ghost, and the anger that dwelt in Paul's mind flowered into a bright sun, strangling his urge to die.

"Will he live?" the nurse asked.

"If the shock is not too much," the doctor replied.

Paul heard the words and cursed. He would live, he swore, until blood rained from the sky.

Through tissue engineering, the bots took the necessary material from one part of Paul's body to repair other parts, destroying and building in a seemingly endless cycle of agony. Paul's skin crawled, and the nurses had to tie Paul down so he would not claw at the raw wounds that appeared on his body as the bots continued in their mindless mission. Destroy, build. Destroy, build. An endless army of tinny machines marching as Paul squirmed like a calf in the final throws of birth, clawing his way back from the darkness, aching and shivering as a black wind called in the well of night while evil things chittered and prayed to the great and angry god they named Retribution. And just when Paul had suffered too much, when his mind threatened to crack and fall into the abyss of insanity, a cool wave, soft as a kiss, slowly rolled from his feet, up his legs and through his groin, flooding his stomach, and then gently crept to his heart, arms, and lungs.

Paul slept.

When he woke, the noise of the ocean broke, leaving the sterile room strangely quiet. Paul heard the beeping of a machine, constant, and equated that to a heart monitor. The steadiness of the beep provided him with confidence, and, with eyes closed, he began testing his body, focusing on each part and carefully moving it: his toes, feet, and legs, then his fingers, hands and arms, and finally he rotated his head and let his eyes flutter open.

The room was dim, and the tiled walls looked cold. Paul pulled his right arm up to where he could see it, noting the clear tube of an IV that ran into the vein at the back of his hand. Slowly swiveling his head to the left, he moved his left arm, flexed his fingers, and tested his dexterity by running through an old finger exercise he had learned as a young man trying to master the art of knife throwing. He felt right though weak. Shifting his head, he looked down at his feet and slowly pulled his legs in and stretched them back out. They felt odd as if his mind were not used to moving them. Paul cleared his throat and winced. It was raw and dry.

"Nurse," he called, but his voice was barely a whisper.

Paul looked around and finally found it, a button on a wire cord, which he pressed, settling down afterward to wait, his thoughts on Jillian and Syrch Corp and the balding man with the snide grin.

In a few minutes, a female nurse entered the room. She cocked her head to the side and studied Paul from a small distance as if afraid he might not be sane, before she smiled brightly and pulled the curtain that separated the room to the side, exposing a sitting chair and a glass panel by the door. The nurse was young, in her midtwenties, yet she carried a confidence that Paul found reassuring.

"You're awake, Mr. Thorne. Well, let me be the first to welcome you back."

"Time?" Paul wheezed. "How long … have I been here?"

"Three days, Mr. Thorne. And to be honest, it was touch and go at times."

"Water?"

"Of course." The nurse helped Paul sit up, and she gave him a small glass of water, holding it to Paul's lips and only allowing him to take a small amount at any time. "Better?"

"Yes. Thank you," Paul replied. "Weak."

"The doctor said you would wake feeling weak as a kitten, but he said that is a normal aftereffect of the juice. You should be hungry too."

Now that the nurse had mentioned it, Paul was starved.

The nurse smiled. "I will bring you some food. But then you need to rest some more. You've been through a lot. There are still some bots in your body, but you will clear some of them in the next forty-eight hours. And the doctor said you will feel 100 percent better in another half day or so."

Paul nodded. "Some of them?" Paul asked. "Did you say I'll clear some of the bots?"

The nurse looked a little confused. "The juice the doctor found was from Lin Corp, Mr. Thorne. It is a very specialized combat mixture—like you requested. The doctor said it was not as powerful as the ones used by Terra's Geist Marines, and the doctor said that most of the bots would pass but several, and to be honest, I do not fully understand what the doctor was saying as it was highly technical, but several of the bots will never leave your system."

Paul was not sure he liked that. But he could not deny the beneficial effects. He was sore and tired, but from what he recalled of his injuries, if Paul had healed naturally, he would have spent months of slow healing and rehabilitation. He just didn't have the time.

"Jillian?" Paul asked.

"Jillian? I'm sorry, Mr. Thorne. I am not sure what you mean. Who is Jillian?"

Was she already on her way back to Papen's World? Paul wondered. Had he failed her? He should have followed his instincts and run from the Banyan Tree the moment the operators were compromised, but Jillian had needed the sleep. Now she would pay for his weakness. There was no time to waste. Paul had to get up. But he felt so tired.

"My daughter," Paul answered. "Have they found my daughter?"

The nurse covered her mouth with her hand, and her eyes grew wide. "Daughter? No, I'm sorry. I don't know anything about your daughter. I thought you were alone."

Paul felt alone. He felt as if the whole of time and space was expanding in his heart, thinning his soul. "I see. I need to go." Paul moved as if to get out of bed.

The nurse pushed him gently back down. Paul could not resist.

"I will talk to the doctor. Maybe they brought your daughter to another hospital, maybe Children's Mercy. And you stay still. You are in no shape to get up out of bed. Even with the juice, your body suffered horribly. It needs time to heal."

But Paul felt he had no time.

Still, there was not much he could do at the moment. If he was too weak to resist the nurse, there was very little he could do if he managed to track Jillian down, only to find he had to deal with three or more thugs.

How much time did Paul have? Really? He tried to think. A week to get a message pony to Papen's World at the least, a few days to mobilize a response, and then another week or so to send either instructions or a group of enforcers to retrieve Jillian—that meant

Paul had what? Between five and eight days? That gave Paul a little time. Paul had never taken juice before, nevertheless combat juice. The idea of it bothered him. But he had heard how quickly juice could heal a beaten body. There was still hope. Perhaps in a day or so he would have some strength back and could go after Jillian. And he already knew how. He would use the same signal that had brought her enemies down on her, the Syrch Corp tracker. The operators who had taken Jillian didn't know who they were dealing with. Paul was a Syrch enforcer. He knew how Syrch operated, and he knew the tracker's broadcast frequencies. He would find them and free Jillian.

And he would do it with extreme prejudice.

26

━━∘⊶∘◉○◉∘⊷∘━━

DOROTHEA

THE LIMP in his left leg was barely noticeable as Paul stood in a recess of the reception lounge at the docking platform where a short time ago he and Jillian had left the *Dorothea* to strike out on their own. Paul had been surprised to find out that the cargo ship, with Captain Gutwein, Azalea, and Faolan, had not departed from the asteroid. The *Dorothea* was still occupying a berth, and Paul felt a thrill of relief as he noticed the lithe from of Azalea, the pilot, disappear into the long ramp that led to the ship's airlock door. She was the key to his having a chance at finding Jillian. But to get Azalea to agree to help, Paul knew he would have to convince Captain Kurt Gutwein and maybe even Faolan, the engineer. They were a small and tightknit group. And though the captain was the captain, he more than often led through consensus versus through the dictatorial authority that most captains held on their ships. Paul therefore had to convince all of them. If he failed, Jillian was doomed.

Paul stepped out of his nook and made his way through the mingle of people toward the ramp, turning down the tunnel and approaching the ship's closed airlock door. Paul did not like the idea of bothering the crew of the *Dorothea*. They owned him nothing. But what choice did he have? Time was running out.

Paul pressed the communicator outside of the door and said, "Paul Thorne for Captain Gutwein." He stood patiently, feeling exposed.

"Paul?" Azalea's voice greeted him through the communicator, and her picture appeared on the small screen. She had a pretty face with soft, brown eyes and a skin tone that spoke of long summer suns near an open sea. Azalea's hair was midlength with jagged ends in a style that was not common on Papen's World, though it seemed a little more common on Plaza One. Azalea was smiling, and her voice was warm, but then a serious expression spread over her face, her eyes growing tight, and Azalea's whole demeanor shifted to one of tension. "Where's Jillian?"

There was no way to sugarcoat what Paul needed. "I need your help," he said. "Jillian was kidnapped by Syrch Corp. I need you to help me save her."

The airlock began to cycle. "We'll meet you in the kitchen, Paul. I'll wake the others."

"Azalea—thank you. I don't ... there's ..." Paul tried to smile.

"No worries," Azalea assured him.

The door opened, and Paul stepped into the *Dorothea* once again. The ship was familiar and comfortable, and he felt as if a weight had been lifted, at least temporarily, off of his shoulders. He found his way to the kitchen where Azalea was waiting for him. Faolan arrived at Paul's heels, and the three shook hands and made small talk until Captain Gutwein arrived, motioning for Paul to sit at the table while Azalea and Faolan got everyone a cup of coffee from the ship's food processor bank.

"I must admit," the captain began, "that I didn't expect to see you again, Paul. And I take it there is trouble? Azalea said something about Syrch Corp kidnapping Jillian? Now why would they do something like that? I knew you were both hot items, but—why don't you fill us in, Paul. The whole story. We deserve that if you intend to get us mixed deeper into your personal business."

Paul took a sip of coffee and placed the cup gingerly back upon the table. "That's fair enough, Kurt."

As the group settled down to listen, Paul began. He told them the whole story: the visit by Dr. Gibson, the coin, the hit on Jillian and how that resulted in Rif's death, the subsequent discovery of the doctor's secret and Jillian's origins, the meeting with Gordon Pepper and Jillian's confined return to school, Paul's kidnapping of Jillian a second time and their rushed escape to the open strip mine. The only item Paul left out was Jillian's strange ability to stun people or force them to fall asleep. Paul didn't understand it, and he was afraid knowledge of it might scare the crew of the *Dorothea* away. People had deep concerns about augmentations to humans. Always a risky subject, like religion and politics, it was better to not raise the issue when trying to make and influence friends. He did tell them about Jillian's enhanced intelligence, which elicited a comment from Azalea, who said she had been impressed by Jillian's natural ability to merge with the *Dorothea's* systems.

"I told you Jillian would make a good pilot," Azalea said to the captain.

"Well, now we know why." The captain looked a little askance at Paul, and his lips were set tightly.

Paul shifted in his chair and winced as his recently healed ribs complained. "I don't know if the tinkering with Jillian's DNA made her smart or if she is just a naturally smart kid. But Syrch will poke and prod her until they find out. What person with enough money wouldn't want to have a child that is a genius? Syrch will look at her as a potential windfall in revenue. Giving her uncle, Dr. Gibson, a new research lab and not holding him accountable is evidence enough for me. They don't mean Jillian well.

"So the tracker," Paul continued, "it must have been detected by some hidden scanner or something. And before I could get the tracker removed, a team of thugs, though I think they were not Syrch enforcers but local heavies, tracked us down. They got the jump on me and beat me nearly to death. I only got out of the hospital this morning."

"I thought you looked a little roughed up. Near death?"

"I had enough money for a special treatment, Kurt. It wasn't pleasant, but it got me back on my feet. Now I figure I have two days to find Jillian again and a day to make the grab."

"What special treatment?"

Paul looked at the crew members and shrugged. "It was juice. They gave me an infusion of juice."

"That stuff costs a small fortune," the captain said.

"I know."

"So you are broke too?"

Paul rubbed at his eyes. "Yeah. But I'll worry about that later."

Azalea reached across and rested a hand on Paul's forearm. "Did it hurt?"

"Yes," Paul admitted, "at least the little I remember about it. But I tell you, I was a bloody mess. Without it, I would still be in the hospital. It was ugly and painful, but it worked."

"How do you figure?" Faolan asked. "About the three days? I don't care about the juice, though to be honest, I don't know if I would take it even if I could afford it. I'd like to know why you think you have three days and that Jillian is still in system."

"Syrch does not have much capacity in Tianjin," Paul replied. "Nobody does. That's the beauty of the system. So the people who grabbed Jillian will have to get a message pony back to Syrch Corp, and then Syrch will have to send instructions back or send a team to get Jillian. And what do they do in the meanwhile? Do they just take her out of the system with no real understanding of her value and with no instructions from Syrch? No. Jillian is still here. And any way you choose to look at it, the guestimate of time is about the same. Ships only travel so fast."

"And what do you want us to do?" the captain asked.

"I remember talking to Jillian about how she and Azalea hooked into the ship's computer system, and Jillian said she found a condenser coil that needed replacement."

"Yes, she did. A great piece of deductive reasoning," Azalea confirmed.

"It got me thinking," Paul said. "Can you use the ship's communication system to search for a signal if I gave you the frequency?"

"Maybe. Does it frequency hop? Is it scrambled?"

"No. It's an open signal. Hopping and scrambling would defeat the purpose of having one installed—so a person or thing can be easily tracked. The alert system is designed to allow people to be able to track down and recover Syrch's property. I thought you could pinpoint the signal for me, and then I'd go and get Jillian. That is all you would have to do."

"Jillian—property?" Azalea sounded angry. "What do you think, Captain?"

Captain Gutwein thought about it for a moment before replying. "Is it something you could do, Azalea?"

"Well, yes and no. I can find the signal—most likely. But that would only give me one reference point. I'd need at least one other reference so I could do a resection and find the girl. If I could get three or more, then that would improve the calculation and reduce the margin of error. We could move the ship about the asteroid, but that would not take into account Jillian being moved. So it would be best to get simultaneous vectors from multiple locations."

"How would you do that?" the captain asked.

Azalea shrugged. "Call a few friends?"

Faolan shook his head. "You want to bring in more pilots to help with the search? You might as well hang out a neon sign for Syrch Corp, giving them the finger."

"Not necessarily," the captain responded. "It's an open signal?"

"Yes," Paul replied.

"That means it would be a passive search too. Am I right, Azalea?"

"You are correct, Captain. We do not have to send a signal out of the ship to get the task accomplished. We just need to listen."

"So there is no need to identify the ship with an active ping. Faolan?"

"It's risky, Captain. Syrch won't appreciate it, and we are not on their good side already. But if what Paul says is true … I don't feel comfortable about it, but I say we take the risk. I liked that kid."

"Me too," the captain admitted. "Then it's settled, Paul." The captain turned back to Paul and said seriously, "We're in. But what will you do once you have the girl? You said you are broke."

Paul took another sip of coffee and, still holding the cup near his mouth, said, "We'll run. Syrch knows she is here. So I'll run to Lin Corp space—anywhere in Lin territory—somehow. I think Lin Corp will take Jillian and protect her."

"Lin Corp? They might at that," the captain said thoughtfully. "You'll bring Jillian back here to the *Dorothea*." The captain's statement was not a question. "And we'll take her to Lin Corp."

"I can't ask you to do that."

"You're not asking, Paul. I'm offering. It is not really an offer either; it's a condition. If we are to help you, then you will bring Jillian here, and we will get her to Lin Corp. There is little practical use in doing anything if you are too broke to buy transit on a space liner, and Jillian still has to get that tracker removed. You can't do that without help. So you're stuck."

Paul looked at the three crew members. Faolan nodded his head slightly. Azalea looked determined. And the captain was a rock of confidence.

"Thank you—all of you. I don't …" Paul struggled.

"Think nothing of it, Paul. Like we said, we all like that little girl. And if half of what you have told us is true concerning Jillian's birth and Syrch using her as an experiment … we want to do this. Screw Syrch! Some things are right. And this is one of those. It's settled? Good." The captain stood up and ran a hand through his hair. "Well, we better get moving. Faolan and I will finish getting the ship ready for transit. You and Azalea—Paul— find the girl."

27

◦—∞—◦—◯—◦—∞—◦

VIOLENCE BEGETS
DEATH

A **SYRCH** Corp battle cruiser, a frigate, and a corvette intruded upon the Tianjin system to the consternation of the system's government and its many patrons. While not a large enough force to blockade Tianjin, the *Ajax* and its smaller companion ships, the *Devastation* and *Valiant*, took up station off Plaza One, effectively hemming the asteroid between their guns as a Syrch party took a small shuttle down to the surface where they met with high-ranking members of the local police and government. The populations of the Tianjin system were tense, and several star ships left the system, anticipating violence, while the remaining people developed a bunker mentality and stayed near their homes or business establishments. It was an unprecedented move by Syrch Corp, but when you had the type of firepower Syrch Corp commanded, you could use a heavy hand, and nobody would complain, at least not openly. Rumors flew as to why Syrch Corp had shown up in force, and, Paul understood, the government of Tianjin had filed a formal complaint with the League of Planets. But this meant little to Paul at the moment, sitting in a car outside of a small house located on a rise of ground in the northern section of Plaza One's interconnected domes.

The house was an unattached, middle-class, geodesic dome with a small yard covered with paving stones and a few raised beds where imported fauna struggled to grow in the chemically altered dirt of the asteroid. Like most homes on Plaza One, there were no windows in the structure, a necessity of survival in case the main dome failed. The house then became a survival pod capable of maintaining oxygen, water, and food for a set period. Though Plaza One dome had never failed, there had been too many tragic instances throughout human space, and the Tianjin system had seen its share of decompression and death. Part of a larger integrated safety system that was complemented by ground transportation that would sustain life for a few hours, public emergency shelters, and mandatory water, food, energy, and oxygen control laws, the home was specifically built to an exacting code. That made it more difficult to break into the house, Paul knew, because the construction material had to be strong and airtight.

"We have a fifth reading, Paul." Azalea's voice was crisp yet low in Paul's ear. "Right rear of the house—that is where the signal is most powerful."

"It's got to be Jillian then," Paul replied into his hidden microphone. The communication system was not as good as the one he and Rif had used on Papen's World, being a bit bulkier, but it got the job done.

Paul extended the butt stock of his rifle, a modified KNR flechette rifle, with its high-capacity magazine, a laser sight with a wide optical aperture for quick sighting, and both an auto and semiauto setting. Keeping the weapon below the sight line of the car's windshield, Paul keyed it for auto fire. He then glanced down in the courier bag that sat on the seat next to him, opening it wide enough to see the explosive that he had rigged to a triggering device. The explosive, a malleable, claylike substance, had a textured surface that encouraged it to cling tightly to most material. Paul was not an explosives expert, but his research indicated that the quarter pound amount he had rigged would be adequate to blow a hole in the wall of the home. Paul had chosen the wall instead of the door because the door was one of the stronger points in the structure, as it was an airlock door. That decision had dictated the shape of the charge too. The U-shaped charge should make a hole large enough for Paul to get through, but it could also kill anyone on the other side of blast. Having an exact location for Jillian was therefore paramount. Getting a more definitive reading from Azalea on the tracker embedded in Jillian and continually checking the target wall for infrared body-heat signatures gave Paul the confidence he needed to move to the next step.

Stepping out of the car, Paul slung his rifle in front of him, using some material he had modified to simulate a combat sling, allowing him to release the weapon with both hands while retaining it in a near-ready firing position. His pistol was in a leg holster that he had borrowed from Captain Gutwein and was low on his thigh, positioned to where his fingertips naturally hung at the same level as the pistol's grip. He wore a pair of clear protective glasses that wrapped around his eyes and fingerless shooting gloves. Paul had ditched his coat and opted for a simple T-shirt with brown, resilient slacks, and a small knife was sheathed on the inside of his left ankle. Paul took the small courier's bag with the explosives out of the car and opened the backseat, grabbing a long, metal pole that would assist in holding the explosive charge in place while at the same time providing just enough forward pressure to help direct the bulk of the cutting blast into the wall. Finally, Paul took a large spray can and held it in his right hand, checking to make sure he had the direction valve in line with his index finger. The home did not have any windows, but it did have closed-circuit television cameras at the apex of each curved wall. The spray, a silicon sealant, would put the cameras out of commission when sprayed on the lens.

The residential area was quiet, it being the heart of the working day, and Paul casually strode up to the house and sprayed first one and then the second camera that provided coverage for the target side of the house. Satisfied, he knelt and began securing the explosive to the wall. When done, the charge resembled a wooden frame with two internal slats, held in place by the metal rod, and was approximately two feet off the ground. That would make the entrance hole low, but Paul preferred that over a higher entry point that would also be a natural aiming point for any defenders. He hoped to avoid a hip-shot burst of defensive fire. Paul took a calculated amount of time to double-check his work, keeping an eye on his surroundings, before he moved back about fourteen feet and lay prone on the ground.

"All set," Paul said into his communicator. "Target's location?"

"It hasn't changed. Far side."

Paul ducked, putting his face into the dirt, and clutching the activator in his hand, he flipped the red safety cover off the detonation toggle and pushed the toggle with his thumb. There was a sharp explosion followed by a wave of heat and the sound of material flying through the air. Paul waited for a count of three and then moved, crouching, toward where a clean, square-cut hole breached the wall. Paul readied his rifle and stepped boldly through the breach, one foot at a time, the smoke that filled the space temporarily blinding him. But Paul moved purposefully forward—heel to toe, heel to toe—in that rolling, measured gait used to minimize the deviation in his site picture and the trajectory of any fired rounds. It was a gait used and perfected by the military and other specially trained operators. It followed the principle that the shooter's body was the firing platform and that the body should emulate a tripod as much as possible, with as many points of contact between the shooter's body and the ground. It was not as fast as a run. It was slow, methodical, and smooth, and it made Paul look almost like he was ice-skating.

Moving through the first interior doorway, Paul fired two quick bursts at a woman who was stumbling down the hall with a pistol in her hands. The woman groaned as the flechette needles hit her and she collapsed to the floor. Paul ignored her and moved left down the hallway toward the rear of the house where the signal indicated Jillian was being held. Though the house was a dome, the interior was built out in right angles, giving the appearance of a rectangular space. The only telltale that the house was circular was the shape of the ceiling that was vaulted, the triangular pattern of the blocks that made up the home clearly visible. Paul expected there would be an open space that took advantage of the vaulted ceiling somewhere in the house, perhaps a living room. But the hallway he was following was cramped and made a slow arc to his right, revealing a bathroom with shower, sink, tub, and commode and a closed bedroom door at the end of the hall. The bathroom was empty, and a careful check of the door to the bedroom found it locked. Paul struck out with his foot, and the door broke open with a loud crash. Pushing his way into the room, Paul saw a bed, vanity, dresser, and a closet door. He did not see Jillian.

"Jillian!"

Paul heard a squeak, and Jillian's head popped above the edge of the bed.

"Are you okay?"

"Paul? Paul!" Jillian got off the floor and ran to him, throwing her arms around the enforcer and crying.

"Did they hurt you? Jillian?" It was difficult to hug the girl with his rifle in the way. Paul put his left hand on her back and squeezed. Then he turned back to face the door. "How many people are there? Jillian, how many people are in the house?"

"I thought they had killed you! And I didn't want to go. They made me. I tried … I tried …"

"It's okay, kid. Look …" Paul knelt down and held Jillian out at arm's length, looking her over for any overt signs of injury. "Were there just the three of them? Jillian! Listen, how many people?"

Jillian nodded. "I only saw three. But I don't know because I've been locked in this room."

"All right, stay behind me." Paul moved to the bed and found Mr. Bunny sitting on a pillow, still wearing the clothing Azalea had made. "Here, don't leave him behind."

Jillian took the stuffed bunny and followed behind Paul as he—heel, toe, heel, toe—moved back down the hall, his rifle in the ready position. He helped Jillian past the body of the dead woman and continued around the hall to where it opened into a large living space. A white couch and matching chairs sat around a small coffee table. Beyond that was an open kitchen where a small, rectangular table stood surrounded by barstools. And to Paul's right was the main door. He opened the door and then stopped suddenly, the banging sound of car doors closing catching his ears. He pushed Jillian back behind the wall and fired several rounds at two men who were stepping out of a black sedan. One man went down, and the other returned fire with a pistol, the rounds imprecisely impacting on the wall. A second car pulled rapidly up the street, and three additional people stepped out of the car, ducking behind it for cover. Paul recognized two of the new people: the bald man who had beaten him and whom Paul had confronted in the Banyan Tree Club, and Shiloh.

Shiloh Trenton in a black skirt, white blouse, with a matching suit jacket, wielding a subgun and wearing dark glasses, glanced over the top of the sedan and made eye contact with Paul. He had her in his sights but held his fire. Instead he swiveled and fired a burst at the first sedan and the man who was now crouched by the rear of the vehicle shooting at Paul. Paul's shots sang and skipped through the air, thudding into the body of the car, forcing the man to back away and stop firing.

"Give it up, Paul! There is no place to run!" Shiloh yelled.

Rotating his shoulder out, Paul quickly leaned out of the doorway and fired several rounds at the bald man who was half-crouched behind Shiloh's vehicle, hitting the man in the chest, neck, and head.

"I owed him that, Shiloh! Now nobody else has to die here. Let me and the kid go."

Paul heard Shiloh curse. "You're outnumbered, Paul. And you're boxed in. I've got ships in orbit, so where are you going to run? I don't think you are in any position to negotiate!"

"I'm not going to argue with you, Shiloh! I'm going to sit in here and wait for the cops. Anyone coming in this door in the meanwhile is going to get their heads blown off. Understand?"

"Damn it, Paul!"

"Move back from the door," Paul told Jillian. As she did, Paul used his foot to swing the door closed. "Now hurry, back down the hall. There's a hole in the wall by the other bedroom. We need to get out of here before they figure out there's another exit to this place."

Jillian took a few steps and stopped, confused. Paul backed away from the door and took her by the hand, guiding her past the dead body and out the hole he had blown in the back wall of the home, and quickly moving her to the waiting car. Paul put Jillian in the passenger-side seat, buckled her in, and told her to duck down out of sight. He was just opening his door when a man carrying an assault rifle appeared around the edge of the house, his attention on the building. Taking quick aim, Paul shot the man dead. That brought the remaining two enforcers running. Paul got behind the wheel and slammed the car into drive, stepping hard on the acceleration pedal as Shiloh and the other enforcer rushed back to their car and gave pursuit.

Paul drove recklessly, ignoring stop signs and narrowly missing another moving car. The two enforcers were coming on fast, Shiloh driving and the other, a man with dark hair and sunglasses, who had his torso out of the open passenger-side window and held a long gun pointed in Paul's general direction. The man fired, but his shots were wild, snapping past Paul's speeding car. The next shots were more accurate, punching into the rear of Paul's vehicle, but neither Paul nor Jillian was hit. Paul knew it was only a matter of time though before one of them was injured. He had to do something.

Paul steered hard to the left, his tires screeching and skidding as he made a sharp turn. Shiloh deftly followed, and Paul began searching for a place to make a final stand. He had to get out of the car and into an area where he could separate from Jillian to remove her from harm and then engage the two Syrch Corp enforcers.

His sudden maneuver with the car had created space between him and his pursuit. He glanced in the rearview mirror, noticing that the male enforcer was fully inside the car now but was positioning himself to make another attempt at shooting Paul. He swerved onto another street and made a dash toward a public area where a few office building domes were arranged in a half-moon shape before a large fountain that trickled water from the likeness of an insanity crystal held in the upraised hand of a statue of Er Quin, the inventor of the frame drive. A few people in business attire were moving between the buildings when Paul screeched to a stop, fired at the pursuing car, and quickly pulled Jillian up the stone stairs toward the entrance of the second building. Paul pushed into the lobby as people scattered and the pursing male enforcer, stepping out of the car, opened fire, shattering the thick glass plating of the lobby windows and cascading shards of glass on the carpeted floor. Paul fired blindly back over his shoulder and led Jillian through a fire escape door. In the stairwell, he picked her up and started moving rapidly up the stairs. On the third landing, he slipped through the fire door and into a hallway with several doors along both sides and an open sitting area and break area to his left.

"See the door at the end, Jillian," he huffed, breathing hard. "Go there and wait for me."

"But, Paul!"

"Do it! I'll be right behind you."

Jillian did not look happy, but she obeyed, sulking her way to the indicated open door and disappearing inside. Paul saw her poke her head around the door and motioned her back inside. Just then a small group of people came from the far end of the hall heading for the break room. When they saw Paul, a woman screamed and dropped a collection of papers, and the group hastily beat a retreat back the way they had come. Paul opened the fire door, stepped out, and peered cautiously into the stairwell. He saw a shadow of movement below and raised his rifle to his eye and patiently waited.

The male enforcer's head popped into view for a second. Paul squeezed the trigger, the hissing sound of his KNR flechette rifle echoing in the enclosed space, but the man jerked out of the line of fire. Paul was sure he had missed. In the quiet that followed, he could hear Shiloh and the other enforcer shuffling up the stairs, hugging the wall. Since the stairs turned at each landing, the two remained hidden though Paul could approximate their location as they climbed to the first and then the second level. Sweat beaded on Paul's forehead, and his eyes were tightly focused on his rifle sights, but he thought he heard something. It was the barely audible bounce of a closing door. Paul concluded that one of the two enforcers had gone through the second landing's fire door and was likely trying to flank Paul, either by using another stairwell or simply by getting on the elevator.

A klaxon suddenly blared. Paul jumped, startled, and a voice came from unseen speakers announcing a security situation and requesting all personnel evacuate the building or lock their doors and hide in place. Paul quickly slipped off his left shoe and stuffed it between the fire door and the wall, propping it open, just in case there was an automated lockdown of the building. He did not want to lose access to Jillian. Then he skirted the wall toward the opening of the stairs, hoping to get a glimpse of either Shiloh or her partner so he could take that person out before the other came up behind him. He could not see anyone. Paul exchanged magazines on the rifle, the combat reload giving him a full magazine for the desperate idea that blossomed in his mind. He kicked off his other shoe and removed his socks one at a time, throwing them on the carpeted floor. He took a deep breath. Aiming at the wall in what he felt was the approximate opposite location from the enforcer below, Paul fired a steady stream of flechettes while running full tilt down the stairs, spraying fire before him, the deadly projectiles zipping and clanging wildly in the enclosed space as they ricocheted every which way. Paul came around the stair and suddenly could see the male enforcer, crouched low against the back corner by the fire door. The man began shooting, but in the chaos, he failed to kill Paul, though several needles flicked through Paul's clothing, and he suffered minor wounds on left hip and thigh. Paul was more accurate, shooting a burst into the floor and guiding the impacts up until they intersected with the man, striking him several times from the bottom to the top of his body. The man slumped forward, but Paul did not pause. He moved back up the stairs and into the hall on the third floor.

The alarm ringing and red emergency lights flashing over the stairwell, Paul ran barefooted to where Jillian was waiting, standing against the back wall of a large office. A desk and chair, faced by two other chairs and a small, round coffee table, stood between Paul and Jillian.

"Come on!"

"Where are your shoes?"

"Come on!"

Paul grabbed Jillian and rushed back to the stairwell, ducking through the fire door and dashing back the way they had come. Jillian looked away from the corpse as Paul picked the little girl up and moved pell-mell down to the ground floor. In the lobby, a shard of glass jabbed into Paul's foot, and he hopped and cursed, placing Jillian on the floor and trying to pull the shard out with one hand as he swung the rifle back and forth between the elevators, stairs, and main door. The only other person in the lobby was a man, crouched against the wall, his hands over his head, muttering something in a frantic voice. He looked up at Paul and shrieked, but he kept still, shaking and staring at the floor directly in front of him. Paul ignored the man, fished the glass out of his foot, and, trailing blood, pulled Jillian out of the entrance and back toward his car. Paul had taken two steps when he heard something and froze.

"It's over, Paul. Drop your weapon!"

Paul turned, slowly. Shiloh Trenton stood by the side of the dome, slightly behind Paul and Jillian, her weapon ready and trained on Paul's heart.

28

---◦○◎○◦---

DARKNESS

PAUL DROPPED his rifle on the ground.

"Shiloh—"

"Don't you dare, and you!" Shiloh shifted her aim to Jillian. "Don't you even think of taking one step nearer to me, little girl, do you hear? I have no qualms killing you. You'd be dead already if Syrch Corp didn't want you back. Freak! She's a freak!"

"Leave her alone."

"And you—stupid. Don't you see what she's doing to you? Don't you understand what she is?"

"What the hell are you talking about, Shiloh? She's a kid, not some laboratory rat. Syrch has no right …"

"Right! God, how deep inside your mind is she, Paul? Do you think that little thing she did back on Papen's World is all she can do? You're a fool. She's … she's *influenced* you! Warped your thinking, twisted your mind!"

Paul held his hands up. "I know what she did to you. Maybe she'll do it again."

Shiloh hissed. "One hint of anything, and I'll drop her."

"Move behind me, Jillian."

"Don't."

"Jillian."

Jillian shuffled slowly toward Paul.

"I said, don't!"

Jillian stopped. Paul set his teeth and took a step toward her. Shiloh's weapon swung back at Paul.

"Paul, listen to me! That ... girl ... she's been modified."

"I know."

"Do you? Do you really? And you think all she can do is stun people with her mind? Is that it? She is smart and can stun people, but she is really an innocent little girl. Is that what you believe?"

"She is an innocent little girl." Paul was suddenly angry. "What Dr. Gibson did to her was inexcusable! And Syrch—taking his side, rewarding him; I'm disgusted."

"Disgusted? Who cares? Paul, don't you get it? You're under her sway. Think about it. Use your limited brains."

"What the hell are you talking about?"

"Dr. Gibson told us more, Paul. After you were cut out of the picture, he came clean. That little monster emanates some type of mind control, Paul."

"That's the stupidest thing I've ever heard."

"Is it? Is it? Ask her. Ask her about Rif. You were going to kill her, weren't you, Paul? I know you. You might not like it, but you would do it. So why didn't you? Why?"

"I thought about it," Paul hissed. "Are you happy? But Jillian is just a little kid, Shiloh. I don't kill little kids."

"Where was she situated when you took her? Rif was driving, wasn't he? Wasn't he? You—you had direct contact with her in the car. Didn't you?" she accused.

Paul looked at Jillian. Her eyes were wide open and clear. Paul took another step toward Jillian.

"Is she doing it now?" Shiloh asked. Her voice was venomous. "Stop it! I swear to god I will kill her, Paul. One more step, and I'll blow her freagin' head apart."

"Doing what? Controlling my mind, Shiloh? Is that the crap the *good* doctor told you?"

"Direct contact … that is what he said. Was she on your lap? Did you hold her?"

Paul thought about it. He had.

Shiloh must have seen the answer on his face. "You did!" she exclaimed. "That is how she does it, Paul. She can't exercise her control without touching you. She ordered you to protect her. She ordered you to kill Rif. And you did. You did! You could have convinced Rif to hold off. You know that. He wasn't very bright. But she—that kid—didn't *know* that. She touched you and implanted the thought in your head. That is what the doctor told us, Paul. That is why he wanted her dead. He was terrified of her. And who else? Who else has she controlled since you took her?"

The crew of the *Dorothea*, Paul thought. She has had contact with all of the crew.

"Jillian?"

"I didn't do anything!" Jillian cried.

Paul took a halting step forward. "Jillian? The crew? I've never seen anyone take so quickly …"

"And how many people have you killed, Paul?" Shiloh continued. "How many people have you killed for her? She is deranged—mad! You're a professional, but everything you have done has been sloppy. That's not you. It's her!"

"Paul?" Jillian said. She looked tiny standing in front of him, her eyes wide and tears sliding down her cheeks.

"Jillian, is that true? Is what Shiloh is saying true?"

"I hate you!" Jillian turned and shouted at Shiloh. "You're a liar! You lie! I didn't do anything to Paul. I didn't do anything to the captain, Azalea, or Faolan either! They're my friends!"

"The doctor told us what you did to *him*. I know what you are."

"He's a bad, bad man!" Jillian shot back. "I told him to leave me alone. He was hurting me."

"Jillian, what are you saying?" Paul suddenly knelt and looked her in the eye. "What are you saying?"

"No, no, no!" Jillian cried. "I didn't do anything. He hurt me. I just told him to stop. I love you, Paul. I love you!"

"Jillian?" Paul's crooked eyebrows lifted and fell, and his face gathered in confusion and hurt.

"She modified your mind, Paul. That is what I am trying to tell you. She's changed you."

Shiloh was right. Jillian had changed Paul. He looked at the little girl, and his heart felt heavy, conflicted, and a sick feeling spread through his chest. Paul reached a hand out to Jillian and pulled it back, studying his fingers in a daze, glancing at Shiloh as she kept her weapon on the girl.

"Get away from her, Paul. I'm taking her back to Syrch Corp where she belongs, where she can't hurt anyone ever again."

"It doesn't matter, Shiloh." Paul spoke softly.

"What? Of course it matters! Syrch has equities."

"Equities? She's a little girl, not a commodity." Paul rose and took two quick steps, shielding Jillian with his body. "Shiloh, you are going to have to kill me to get to Jillian. I don't care if she has some type of psychic power or not. I know how I feel. And the system sucks. Syrch Corp sucks. Jillian is more than just a chit, a piece of stock in a mutual fund. She's human. Human. So you're going to have to make a decision, Shiloh. You're going to have to decide, but it doesn't have to be this way. Let us go."

"I can't do that, Paul."

"The difference between me and you, Shiloh," Paul said sadly, "is that I don't believe Syrch is infallible. They don't know everything. I don't recognize Syrch Corp as God."

"Paul, don't make me do this."

"I am not making you. Make the right choice."

"I am, Paul." Shiloh's voice became hard. "But are you?"

Paul drew his pistol from his leg holster, and Shiloh fired. His hand was a blur of speed as his Mouser cleared the holster and rotated toward Shiloh. Paul fluidly shifted his body to the left as his gun went off, and a needle of hot pain exploded in his shoulder. The shoulder shattered, and a spray of blood peppered the ground behind him. The dome spun and blurred, and Paul fell to his left knee. He coughed up blood. It smeared across his lips, dark red, syrupy, and dribbled down his chin. It took all of Paul's concentration to keep his pistol extended, aimed at Shiloh who had crumpled to the ground, her life already ended, a clean yet ghastly hole punched through her cheek, through the grit and cartilage, exiting from the back of her skullcap in a blob of blood, brain, and bone.

Paul let his pistol drop.

Turning, Paul focused on Jillian, who stared at him as if she had just realized what type of man Paul was, and in that moment, Paul saw fear in Jillian's eyes. A deep welling pain crushed Paul.

Slavery has many subtle faces. Syrch had lost faith, faith that humanity could be better than the primal creatures that had shuffled through a million years of evolution. Syrch had reduced the meaning of life to values on a spreadsheet, accountants' tricks, and greed. But for Paul, all of humankind's suffering and sacrifice, the blind corners and dead ends, had to mean something. His life had to have meaning. Even the horror and fear in Jillian's eyes could not dissuade Paul from that truth. If Jillian feared him, that was the price Paul had to pay.

Paul realized at that moment that he loved her. She was the child he had never had. Didn't she know? He had done it all for her, to protect her, to give her a chance at a normal life. How or why that love had grown did not matter. He loved Jillian like a man damned to live in shadow might worship a distant star. Without Jillian's love, Paul had been a slave to the corporations, a deadly tool that now had outlived its purpose. And the life he had led to this slim moment was nothing. Without Jillian's love, Paul knew, he was but a stone in an endless universe.

Jillian reached out a hand and touched Paul. It was soft, a blessing and benediction, and the fear that Paul had seen in her eyes changed. Paul realized Jillian did not fear him; she was afraid for him. Paul's doubt evaporated, and for the first time in his life, Paul felt true joy.

"I'm okay, little one," Paul managed, "though I don't know if I can get you to the *Dorothea*. You need to go. It's now or never, kid."

"She was your friend too. I think she loved you."

"Maybe, but she was wrong."

Jillian helped Paul to the edge of the building. He flinched as his torn shoulder felt the pressure of the wall behind him, and he coughed up more blood.

"I don't want you to die," Jillian pleaded.

"It's not about life, kid. It's about the kind of life we choose." He tried to smile but felt dizzy, and his body seemed confused and clumsy as he fought to hold down the vomit that threatened to spew from his mouth. "You have to go, kid. Did you hear me? Jillian, you have to go."

"I'm not leaving you." She held Mr. Bunny in her left hand. The stuffed animal shook as she gesticulated in frustration.

"I can't make it," Paul said. "You can. You have to go or they will catch you."

"No! You have to come with me. You have to fight. I won't leave you!"

Paul laughed softly. "I tell you what. I'll make a deal with you." He spoke haltingly, his breath rapid and shallow. "Go and get the captain. He'll help." Paul tried to sound nonchalant. "I'll wait here. I promise. I will wait for you."

"Get help?"

"That's right."

Jillian looked at Shiloh's body then turned back, and a new look of determination crossed her cherub face. "I didn't mean—I didn't know ..." She hugged Paul, getting a smear of Paul's blood on her dress, and then kissed the enforcer.

"I'll be right back."

"Sure. See you, kid."

Jillian darted into the door of the building, repeating her promise, her feet moving as quickly as her little legs could churn. Paul could hear her yelling frantically for a videophone. He watched her go. He knew he would never see her again. It hurt—that knowledge.

Paul had never died before, but he felt the hand of death. He knew it was coming. Yet the jagged hole in his foot hurt more than the wound that was killing him. It made no sense. It was irritating. His foot burned and throbbed while the other wound felt cool and distant. He thought dying should be more dramatic. But it was silly, stupid even. Paul suddenly wondered if his mother had loved him at all, all those years ago. She was a blurred memory, something warm and comforting in the dark, but she had given Paul away. Even now as he felt the blood roll down his back, the raw hurt of that moment resonated. He had been about Jillian's age when his mother dropped him off at the orphanage—or had he been younger? Yes, he was maybe a year or two younger. Paul had wanted so badly for his mother to stay. He still didn't understand what he had done so wrong that his mother abandoned him to strangers, cruel in their discipline and cold. And the anger came again. Deep and pure and filled with longing that bespoke of empty nights and an empty life, it rose up and threatened to sweep everything else aside. Jillian had been the only person ever to show Paul any feeling. He could see it in her face, her smile, and hear it in her voice. Even if Shiloh had been right, even if it was all a construct of some arcane power, that did not change the simple fact that Jillian felt like his child, like his own daughter. Paul reached through the long dark where his innermost self hid and allowed himself the luxurious weakness of unadulterated love. But the old scar was still there, lurking, his mother's betrayal and condemnation.

Nobody had loved Paul except Jillian—well, there was Shiloh, in her odd way.

Paul and Shiloh had never been more than distant acquaintances with possibility, but Shiloh had been the closest Paul had ever come to having a true lover. Conditioned since birth to rules and Syrch Corp's brand of honor, Shiloh couldn't see Jillian in the same light Paul did. But in a way, Paul admired Shiloh that. She had lived the life she wanted to the very end. She was a Syrch Corp enforcer, blood and bone.

In contrast, Paul had failed in everything. He had failed as an enforcer. He had murdered Rif and Shiloh. He had failed to protect Jillian and get her to Lin Corp. Yes. Maybe this was where Paul should be, on an open field beneath a dome at the end of the universe with Shiloh's cooling corpse as his only companion.

Paul fell to his right side and with effort crawled the short distance between the blood-smeared wall and Shiloh's body. It was difficult to pull himself across the grass with one arm, his legs kicking. But he finally reached her and placed his head just under Shiloh's chin.

"I'm sorry."

The smell of flowery perfume mingled with the iron tang of blood. The grass, nurtured carefully and grown on this distant land far from the planet of its origin, felt sharp and crisp. A slight breeze tickled the hairs on Paul's arms. And far above, the emerald, jadeite green of Plaza One's dome sparkled while beyond starships plied the vastness of space. A deep, stabbing fear filled Paul's confused brain, and he called for his mother, but his mother was long lost, and Paul felt his death as a lonely one.

And that is when the universe turned dark.

29

⊶∘⊶○◉○⊷∘⊷

THE FRAME

THE ***DOROTHEA*** framed quietly out of the Tianjin system. The small cargo ship was still and quiet as Azalea, deep in her pilot's trance, explored the universe using the ship's sensors, feeling the solar wind kissing the ship as it left the outer heliosphere and sensing the interstellar wind as it moved across the ship's field of lateral travel. Captain Gutwein sat quietly in the command chair, rereading the cargo manifest and doing last-minute calculations on cost and potential earnings. Faolan was somewhere in the bowels of the ship, tinkering on the water reclamation system, trying to discover the source of the metallic taste the water recently developed. The source of the impurity had to be somewhere in the system after the distiller, which reduced possible areas of concern by two-thirds. The *Dorothea's* escort, the majestic Lin Corporation battleship *The Swan*, bounded beside the smaller ship, its presence enough to warn off the Syrch Corp ships that slunk angrily back toward Papen's World. As much as Syrch Corp wanted Jillian back, they were not about to tangle with Lin Corp and begin a war that could destroy them. Together, the two interstellar ships framed through the dark expanse of space on a course for the Romeo system, the home of Lin Corp.

Jillian stood in a hallway on the second deck, staring sullenly at a closed door, her shoulders hunched as if vexed and her little face slightly twisted. She stamped her foot on the cold, metal flooring and harrumphed.

"I'm mad at you," she said as she entered the room. Jillian placed her hands on her hips and looked sternly at Paul. He was lying on a bed with Mr. Bunny next to him, propped against a pillow. All the intravenous tubes were gone, having been removed by the automated medic in the *Dorothea's* medical bay. Paul still looked wan and had lost a lot of weight. But he was alive.

"Why?" Paul put down the digital reader and looked down at Jillian, an amused look on his face. "Why are you angry at me now, Jillian?"

"I don't understand why I can't stay on the ship."

"You want to go to school, don't you? You want to learn and become a pilot like Azalea. You can't do that here. And besides, I'm not staying here either."

"What?" Jillian looked confused. She approached the bed and sat on the edge, looking down at her hands. "I thought—you said you couldn't go back home."

Paul nodded. "That's right. I can't go back to Papen's World or to Telakia for that matter. I burnt those bridges too."

"Will you stay on Romeo Five?"

Paul could hear the hope in her voice. "No, kid. I can't stay there. The Lin Corp folks won't allow it. I am bringing them enough trouble."

"Trouble?"

"You."

"Me?"

"Come up here." Paul padded the pillow by Mr. Bunny. Jillian scooted up there and held the stuffed bunny in her lap. "Let me see if

I can explain this to you. Lin Corp and Syrch Corp are not friendly with each other."

"They're enemies?"

"Yes. They are. And Syrch Corp thinks of you as their personal property, and they think they can study you and learn how to make more people like you, and then they can sell that knowledge for money. Got that? Good. But Lin Corp is at least as strong as Syrch, maybe stronger, so Syrch Corp can't bully them and just come in and take you. Once you are a citizen of Lin Corp, you are off-limits. And if Syrch Corp complains, then the truth would come out, and that would give them problems with the League of Planets, Terra, and Lin Corp. So they may not like it, but Syrch Corp will have to let you go. I suppose they could try to kill you ..."

"Kill me?"

"But you're a little girl—"

"I'm not so little."

"Like I was saying, it would be really bad press—really, really bad press—if they were to go after you in that way. So once we get you to Lin Corp space, you'll be safe. And you'll go to their best school and grow up and learn how to protect yourself, and you will live a free life. But that is not the case for me."

"Why not?"

"I was an enforcer, Jillian. I am not lily white, and, to be honest, nobody likes me. I've done some bad things. Really bad things. And I betrayed Syrch Corp. They can't let that stand. They will be sending people against me all the time, and if you are nearby, then you'll get caught in the crossfire."

"Are they going to try to kill you?"

Paul thought about his answer for a while. "I'm not going to lie to you, Jillian. I broke their contract and killed their people. Yes. They will come after me."

"I don't want them to kill you."

"Now, kid, don't worry about that. I'm a tough guy. Didn't I just live through a beating and a shooting that would kill a normal person?"

"That's the nanos."

"Yep. First-grade Lin Corp combat juice. And those things are still inside of me. I can handle myself."

"I can too!"

"I know you can, kid. But it's too early in your life for you to spend all of your time trying to fight off the bad guys. You need to go to school. You need to use those smarts and make me proud."

"I don't want to leave you," Jillian said.

"Did you know kids back on Papen's World who lived at the school? You did? Now you will live at a school too. You'll run around and learn the area, and it will become your home. It will be the first place where you can be safe. It is where you belong."

"But I won't see you."

"Maybe you will. I can't make you promises, Jillian. But I will see you when I can and keep in touch other ways too."

"But where will you go?"

Paul rubbed at his jaw. "I'm not sure, kid. I guess I am going to have to figure that out. Syrch Corp space is out of the question, and I probably am not welcomed back to Tianjin either, so maybe I'll try Terra or the League of Planet's space. And there's a nasty little war going on in the Federation system; they might need someone with my experience."

"Federation?"

"A small independent part of space. It's out on the edge of inhabited space. I'll probably work my way out there."

"And you'll be safe?"

"Of course I will."

"But I'll miss you."

"I'll miss you too, kid. But you'll work hard and make me proud?"

Jillian nodded. She leaned up against Paul, and he put an arm around her shoulder.

"How long before we get there?" Jillian asked.

"Romeo Five? Oh, I guess a couple of weeks. We have time to relax."

"Will you read me a story?"

"Sure, kid. Here." Paul picked up the digital reader and scanned through the ship's library. "How about ... this one?" He showed her the title, and Jillian agreed.

"Okay."

Snugging close, Paul began to read. The pain in his shoulder was receding as the nanos steadily continued their repairs. If it had not been for the combat juice, Paul knew, he would never have survived. He felt a pang of guilt about Shiloh. She wouldn't get the same second chance, and neither would Rif. Both of them would be dumped into a reclamation vat, and nobody would mourn their passing. What rankled Paul the most is that Dr. Warner Gibson had gotten away with it. The doctor had murdered Jillian's symbiont parents—his own sister and her husband—and carried out his heinous experiments on Jillian doing untold damage. Paul had explained to the Lin Corp representative the little he knew about Jillian's life. He hoped Lin Corp clinical psychologists were up to the task of helping Jillian come to terms and deal with her abuse. How does someone get over being scientifically tortured as a little kid? Paul didn't know. And there were the other people, the independent operators and Syrch Corp enforcers Paul had killed. The doctor was to blame for those as well. Yet Syrch Corp had promoted him and given the doctor a full laboratory where the man could carry out new experiments on yet unborn children in the hopes that his cruelty created a marketable product. Paul was no believer in justice. He had seen too much in his life to believe there was some type of moral and ethical code of behavior that would ensure that Dr. Gibson was adequately punished. And Paul did not believe in God, at least not the old God that would reward or punish a person upon their death in an ultimate and permanent exercise of justice. There was nothing when you died. Not even darkness. Yet the idea that the doctor had gotten everything he had wanted made Paul's blood boil.

Paul looked down at Jillian. She was dozing off, startle, and doze again. Paul hoped he was doing the right thing. Syrch Corp would hunt him down. And Lin Corp had no use for him. He could not stay in Lin-controlled space. He had asked and had been, not so politely, told no. Lin Corp citizens were very suspicious about strangers. Though Paul had no love for Terra Corp—Lin Corp's arch nemesis with a few massive wars and several skirmishes between them—and that distrust was always lurking behind the serene façade of Lin Corp's corporate soul. Distrusting strangers was a blind part of their culture.

The corporations were at war. They had been since Lin Corp formed from the ashes of Second Resource War when the seeds for all three of the mega corporations were sown. The war continued as humans expanded into their home system, with Lin and Terra attacking each other on Mars and in the outer planets; the war stopped being one of intrigue and dirty deeds with the outbreak of direct conflict in the First Trade War. The aftermath of that war did little to dispel the building pressure as Lin and Terra corporations clashed one hundred years later, a violent war that established the current disposition of territory and trade zones. But humanity kept pouring into space, and new planets, farther and farther away from Sol, led to the establishment of the independent League of Planets and, much more recently, the founding of the upstart and insatiable Syrch Corporation. Wherever humans traveled, it was always the same story, repeated since the time the first protohuman spied a berry bush in adjacent lands and fought and killed his neighbor for access and control of that resource. For humans consume all and demand all, and not even the limitless expanse of the universe and its countless resources could satisfy humanity's appetite.

Paul looked down at Jillian. She was finally asleep, her mouth slightly open, one hand lightly holding Mr. Bunny and one draped over Paul. He thought of her as his daughter. And Paul had killed people he admired and foes alike to keep Jillian safe.

Would she inherit the war? Could men somehow evolve and become something more? Perhaps, Paul mused, that was what Jillian represented. Maybe she was the first in an evolution of humankind in a new generation that would finally put conflict behind them and build a better future. But to believe that, Paul would have to have faith in humanity. And he had seen too much of human cruelty to think that people would ever change. There would always be war—between the corporations or between governments—until after the final hour of humanity's existence.

Kissing Jillian on the head, Paul dimmed the room lights. He carefully settled onto the bed and closed his eyes.

30

───◦◦◦◯◯◯◦◦◦───

THE LONG CLIMB

IT WAS a long climb up steep stone stairs that lined the circuitous route up the side of the mountain to the towering walls of Dong Zhongshu Taixue, Lin Corp's premier school for the gifted that lay nestled within the bosom of the holy mountain. Mount Lie Shanqu soared over thirty-five thousand feet above the Ruan Ji River valley, a lush land of rhododendron, with their delicate flowers of white, pink, and blended rose, and bayberry with their flat, green leaves and pearly, grapelike fruit. Lofty, majestic juniper trees, with their thick, soft pine needles dotted with berries, swayed in the soft breeze along tributary streams that crisscrossed the valley, feeding into the mighty river, the Ruan Ji. In the meadows and hollows that surrounded the snow-covered peak, transplanted rhino shared the landscape with occasional lions, snow leopards, and musk sheep and lived their lives unaware of the great forces that had brought them back to life from the edge of extinction on a planet light-years from earth. Flights of birds, flameback woodpeckers, orange bullfinches, hoary-throated barwings, and a myriad of other exotic species shared the sky with golden eagles, large and powerful hunters that skittered with suddenness like arrows shot from the sun. Scores of bearded vultures, with their rust-brown and white-speckled bodies, circled above, scavenging for bones, which they broke with powerful beaks, or hunting the lesser creatures of the ecosystem: hares, marmots, and the occasional larger steenbok deer. Stretching two thousand miles, from east to west, the great Nanga range was the greatest mountain range on Romeo Five, the venerable home world of Lin Corporation. Yet it was Mount Lie Shanqu, proud in its jagged youth, that held court within the billow of clouds and snow that floated through the alien, azure sky.

Paul held Jillian's hand as the two of them slowly ascended. Jillian's grip was tight, and her breath came in little puffs as she exerted herself. Her coat, charcoal gray with embroidered roses of red, yellow, and white, was soft in the light of the system's star. Beneath it she wore a new lilac-colored, organdy dress with a sash around her waist that ended in a fine, flowered bow. The dress was lined with the latest high-tech fabric, a lush, soft-as-silk concoction that moved with her tiny body but whose molecules swam together tightly, trapping warm air in layers of fibers that gave the otherwise light-weather dress the same comfort of thick wool on a cool day.

Pausing on a landing of migmatite, a textured gray stone with folded swirls of white, pink, and orange leucosome, Paul let the girl rest. Jillian had been quiet since they had arrived at the base of Mount Lie Shanqu. She had grown sullen the further up the mountain they climbed, but her face was furrowed with self-determination, as if she had resolved not to allow herself to feel sad and abandoned. Yet Paul felt uneasy too. The surrealist beauty of the vista below, the solemn wonder of rising peaks, half-hidden by snow and cloud, and the fresh breeze that rustled through the opulent air made him feel like a Neanderthal, having roamed too near a magic stream, suddenly transported into a garden where the rules of the brutish life it had led were far and distant and rudely insignificant. The serene quiet left Paul feeling restless, nervous, and ready to bolt.

"How much more?" Jillian tried to judge the length of the remaining stair, one hand keeping her fur-lined hood from falling to her shoulders as she looked up into the looming sky.

"Not much, kid. Just around the next corner."

"You've been saying that for a while."

"One of these times, I'll be right. Don't think about it, and it won't be such a bother."

"But … never mind." Jillian sat down on a bench that overlooked the valley.

"I promise it won't be long now, Jillian."

"Why do I have to come here?"

"We've talked about this."

"But I want to go home."

"You know you can't. It isn't safe."

"They didn't hurt me."

"No. Not now. But later? When you are grown? I didn't like the way they were looking at you, as if you were some prize experiment. You need to live a real life."

"Can't you stay with me?"

"I wish I could, kid. But we talked about that too."

"Why won't they let you go?"

"I'm an enforcer, Jillian. Was … that comes with certain baggage."

"I don't understand."

"I know."

"I don't want to go!"

Paul dropped a protective hand across her shoulder and held Jillian for a moment. Looking out at the land, he followed the path of the river, a distant ribbon flowing through wood and field. For the first time in his hard life, Paul had someone. But he knew what that meant. He knew it could not last. How could he explain it to a little girl? Her hurt became his hurt, and his eyes watered though he willed them to stop. He blinked and wiped at his eyes, irritated at himself yet unable to bring the surge of emotion into check. When had he become so weak? Why did this ache so much? A flood of grief poured through him, and he had to look away, close his eyes, push the image of the verdant garden-world away, and focus on the dark pool that ebbed in his mind. He let the inner shadows still him. The tightness in his chest and along his throat began to unwind, and he once again clearly saw the path to Jillian's destruction roll outward through time—if Paul were to fail here, at this moment, with the stone path of a longer, happier life within reach. Paul would not allow his weakness to deny Jillian a real future. Though Paul felt cold, he would not pull the child back into the murk just to ease his own loneliness.

Paul knelt down. Taking Jillian's head in both his hands, he forced the child to look at him: his gruff features, the day-old beard, crooked eyebrows, and deep-set eyes. He looked at Jillian for a moment, silent, longing, and suddenly pulled the girl to him and hugged her dearly. He knew she was an illusion of what could not be.

"Come." He stood. "They will be waiting."

"Don't you love me?"

"It's not a matter of love, kid."

Paul pulled Jillian along as they once again began the long climb toward the walls of the school. Behind the walls but invisible from view were the spiraling towers and domed buildings of Dong Zhongshu Taixue. The precepts of the school would protect Jillian from Syrch Corp, nurture and instruct her. And above, in the inter-system space, Lin's battle fleet and listening posts cast a protective net over Jillian like nothing Paul could hope to emulate. She was special. And if she hoped to have any life of her own, she would have to find it here, nestled in the bosom of the holy mountain, far away from the ravaged space where Syrch Corp carved up lives and resources in the name of the one god, profit.

It was an arduous climb. The system's sun was in dusk, throwing streaks of color through the sky when Paul and Jillian arrived at the heavy wooden doors set into the wall. To the left of the closed doors, a bronze gong on a spirit-guide, ebony frame stood. A long-handled mallet hung from its side. Paul picked the mallet up and, after quickly glancing down at Jillian, who refused to meet his eyes, gently rapped at the gong, creating a deep, reverberating note that echoed down the mountainside. Paul rehung the mallet, took Jillian's hand, and stood facing the door.

After a minute, one of the two halves of the great door opened, a withered, old hand grasping it around the door's edge, pushing the door outward. An older man with a kind face stepped through the opening. He wore a monk's robe of orange, and his hair was shorn close. A metal disc hung on a thin chain around his neck.

"You are late." The monk's voice was soft and welcoming.

"I'm Paul Thorne, and this is Jillian Caldwell."

"I know who you are, Mr. Thorne. My name is Wang Tao. I am the master here at Dong Zhongshu Taixue. We have been expecting you—both of you. Won't you come in?"

"No. No. I don't think I will. It would be better to let Jillian start her new life right now. I … I don't want to drag this out."

"I understand, Mr. Thorne."

"Now?"

"Yes, Jillian. I need … It's better this way, kid. Really."

"Okay."

"Come here, kid." Paul hugged her. "You be good, hear? Don't cause the prefects any trouble."

"Will I see … see you again?"

"You never know, kid. But I think so. I will try." Paul let Jillian go and walked to the edge of the winding stairs that led into a darkening valley.

Stepping off the landing, Paul slipped down into the growing gloom, leaving Jillian alone with the old monk.

"Don't cry, little sparrow. We must never impose upon someone else a character not their own. Mr. Thorne is what Mr. Thorne is. Rejoice in that."

"But … but …"

The monk looked down at Jillian and brushed tears from the girl's face. "I think Mr. Thorne is smarter and cares about you more than you give him credit for, little sparrow. It is better to light one small candle than curse the darkness."

"I don't understand."

"No, young one. But you will. Someday."

THE DOORBELL rang. Dr. Warner Gibson stretched lazily and stood up. Turning the holo-vision off and scooting down the marble floor, he reached for the door.

"Who is it?" he asked through the security system.

"Courier."

The female voice was not familiar. Dr. Gibson looked at the video monitor and saw a young woman standing outside his apartment door in his private elevator. She held an envelope in one hand, and she was looking down at her high-heel shoes.

"Okay, wait a moment."

Ever since he had started as the lead to a new genetics project last year, the doctor had received packages at all hours of the day and night. He supposed it was a small price to pay—considering. The doctor pressed a button, and the doors to the elevator swooshed open.

"I'll take it ..." Dr. Gibson's voice trailed off. Where before a young woman had been, there stood the gruff figure of a man. "How did you?"

The man held up a tiny piece of electronic gear. On the device's screen, the woman that Dr. Gibson had seen through his security video monitor appeared, just as the doctor had seen her.

"I don't understand. Don't I know you?"

"I'd say so."

"But ..."

"My name is Paul. Paul Thorne. I had a partner once. Rif Slater." The doctor stumbled back into the foyer. Paul followed.

"Wait ... You can't ..."

"Someone has to pay."

"I'm protected! You can't come in here!"

Paul pulled out his flechette pistol.

"But you can't! I'm protected!"

"Sure I can."

The doctor held up his hands, trying to shield himself from the barrel of Paul's gun. Paul fired—two to the chest and one to the head. The doctor crashed into the table and knocked the pewter statuette to the floor. Fresh flowers from the statuette's bowl fell over the doctor's corpse.

Paul calmly turned and left the apartment. He holstered his pistol and waited for the elevator to reach the lobby. A pleasant bell rang, and the elevator opened. Paul walked to the front door. The rain was falling like a swell, thick and hard in the night. Paul drew the collar of his coat up around his neck and stepped into the shadows that pooled around the inadequate amber lighting along Capital Street. His woolen Homburg hat pulled close across his brow, Paul slipped into the storm, moving quietly up the street and into the dark.

People, Places, and Things

CREATURES

Ligmi wasp-spiders. Found in the Ligmi system, Ligmi wasp-spiders are a large, native alien species that live in packs like hounds but build nests that resemble giant bees' nests on earth. They lay their eggs inside their victims, which hatch after a gestational period of five months, the baby wasp-spiders attacking and killing the host, using the host as a food pantry while the wasp-spiders establish a new nest.

CORPORATIONS

Lin Corporation. One of the "big three" corporations, Lin Corp is credited with development of the original frame drive. Lin Corp was established by Er Quin on the planet Mars and later relocated to Romeo Five, second planet in the Romeo system. Lin is known for its attention to harmonizing its workforce and products with the environment. The CEO of Lin is responsible for easing inter-system conflict between the various Lin Corp entities. Lin Corp has a robust bureaucratic apparatus and directly administers its territory. People who manage Lin Corp work in cones, or specialties that include all disciplines, including governance. The corporate culture is *balance*.

Militan Corporation. Militan Corp is a subsidiary of Syrch Corp operating in the Telakia system. Militan Corp is known for mining high-quality material used to make spacecraft and other carbon-based technologies.

Syrch Corporation. One of the big three corporations, Syrch is known for its lack of concern for its workers and the environment and for its massive construction projects. It is the newest of the big three and is ruled by a CEO, a board of directors, in-system governors and governors' boards, and planet administrators. The Syrch corporate structure is overlain over local, civilian government structures. The corporate culture is *survive to dominate*.

Terra Corporation. The largest of the big three corporations, Terra Corp controls Earth and the Sol system. Terra is known for its prowess in maximizing production value while shouldering its self-assigned mission of leading the human race to the next level of evolution. Renowned for its powerful naval fleet, backed by the incomparable Geist Marines, Terra's internal structure is a hierarchal corporate-military structure overlain on multiple democratic governance models—system dependent. The corporate culture is *born to lead*.

PEOPLE

Caldwell, Jillian. The product of an unsanctioned experiment by a Syrch Corp scientist, Jillian has illegally modified DNA that makes her extremely intelligent but also bestows upon her limited psychic abilities. She can influence people within her close circle (an uncontrolled power), making people want to protect her, and she can temporarily disrupt neural transmitters in the brain, causing the victim to "sleep." She is the niece of Dr. Warner Gibson.

Curry, Anabel. Anabel Curry is the office manager and personal assistant to Syrch Corp's director of security, Gordon Pepper.

Fletcher, Jerry. Dr. Jerry Fletcher is the primary scientific adviser to Syrch Corp's Security Division.

Gibson, Warner. Dr. Warner Gibson is a biochemist who leads Syrch Corporation's biological-based research. He is Jillian Caldwell's uncle.

Gutwein, Kurt. Captain Kurt Gutwein is the captain of the *Dorothea*, a small cargo ship that deals in both legal and illegal trade.

Kase, Everret. Dr. Everret Kase is a knowledgeable computer specialist in Syrch Corp's Security Division. He has a cybernetic left eye.

Pepper, Gordon. Director Gordon Pepper is the chief of Syrch Corp's Security Division.

Slater, Rif. An enforcer for Syrch Corp, Rif is Paul Thorne's partner.

Taljaard, Masopha. Captain Masopha Taljaard is the captain of the Syrch Corp battleship *Dominator*.

Tao, Wang. Dr. Wang Tao is a monk and the master at Dong Ahongsh Taixue, the premier school for gifted children for Lin Corp, which is located on the slopes of the holy mountain, Mount lie Shanqu. The school is located on Romeo Five, the home planet for Lin Corp.

Thorne, Paul (a.k.a. Paul Harlamor). An enforcer for Syrch Corporation, Paul was hired into the Syrch Corp family. He did not grow up on a Syrch world and is therefore an outsider.

Trenton, Shiloh. Shiloh Trenton is a senior Syrch Corp enforcer.

Unknown, Azalea. Azalea is the pilot of the star ship *Dorothea*.

Unknown, Freddy. Freddy "The Fix" is a midlevel criminal expeditor on Papen's World. An expeditor is the middleman in criminal exercises, matching talent to specific needs.

Unknown, Faolan. Faolan is the flight engineer aboard the star ship *Dorothea*.

PLACES

Armory Building. It is located on Capital Street on Papen's World, the home of Syrch Corporation. It is a luxury apartment building in art-deco style.

Banyan Tree Club. The Banyan Tree is an exclusive club and casino located on Plaza One in the Tianjin system.

Bektov Island. Located on Papen's World in the Great Ocean, it is one of forty islands in the chain.

Carl Nyberg Square. Carl Nyberg Square is located in the downtown area of Syrch City on Papen's World. It is a well-known and posh shopping, restaurant, and entertainment district.

Frederick Taylor Industrial School for the Gifted (FTISG). The school is located on Papen's World in the capital city. FTISG is one of the most elite schools in Syrch Corporation's education system.

Forest Tower Dome. The building is located on Papen's World. It is a domed building where Syrch Corporation carries out its most secretive scientific research and development.

Gravesande. A city located on Heyerdahl plateau just south of the equatorial edge of the central continent on Papen's World. It is unpleasantly hot and humid.

Great Ocean. Papen's World's largest ocean is called the Great Ocean.

Kuchin City. A resort city located on one of forty islands found in the Great Ocean of Papen's World.

Mekajiki. Nestled in the Bay of Joy, in the Great Ocean of Papen's World, this tiny village offers a simpler life away from the rush of Syrch Corp's operations.

Mount Lie Shanqu. A soaring mountain rising thirty-five thousand feet above the Ruan Ji River valley on Romeo Five, the home world for Lin Corporation. Part of the Nanga mountain range, Mount Lie Shanqu is considered a holy mountain. It is a place where leaders of Lin Corporation come to climb to its summit and contemplate their place in the universe. It is also home to Lin Corp's premier school for the gifted, Dong Zhongshu Taixue.

Read Building. The Read Building is a modern building of silver-steel and glass in Papen's World's capital city. It rests on Capital Street.

Syrch City. The capital city of Syrch Corporation located on Papen's World.

Traitor's Point. A promontory of land on Kendrack Bay on Papen's World's northern continent, Traitor's Point is a short drive from the Syrch City and Syrch Corporation headquarters.

STAR SHIPS

Ajax. The *Ajax* is a long-range Syrch Corp battle cruiser.

Devastation. The *Devastation* is a Syrch Corp battle frigate.

Dominator. The *Dominator* is a state-of-the-art Syrch Corp battleship captained by Captain Masopha Taljaard. Its home hunting ground is in Syrch's home system, Papen's system.

Dorothea. The *Dorothea* is a small intergalactic cargo ship owned and operated by Captain Kurt Gutwein. It has enhanced in-system nuclear engines and a third-generation frame drive.

Swan. The *Swan* is the largest and most powerful battleship owned by Lin Corporation.

Valiant. The *Valiant* is a Syrch Corp battle corvette.

SYSTEMS, PLANETS, AND PLANETOIDS

Eper system. The Eper system is in Syrch-controlled space. Syrch Corp began heavily mining the system to prevent Terra Corp from expanding into the system. Syrch's Corp's rush to lay claim to the system through strip mining resulted in the destruction of an evolved alien life form. Syrch Corp denies the alien life form ever existed.

Papen's system. Papen's system is the home system for Syrch Corporation, with thirteen inhabited planets. The main planet is Papen's World, the fourth from the system's star. There is a massive blue-giant, super-luminous star, a class O star, twenty-two light-years away from Papen's system. The nearness of this massive blue giant causes increased ultraviolet radiation that requires special terraforming techniques that result in very hot and humid planets.

Papen's World. The capital of Syrch Corporation, it is the fourth planet located in the system of the same name. It is an industrial world. Papen's World has six continents and a Great Ocean.

Plaza One. The largest asteroid in the Tianjin system, it is home to the largest domed living area in the Tianjin system. It has seven standard Earth-hour days and nights as it rotates around its weak sun as part of the asteroid field.

Romeo Five. The home world for Lin Corporation, Romeo Five is located in the Romeo system.

Romeo system. The home system for Lin Corporation is the Romeo system. It has nine planets, all of which have some type of human colony.

Telakia. A desert world renowned for the Great Desert and its prosperous mines of moissanite used in star ship construction.

Tianjin system. The Tianjin system is located outside of the control of the corporations and the League of Planets. An independent system, it has no planets; rather, a large asteroid field orbits a dim and weak star. The Tianjin system is a place where the avant-garde mingle with the ultra-rich and criminal classes. Tianjin system is a tax haven, a place to hide from the law and a place where entertainments of all types are sought and normally found.

TECHNOLOGY

communication drones. Drone ships that use framing drives to pass information between systems by emitting high-burst transmissions to communication buoys.

communication buoys. Communication buoys are the backbone for interstellar communication. Drones frame into a system at designated drop spots where they exchange information with communication buoys. The drones then frame to the next system and repeat the process.

cranial mesh. The cranial mesh is a high-tech implant device for interfacing with computers. The device is implanted in the cranial cavity where it slowly grows until it intertwines with the brain. Once installed, it cannot be removed without killing the host. Unlike conventional and much less expensive interfaces, a cranial mesh does not reach its full potential for years as it slowly expands into the mind's gray matter. Cranial meshes are illegal in some systems.

data crystal. A data crystal is a data storage device with huge capacity.

frame drive. The frame drive is the engine that allows for interstellar travel at light and, depending on the model, faster than light speeds. At its heart is the insanity crystal. However, a frame drive cannot be used near large celestial objects, as those objects, like planets, stars, and large asteroids, create natural flat spots within space-time, where it is not possible to jump from one fold of space-time to another.

insanity crystal. The insanity crystal is the device that allows a frame drive to function and is the backbone technology for interstellar space travel. It was invented by Dr. Jordan Mackley in 2063.

Kirlov's radiation. The radiation caused by use of an insanity crystal within a frame drive. The radiation is visible as a golden hue that surrounds the object that is framing.

Syrch coin. Also known as a golden coin, a warrant coin, or simply a coin, a Syrch coin is a special technological device. It is issued by the Syrch CEO or in-system governor to an enforcer or contractor. The coin contains the information of people targeted for assassination.

TERMINOLOGY

drop spots. The location within a given system where communication buoys are posted. These locations are kept clear so communication drones can quickly frame in and out of a system, exchanging information.

enforcers. An enforcer is a person who works for Syrch Corp and does the company's dirty work—threatening, injuring, or killing those deemed enemies by Syrch Corp. They typically use less advanced weapons than their counterparts in Lin and Terra Corp. Individuals from other corporations with similar professions are also commonly called enforcers.

flat spots. Artificial gravity wells created by ripplers that, when detonated, make it impossible for ships and weapons within their reach to use their frame drives.

folded space. Framing drives use the folds in space to "jump" or "frame" a ship between folds. This allows interstellar ships to traverse the stars.

heavies. A term used to refer to physically powerful men and women who specialize in the use of force. Often used when talking about Terra Corp Geist Marines but also used when talking about Syrch enforcers.

T-lines. T-lines are lines of anticipated trajectory for objects (ships, missiles, drones) moving through space.

WEAPONS AND GEAR

Malcolm Mouser. A double-action flechette pistol with no metal that is difficult to screen for, the Malcolm Mouser is favored by criminals and assassins.

Raven. A raven is a type of ship, not the name of a specific ship. It is an ultrafast gyrocopter used routinely by Syrch Corporation as attack and scout ships on planets with atmospheres. It is not a space-going ship.

ripplers. A space-to-space torpedo or stationary mine that creates an artificial flat spot in space-time. Once caught within a rippler's golden hue (from Kirlov's radiation), an interstellar ship cannot use its framing drive and must travel at in-system speeds. The caught ship is "trapped" within the flat spot while enemy ships, still using their frame drive, maneuver upon and can destroy the trapped ship.

Elemental Spider. A sleek, finely engineered and expensive car, the Elemental Spider is manufactured by Lin Corp.

Dryden Universe Time Line V2.1

2035   Primer Époque begins.

2037–2054   First Resource War, also known as the Extermination War. Nuclear and chemical weapon exchanges leaves much of North America and Eurasia depopulated. Some land areas remain uninhabitable for centuries. Establishment of the North American Union, the immediate precursor to the more formalized New American Federation.

2053   Events of "A Season for Killing" take place—the Battle of Washington.

2056   "Qin," the first permanent lunar colony, founded by Chinese.

2063   Dr. Jordan Mackley, the inventor of the insanity crystal, finishes her master's thesis at the newly constituted University of Antarctica. Entitled "The Insanity Crystal: Icosahedral Quasicrystal Lattice Growth and Advanced Crystalline Design," Dr. Mackley never realizes the significance of her discovery ("A Season for Killing").

2089   First attempted manned mission to Mars ends tragically when Dr. Adelchi Werner goes insane aboard the ship *First Hope*, killing the crew and crashing the ship into Mars's moon Deimos ("Revenge").

2099   First successful manned Mars Landing, China.

2106   First manned Venus landing, New American Federation.

2110   First Mars colony, International Space Association.

2108–2117   Second resource war. Chinese moon base "Qin" destroyed. Rebuilt, named, "Er Qin"

2118–2175   Period of global depression following Second Resource War. Referred to as "Earth Twilight" because Earth's resources past peak.

2175   The dawn of regular spaceflight. Gravity well generators invented, making ground-based space launches inexpensive and providing shipboard gravity for long-distance space flight. Trade across planets within the solar system commercially feasible for the first time.

2180–2210   Period of rapid expansion within the solar system.

            Venus colony in 2184; Europa Colony 2188; Jupiter Cloud colony in 2210; many asteroids settled.

2184   University of Antarctica grad student Lachmi Dryden publishes doctoral thesis titled "The Effects of Natural State Frame Fluctuations on Massed Objects," which outlines the principles for moving an object from one point in space to another without passing through the points in between, effectively allowing faster than light travel without violating e=mc2. The paper receives little attention.

2208   Events of "Star Dust" take place.

2211   Er Qin (precursor to Lin Corp) purchases a majority of Mars, Venus, and several asteroids and becomes the first extra-terran mega corp.

2212   Terra Corp formed. Terra Corp consolidates the majority of Terra's (Earth's) economy, with Europa Colony, Mercury Base, the Jupiter Cloud Colony, and several asteroids. Earth is effectively one economy.

2215   Er Qin tests PTB 94, a prototype framing drive, based on the synthesis of Dr. Jordan Mackley and Dr. Lachmi Dryden's research. While the engine's failure is visible across the solar system, results indicate that the device "jumped" between points 2.3 light seconds apart before destroying itself. Media popularizes the term "insanity crystal," invented by Dr. Jordan Mackley 152 years ago.

2216–2223   Terra Corp and Er Qin (precursor to Lin Corp) race to develop stable framing drives. Both claim success in 2223.

2219   First contact is established between researches at the University of Antarctica and Cetaceans. Over time, the bond between Cetaceans and the UoA leads to the building of a secret research station at lake Vostok, Antarctica. Genetic modification of Cetaceans results in the Ile Soltaire.

2240   Captain Othall of Er Qin (precursor to Lin Corp) successfully pilots the *Hai Ou* (*Seagull*) from Mars to Earth and back using the framing drive. While his average frame-to-frame jump is only 3.6 light seconds, he completes the journey in eighty-four hours, hundreds of times faster than conventional ships.

2243   Threat of war forces Er Qin off of the moon. They reorganize on Mars as Lin Corp.

2247   Undersea Ocean on Europa reached for the first time. Intense pressure and extreme temperatures slow exploration.

2250–2296   First Trade War. Intense competition between Terra Corp and Lin Corp occasionally boils over to open combat.

2253   First space flight by a Cetacean. A bottlenose dolphin named Hides-in-Ferns secretly pilots a University of Antarctica craft to Earth's moon and back.

2297   Lin Corp stuns the solar system by announcing that it has colonized a fourth planet in Proxima Centari system and has explored three other systems. They reveal a secret base on "1st Stone" a hundred-kilometer-wide object in the Oort cloud from which they have built and launched ships capable of travels at speeds up to one light-year per five hundred hours.

2298   Without warning, the humans and cetaceans of Lake Vostok, now referring to themselves as Ile Soltaire, leave Earth in a ship of their own design.

2301   Terra Corp establishes its primary space naval base, Callirrhoe Station, in the Oort cloud on the dwarf planet 90377 Sedna.

2305   Theiana Mason born in the city of New Paris on Mars, to Derrik Markowitz and Patricia Mason. Markowitz is a hydroponics engineer. Mason is a classical musician. Theiana is trained as a musician. However, she is captivated by the discovery of life on Ninus 7 and enters the Sea of Tranquility University on the moon as a biologist with a specialization in exobiology.

2315   Lin Corp announces the discovery of a life-bearing planet in the Ninus system. There have been three previous life-bearing planets found. Ninus 7 is the first bearing complex multicellular life.

2317   Terra Corp announces colonization of Tennus Star system.

2320–2329 Second Trade War: A series of nuclear "accidents" on Mars, Earth, and the Ingus asteroid result in Lin Corp relocating to newly colonized Romeo system. This change gives Terra Corp control of the Sol system.

2325	Tennus system declares independence from Terra Corp; Parmer system is charted by upstart Pim Corp.
2328	First contact with the Europan, which resides beneath the frozen oceans on Europa. The Europan is the first clearly sentient exo-species.
2331	Events of "Revenge" take place.
2338	League of Planets formed. League of Planets is a loose confederation of planets that join together to resist the ever-increasing power of the mega-corporations.
2341	Contact lost with colony Olive i-4. An investigation reveals that a mutated Terran Flu virus, usually carried by canines, infected the local environment. The virus infected all organisms on the planet, destroying the ecosystem.
2341	Theiana Mason and others form the Interspecies Defense Fund (IDF). The IDF establishes protocols for the identification and protection of life-bearing worlds.
2341	Facing hostile takeover by Lin, Pim Corporation dissolves itself, giving the League of Planets full control of the Parmer system. They rename the second planet in the system League Prime.
2346	The League of Planets launches a series of deep-space exploration craft. Among them is the legendary *Duster*.

2355	Syrch Corporation is founded on Papen's World. Civil war breaks out between the independent Federation and Consortium planets.
2358	Lin Corp charters the Genrith system.
2360	Events of "Alder's World" take place.
2370	First sighting of an Ile Soltaire spaceship in deep space.
2375	Events of "A Lucky Man" take place.
2377	Events of "A Step Too Far" take place.
2380	The Interspecies Defense Fund (IDF) adopts "The Charter" allowing for the use of violence to protect alien species.
2385	Events of "The Eclipsing of Sirus C" take place.
2387	End of the civil war between the Federation and Consortium with a Federation victory.
2398	The first recorded attack on corporate interests by Theiana Mason's ship, the *Moth*.
2404	Ile Soltaire ship orbits League Prine and issues a short statement declaring thousands of star systems toward galactic center off-limits to all humans.
2414	Syrch Corp secretly begins the development of a ring world around Skeelar's Star, at the edge of Ile Soltaire's no-fly zone.

2435	Events of "Threshold" take place.
2503	Start of Big Damn Dryden Role Playing Game. Events of "Skye Goddesses of Dryden" take place.
2700–2720	The Battle for Sol. Events of "Rise of the Europan" take place. The Europan takes control of the Sol system.
2720	End of the Primer Époque. Beginning of the Belle Époque.
BE 20,000	Events of "Demon's Eyes" and "A Matter of Trust" take place.
BE 40,000	Technoprey awake and begin their destructive swarm. End of the Belle Époque. Beginning of Codex 2.0.

Afterword

THE CHARACTER Paul Thorne first appeared in the story "A Lucky Man," which is featured in my collection of Dryden Stories called *Origins: A Dryden Universe Collection*. While Paul was a minor albeit important character in that story, he is really the type of character I have always felt was at the heart of the Dryden multiverse. In the Dryden multiverse, corporate power has reached its zenith. The big three—Terra, Lin, and Syrch Corporations—all have spheres of influence where they dominate. Within that context, the corporations manipulate the governments of their star systems, and all the corporations have an expansionist view. Expand or die is their mantra. This is not so different from what we have seen in our past and in current times, and I think it is what makes these futuristic stories, to include Paul's story, so interesting.

Science fiction is, perhaps more than other literary genre, a powerful mechanism where we can consider the ethical and moral implications of humans controlling more and more of the natural world. Through the mechanism of Terra, Lin, and Syrch corporations the authors and artists of Dryden contemplate the impact of science and how science changes social structures, pushing and pulling people and societies into and out of conflict. The stories, it is hoped, ask the reader to decide if the worship of industrial economics, hidden under the thin veneer of what has been termed the information age, with science as its lodestar, is something that humanity really should follow at all costs, or if we should curb our enthusiasm for our industrial-based system for some other, less singular notion of human existence. For it is within this examination that our hope for a better future resides.

The universe that my antihero, Paul Thorne, inhabits is therefore reflective of our own. Paul is a brutal man, but his brutality is derived from being abandoned and unloved and being unprotected. Paul is constantly perched on the edge of poverty as he struggles against forces greater than himself in the hopes of finding self-realization. As a fighter, Paul responds to the world through violence, and though he has convinced himself that his actions are necessary, deep within him he is troubled. He reflects on what he has done, and he does not like what he sees. In some ways, Paul feels helpless, as if he is caught in an irresistible storm wave. In turn, Paul drinks to distort the truth, to forget, yet he still lives by a code of conduct that, though dark and hard, gives him a sense of his place in the universe and explains the greed and violence that he sees all around. It is this internal conflict that brought me back to Paul Thorne.

Paul's journey is reflective, in some ways, of my own. He too wonders about the direction of our society and about our responsibilities to one another. Paul struggles to determine where those responsibilities start and end. For within *that* question are the greatest questions of all: Why are we here? Why do we struggle? What do we hope to gain? What does it all mean? Is there any meaning at all?

I hope you have enjoyed this story and that you find these questions and historic forces, reflected in and through Paul Thorne, interesting to contemplate within the context of your own life. I expect we shall see Paul again on another adventure. For the corporate wars rage on through the stars of our collective future.

Printed in the United States
By Bookmasters

Printed in the United States
By Bookmasters